RAVES FOR JAMES PATTERSON

"THE MAN IS A MASTER OF HIS GENRE. WE FANS ALL HAVE ONE WISH FOR HIM: WRITE EVEN FASTER."

—Larry King, *USA Today*

"WHEN IT COMES TO CONSTRUCTING A HARROWING PLOT, AUTHOR JAMES PATTERSON CAN TURN A SCREW ALL RIGHT."

—*New York Daily News*

"JAMES KNOWS HOW TO SELL THRILLS AND SUSPENSE IN CLEAR, UNWAVERING PROSE."

—*People*

"PATTERSON HAS MASTERED THE ART OF WRITING PAGE-TURNING BESTSELLERS."

—*Chicago Sun-Times*

"PATTERSON KNOWS WHERE OUR DEEPEST FEARS ARE BURIED . . . THERE'S NO STOPPING HIS IMAGINATION."

—*New York Times Book Review*

"JAMES PATTERSON WRITES HIS THRILLERS AS IF HE WERE BUILDING ROLLER COASTERS. He grounds the stories with a bare-bones plot, then builds them over the top and tries to throw readers for a loop a few times along the way."

—Associated Press

"A MUST-READ AUTHOR...A MASTER OF THE CRAFT."

—*Providence Sunday Journal*

"THE PAGE-TURNINGEST AUTHOR IN THE GAME RIGHT NOW."

—*San Francisco Chronicle*

"JAMES PATTERSON ALWAYS DELIVERS A FASCINATING, ACTION-PACKED THRILLER."

—*Midwest Book Review*

"PATTERSON IS A MASTER."

—*Toronto Globe and Mail*

NEVER NEVER

A complete list of books by James Patterson is at the back of this book. For previews of upcoming books and information about the author, visit JamesPatterson.com, or find him on Facebook or at your app store.

NEVER NEVER

JAMES PATTERSON
AND
CANDICE FOX

GRAND CENTRAL
PUBLISHING

NEW YORK BOSTON

The characters and events in this book are fictitious. Any similarity to real persons, living or dead, is coincidental and not intended by the author.

Grand Central Publishing
Hachette Book Group
1290 Avenue of the Americas, New York, NY 10104
grandcentralpublishing.com
twitter.com/grandcentralpub

Originally published in Australia by Century Australia, a division of Penguin Random House Australia, August 2016
First North American hardcover edition published by Little, Brown and Company in January 2017
First North American trade paperback edition: July 2017

Grand Central Publishing is a division of Hachette Book Group, Inc. The Grand Central Publishing name and logo is a trademark of Hachette Book Group, Inc.

The publisher is not responsible for websites (or their content) that are not owned by the publisher.

The Hachette Speakers Bureau provides a wide range of authors for speaking events. To find out more, go to hachettespeakersbureau.com or call (866) 376-6591.

Library of Congress Control Number: 2016953523

ISBNs: 978-1-4789-4477-5 (trade paperback), 978-0-316-43472-0 (ebook)

Printed in the United States of America

LSC-C

10 9 8 7 6 5 4 3 2 1

NEVER NEVER

CHAPTER 1

"IF YOU REACH the camp before me, I'll let you live," the Soldier said.

It was the same chance he allowed them all. The fairest judgment for their crimes against his people.

The young man lay sniveling in the sand at his feet. Tears had always disgusted the Soldier. They were the lowest form of expression, the physical symptom of psychological weakness. The Soldier lifted his head and looked across the black desert to the camp's border lights. The dark sky was an explosion of stars, patched here and there by shifting cloud. He sucked cold desert air into his lungs.

"Why are you doing this?" Danny whimpered.

The Soldier slammed the door of the van closed and twisted the key. He looped his night-vision goggles around his neck and strode past the shivering traitor to a large rock. He mounted it, and with an outstretched arm pointed toward the northeast.

"On a bearing of zero-four-seven, at a distance of one-point-six-two kilometers, your weapon is waiting," the Soldier barked. He swiveled, and pointed to the north-west. "On a bearing of three-one-five, at a distance of one-point-six-five kilometers, my weapon is waiting. The camp lies at true north."

"What are you saying?" the traitor wailed. "Jesus Christ! Please, please don't do this."

The Soldier jumped from the rock, straightened his belt and drew down his cap. The young traitor had dragged himself to his feet and now stood shaking by the van, his weak arms drawn up against his chest. *Judgment is the duty of the righteous,* the Soldier thought. *There is no room for pity. Only fury at the abandonment of honor.*

Even as those familiar words drifted through his mind, he felt the cold fury awakening. His shoulders tensed, and he could not keep the snarl from his mouth as he turned to begin his mission.

"We're green-lighted, soldier," he said. "Move out!"

CHAPTER 2

DANNY WATCHED THE Soldier disappear in the brief, pale light before the moon was shrouded by clouds. The darkness that sealed him was complete. He scrambled for the driver's side door of the van, yanked it, pushed against the back window where a long crack ran upward through the middle of the glass. He ran around and did the same on the other side. Panic thrummed through him. What was he doing? Even if he got into the van, the keys were gone. He spun around and bolted into the dark in the general direction of northeast. How the hell was he supposed to find anything out here?

The moon shone through the clouds again, giving him a glimpse of the expanse of dry sand and rock before it was taken away. He tripped forward and slid down a steep embankment, sweat plastering sand to his palms, his cheeks. His breath came in wild pants and gasps.

"Please, God," he cried. "Please, God, please!"

He ran blindly in the dark, arms pumping, stumbling now and then over razor-sharp desert plants. He came over a rocky rise and saw the camp glittering in the distance, no telling how far. Should he try to make it to the camp? He screamed out. Maybe someone on patrol would hear him.

Danny kept his eyes on the ground as he ran. Every shadow and ripple in the sand looked like a gun. He leapt at a dry log that looked like a rifle, knelt and fumbled in the dark. Sobs racked through his chest. The task was impossible.

The first sound was just a *whoosh,* sharper and louder than the wind. Danny straightened in alarm. The second *whoosh* was followed by a heavy *thunk,* and before he could put the two sounds together he was on his back in the sand.

The pain rushed up from his arm in a bright red wave. The young man gripped his shattered elbow, the sickening emptiness where his forearm and hand had been. High, loud cries came from deep in the pit of his stomach. Visions of his mother flashed in the redness behind his eyes. He rolled and dragged himself up.

He would not die this way. He would not die in the dark.

CHAPTER 3

THE SOLDIER WATCHED through the rifle scope as the kid stumbled, his remaining hand gripping at the stump. The Soldier had seen the Barrett M82 rifle take heads clean off necks in the Gaza Strip, and in the Australian desert the weapon didn't disappoint. Lying flat on his belly on a ridge, the Soldier actioned the huge black rifle, set the upper rim of his eye against the scope. He breathed, shifted back, pulled the trigger and watched the kid collapse as the scare shot whizzed past his ear.

What next? A leg? An ear? The Soldier was surprised at his own callousness. He knew it wasn't military justice to play with the traitor while doling out his sentence, but the rage still burned in him.

You would have given us away, he seethed as he watched the boy running in the dark. *You would have sacrificed us all.*

There was no lesser creature on Earth than a liar, a cheat and a traitor. And bringing about a fellow soldier's end was never easy. In some ways, it felt like a second betrayal. *Look what you've forced me to do,* the Soldier thought, watching the kid screaming into the wind. The Soldier let the boy scream. The wind would carry his voice south, away from the camp.

The cry of a traitor. He would remember it for his own times of weakness.

The Soldier shifted in the sand, lined up a head shot and followed Danny in the crosshairs as he got up one last time.

"Target acquired," the Soldier murmured to himself, exhaling slowly. "Executing directive."

He pulled the trigger. What the Soldier saw through the scope made him smile sadly. He rose, flicked the bipod down on the end of the huge gun and slung the weapon over his shoulder.

"Target terminated. Mission complete."

He walked down the embankment into the dark.

CHAPTER 4

IT WAS CHIEF Morris who called me into the interrogation room. He was sitting on the left of the table, in one of the investigators' chairs, and motioned for me to sit on the right where the perps sit.

"What?" I said. "What's this all about, Pops? I've got work to do."

His face was grave. I hadn't seen him look that way since the last time I punched Nigel over in Homicide for taking my parking spot. The Chief had been forced to give me a serious reprimand, on paper, and it hurt him.

"Sit down, Detective Blue," he said.

Holy crap, I thought. *This is bad.* I know I'm in trouble when the Chief calls me by my official title.

The truth is, most of our time together is spent far from the busy halls of the Sydney Police Center in Surry Hills.

I was twenty-one when I started working Sex Crimes. It was my first assignment after two years on street patrol, so I moved into the Sydney Metro offices with more than a little terror in my heart at my new role and the responsibility that came with it. I'd been told I was the first woman in the Sex Crimes department in half a decade. It was up to me to show the boys how to handle women in crisis. The department was broken; I needed to fix it, fast. The Chief had grunted a demoralized hello at me a few times in the coffee room in those early weeks, and that had been it. I'd lain awake plenty of nights thinking about his obvious lack of faith in me, wondering how I could prove him wrong.

After a first month punctuated by a couple of violent rape cases and three or four aggravated assaults, I'd signed up for one-on-one boxing training at a gym near my apartment. From what I'd seen, I figured it was a good idea for a woman in this city to know how to land a swift uppercut. I'd waited outside the gym office that night sure that the young, muscle-bound woman wrapping her knuckles by the lockers was my trainer.

But it was Chief Morris in a sweaty gray singlet who tapped me on the shoulder and told me to get into the ring.

Inside the ropes, the Chief called me "Blue." Inside the office, he grunted.

There was none of the warmth and trust shared by Blue and Pops in the ring here in the interrogation room. The Chief's eyes were cold. I felt a little of that old terror from my first days on the job.

"Pops," I said. "What's the deal?"

He took the statement notepad and a pencil from beside the interview recorder and pushed them toward me.

"Make a list of items from your apartment that you'll need while you're away. It may be for weeks," he said. "Toiletries. Clothes. That sort of stuff."

"Where am I going?"

"As far away as you can get," he sighed.

"Chief, you're talking crazy," I said. "Why can't I go home and get this stuff myself?"

"Because right now your apartment is crawling with Forensics officers. Patrol have blockaded the street. They've impounded your car, Detective Blue," he said. "You're not going home."

CHAPTER 5

I LAUGHED, HARD, in the Chief's face.

"Good work, Pops," I said, standing up so that my chair scraped loudly on the tiles. "Look, I like a good prank as much as anyone but I'm busier than a one-armed bricklayer out there. I can't believe they roped you into this one. Good work, mate. Now open this door."

"This isn't a joke, Harriet. Sit back down."

I laughed again. That's what I do when I'm nervous. I laugh, and I grin. "I've got cases."

"Your apartment and car are being forensically examined in connection with the Georges River Three case," the Chief said. He slapped a thick manila folder on the table between us. It was bursting with papers and photographs, yellow witness reports and pink Forensics sheets.

I knew the folder well. I'd watched it as it was carried

around by the Homicide guys, back and forth, hand to hand, a bible of horror. Three beautiful university students, all brunettes, all found along the same stretch of the muddy Georges River. Their deaths, exactly thirty days apart, had been violent, drawn-out horrors. The stuff of mothers' nightmares. Of my nightmares. I'd wanted the Georges River Three case badly, at least to consult on it due to the sexual violence the women had endured. I'd hungered for that case. But it had been given to the parking-spot thief Detective Nigel Spader and his team of Homicide hounds. For weeks I'd sat at my desk seething at the closed door of their case room before the rage finally dissipated.

I sank back into my chair.

"What's that got to do with me?"

"It's routine, Blue," the Chief said gently. He reached out and put his hand on mine. "They're just making sure you didn't know."

"Know what?"

"We found the Georges River Killer," he said. He looked at my eyes. "It's your brother, Blue. It's Sam."

CHAPTER 6

I SLAMMED THE door of the interrogation room in the Chief's face and marched across the office to the Homicide case room. Dozens of eyes followed me. I threw open the door and spotted that slimeball Nigel Spader standing before a huge corkboard stuffed with pinned images, pages, sketches. He flinched for a blow as I walked over but I restrained myself and smacked the folder he was holding out of his hands instead. Pages flew everywhere.

"You sniveling prick," I said, shoving a finger in his face. "You dirty, sniveling... dick hole!"

I was so mad I couldn't speak, and that's a real first for me. I couldn't breathe. My whole throat was aflame. The restraint faltered and I grabbed a wide-eyed Nigel by the shirtfront, gathering up two fistfuls of his orange chest hair as I dragged him to the floor. Someone caught my fist before I could land a punch. It took two more men to release my grip. We struggled backwards into a table full of coffees and plates of muffins. Crockery shattered on the floor.

"How could you be so completely wrong?" I shouted. "How could you be so completely, *completely* useless! You pathetic piece of—"

"That's enough!" The Chief stepped forward into the fray and took my arm. "Detective Blue, you get a fucking hold of yourself right now or I'll have the boys escort you out onto the street."

I was suddenly free of all arms and I stumbled, my head pounding.

And then I saw it.

The three girls, their autopsy portraits beside smiling, sunlit shots provided by the families. A handprint on a throat. A picture of my brother's hand. A map of Sydney, studded with pins where the victims lived, where their families lived, where my brother lived, where the bodies of the girls were found. Photographs of the inside of my brother's apartment, but not as I knew it. Unfamiliar things had been pulled out of drawers and brought down from cupboards. Porn. Tubs and tubs of magazines, DVDs, glossy pictures. A rope. A knife. A bloody T-shirt. Photographs of onlookers at the crime scenes. My brother's face among the crowd.

In the middle of it all, a photograph of Sam. I tugged the photo from the board and unfolded the half of the image that had been tucked away. My own face. The two of us were squeezed into the frame, the flash glinting in my brother's blue eyes.

We looked so alike. Detective Harry Blue and the Georges River Killer.

CHAPTER 7

I'VE HAD TWO cigarettes in the past ten years. Both of them I smoked outside the funeral home where a fallen colleague's body was being laid to rest. I stood now in the alleyway behind headquarters, finishing off the third. I chain-lit the fourth, sucked hard, exhaled into the icy morning. Despite the chill, my shirt was sticking to me with sweat. I tried to call my brother's phone three times. No answer.

The Chief emerged from the fire exit beside me. I held up a hand. Not only did I not want to talk, I wasn't sure that I could if I tried. The old man stood watching as I smoked. My hands were shaking.

"That... that rat... that stain on humanity Nigel Spader is going to go down for this," I said. "If it's my last act, I'm going to make sure he—"

"I've overseen the entire operation," the Chief said. "I

couldn't tell you it was going on, or you might have alerted Sam. We let you carry on, business as usual. Nigel and his team have done a very good job. They've been onto your brother for about three weeks now."

I looked at my chief. My trainer. My friend.

"I've thought you've been looking tired," I sneered. "Can't sleep at night, Boss?"

"No," he said. "As a matter of fact, I can't. I haven't slept since the morning the Homicide team told me of their suspicions. I hated lying to you, Blue."

He ground a piece of asphalt into the gutter with his heel. He looked ancient in the reflected light of the towering city blocks around us.

"Where is my brother?"

"They picked him up this morning," he said. "He's being interrogated by the Feds over at Parramatta headquarters."

"I need to get over there."

"You won't get anywhere near him at this stage." The Chief took me by the shoulders before I could barge past him through the fire door. "He's in processing. Depending on whether he's cooperative, he may not be approved for visitors for a week. Two, even."

"Sam didn't do this," I said. "You've got it wrong. Nigel's got it wrong. I need to be here to straighten all this out."

"No, you don't," he said. "You need to get some stuff together and get out of here."

"What, just abandon him?"

"Harry, Sam is about to go down as one of the nastiest sexual sadists since the Backpacker Murderer. Whether you think he did it or not, you're public enemy number two right now. If the press gets hold of you, they're going to eat you alive."

I shook another cigarette out of the packet I'd swiped from Nigel's desk. My thoughts were racing.

"You aren't going to do yourself any favors here, Harry. If you go around shouting in front of the cameras the way you did in that case room just now, you're going to look like a lunatic."

"I don't give a shit what I look like!"

"You should," the Chief said. "The entire country is going to tune in for this on the six o'clock news. People are angry. If they can't get at Sam, they're going to want to get at you. Think about it. It's fucking poetry. The killer's sister is a short-tempered, frequently violent cop with a mouth like a sailor. Better yet, she's in Sex Crimes, and has somehow managed to remain completely oblivious to the sexual predator at the family barbecue."

He took a piece of paper from the breast pocket of his jacket and handed it to me. It was a printout of a flight itinerary. He untucked a slim folder from under his arm and put it in my hands. I opened it and saw it was a case brief, but I couldn't get my eyes to settle on it for more than a few seconds. I felt sick with fear, uncertainty.

"What's this?" I asked.

"It's an Unexplained Death case out on a mining camp in the desert near Kalgoorlie," the Chief said.

"I'm Sex Crimes, Pops. Not cleanup crew."

"I don't care what you are. You're going. I pulled some strings with some old mates in Perth. The case itself is bullshit, but the area is so isolated, it'll make the perfect hideout."

"I don't want to go to fucking Kalgoorlie! Are you nuts?"

"You don't get a choice, Detective. Even if you don't know what's best for you right now, I do. I'm giving you a direct order as your superior officer. You don't go, I'll have you locked up for interrogative purposes. I'll tell a judge I want to know if you knew anything about the murders and I'll throw away the key until this shitstorm is over. You want that?"

I tried to walk away. The Chief grabbed my arm again.

"Look at me," he said.

I didn't look.

"There is nothing you can do to help your brother, Blue," the old man said. "It's over."

CHAPTER 8

I DIDN'T KNOW which genius from Sydney Metro packed my bags for me, but they'd managed not to find the suitcases in the wardrobe of my tiny apartment in Woolloomooloo. I exited the baggage claim area in Kalgoorlie airport with three black garbage bags of possessions in tow. From what I could see in the pale light of the car-hire lot, some of the items I'd asked for were there, and quite a few I hadn't, too. I recognized my television remote among the fingerprint-dusted mess.

The numbness that had descended on me about my brother's arrest began after my first glass of wine on the flight. Now it was affecting my movements. I realized I had been standing at the hire car counter in a silent daze when the attendant clicked his fingers loudly in my face, snapping me back to reality.

"Miss? Hey! Miss!"

I frowned, reached out and pushed over a canister of pencils standing on the edge of the counter. The pencils scattered over his keyboard.

"So you're awake, then," he sighed dramatically, gathering up the pencils.

"I'm awake."

"What's the name?"

"Blue."

He did some tapping on the keyboard. Printed and presented me with a demoralizingly long form to fill in and a set of car keys.

"Blue and Whittacker. You've got the little red Camry."

"Who's Whittacker?"

"I am," said a voice from behind me. I turned around as a lean, broad-shouldered man was carefully setting down two immaculate leather Armani suitcases on their little golden feet. He put out a long-fingered hand. "Edward. You must be Harriet?"

"Harry. You're the driver?" I asked.

"I'm your partner, actually," he said, smiling.

CHAPTER 9

I CALLED THE Chief first, sitting in the backseat of the car, to tell him I'd arrived and see if there was any more news on Sam. There was no word on my brother. I called a contact I had in the Feds, and when that route failed, I called some journalists I could trust to see if they had the inside scoop. A cocoon of silence had descended around Sam. By the time I'd given up calling his friends and neighbors, only hearing the same shock and horror I already felt myself, Whittacker had driven us out of the town and onto the highway.

"Everything all right?" he asked.

"You just mind the road, Whitt, and leave me to me."

"Actually, I prefer Edward," he said.

"You say 'actually' a lot."

His brow creased in the rearview mirror. I leaned on the windowsill and watched the featureless desert rolling by. When I couldn't stand thinking about my brother being in prison any longer I climbed through the gap between the seats and landed in the front beside Whitt. On the floor I found his copy of the case brief, which was bigger than mine.

"Remind me why I'm working with a partner," I said. "I never requested a partner."

"I had a back injury about a month ago. Compressed a disc in my lower spine. So I'm on light duties. I used to be Drug squad, but there's a lot of kicking down doors in Drug squad, as you can imagine." He smiled.

"Give me the rundown on this case, Whitt," I said. "Where are we headed?"

"To the very edge of nowhere."

"We were just there." I jerked my thumb toward the highway behind us, the tiny town in the middle of a sandy abyss.

"Oh no, there's plenty more oblivion to come. Right now we're on the outskirts of the Great Victoria Desert. It's as big as California, and largely uninhabited. Bandya uranium mine is smack-bang in the middle of it. It'll be another five hours of this." He gestured to the bare landscape.

"Five hours? Christ almighty." I slumped back in my seat.

"We're on the hunt for one Daniel Stanton, twenty-one years old."

I opened the file and found a photograph of a tanned

young man with blond, shaggy hair. A big, infectious smile. In the picture, he had his arm slung around the neck of a black Labrador.

"Cute. What did he do?"

"He died."

"Well, that was a poor choice." I sighed.

"His divisional manager at Bandya reported Stanton missing about eleven days ago," Whitt said. "It wasn't a huge deal at first. Guys go missing from the mine all the time, so he tells me."

"They do?"

"Well, I mean, they usually turn up. These mines are so isolated that they're operated by workers who fly in from cities all over the country. They work three weeks, then they fly out again and get a week off back in their hometown. Young guys sign up to do it because the money is incredible."

"How incredible?"

"Are you sure you want to know?"

"I'll ask the questions here, Detective Whittacker."

"Entry-level positions at this mine are about three times our salary as detectives," he said.

I couldn't reply. I just stared at my new partner, my mouth hanging open.

"Yeah," he laughed.

"So why the hell do they go missing?"

"Well, there's a reason the money is so great. The work is hard, dangerous, and for three weeks of the month they're stuck in the middle of the desert away from their families. They're young and impatient, most of them. When they get tired of it, they just go on leave and never come back. Or they drop their tools, hitch a ride into town and go home. It breaks down even the toughest guys after a while, apparently."

"So what happened to Danny Stanton? Did he just walk off the job?"

"Well if he did, he went the wrong way entirely." Whitt glanced at me. "Straight out into the desert."

CHAPTER 10

"FLIP FORWARD A couple of photographs," Whitt said. I shuffled through and found a Forensics-lab shot of a decomposing foot.

"Oh, hello," I said, holding the picture close to my face in the dim light of the car. "Never leave home without both feet, Whitt. You won't get far."

"The foot was actually found on the camp," he said. "Three days after Danny went missing, a couple of miners found a dingo inside the fences dragging a steel-capped boot around, trying to get at what was inside. The camp is plagued by dingoes scavenging for food scraps, so it didn't raise any alarms at first. Inside the boot, the guys found the foot, and the foot is Danny's. Was Danny's. Whatever."

I squinted at the picture. The foot had been severed

at the ankle joint. The photograph was good enough quality that I could see shredded bits of white material stuck to the hairy skin at the ragged incision. His sock.

"Forensics in Perth say the foot became disconnected from Danny's body postmortem, by animal predation."

"So the kid was already dead by the time the dingoes started to pick him to pieces."

"Indeed."

"Well, I can't see a dingo carrying a boot very far," I said. "The body must have been within boot-carrying distance of the camp, right?"

"Wrong," Whitt said. "That's the interesting part. They haven't found the body yet. The mine operators and police in Perth sent out aerial and ground search teams for two days. Nothing. No trace."

"That doesn't make any sense."

Whitt shrugged.

"Don't shrug at me, Whitt. I want answers."

"I don't have any answers for you," he said. "I haven't even reached the camp yet."

I sat back and looked at the photograph of Danny's foot. Why would the kid walk out into the desert if he wanted to go AWOL? Why wouldn't he just get a ride back into town? If he'd walked out into the desert on his own and got lost, maybe died from dehydration trying to find his way back, why wasn't the foot covered in blisters from the sweat running down his ankles into the boot?

I stared at the foot until I fell asleep with my head

against the window. The sun was setting, warm on the back of my eyelids. The Chief had been right. Suddenly, blissfully, my mind was full, even if it was only because one darkness in my life had been replaced by another.

CHAPTER 11

"WHAT'S THIS NOW?" Whitt said, slowing the car.

I snapped awake.

Ahead of us on the isolated dirt road a sedan came into view, its hood popped and cabin lights on. A lanky figure stood beside it, waving his arms.

"Where are we?"

"We just came through Bandya," Whitt said. "Looks like this guy's broken down."

As we came alongside the man's vehicle our headlights lit the bottom half of his face. A dark cap was pulled over his eyes. He stuck his head almost through my window. I smelled cigarette smoke.

"What's the trouble?" Whitt asked.

"No trouble, mate." The man gave a wide smile jammed with too many teeth. "Just get out of the car."

From the darkness, six men appeared, surrounding us.

The tall man wrenched my door open and reached across me, unbuckling my seat belt.

"Hey!" I yelled. It only takes seconds for my fight reflex to kick in. The Chief had smacked me in the face and ribs and stomach enough times in the ring to develop a kind of trigger-rage in me. *Wake up, Tiger!* he'd yell.

The tall man had woken the tiger.

As he pulled me from the car by my wrists, I used the momentum to surge upward and butt him in the face with my forehead. He leaned back and I hooked a leg around his knees, pushing him in the chest with both hands, sending both of us sprawling in the dirt. The reaction around us was one of joyful surprise. Someone grabbed my arms and pulled me off the man, but not before I landed a right hook into his ear.

"Y'all right, Richie?"

"Fuck!" Richie got to his feet, touching his bleeding lip. "I didn't see that one coming!"

The men laughed. I was shoved against the car beside Whitt. A rough hand held my head against the top of the warm vehicle. Whitt was looking at me. There was no panic in his face. He seemed almost curious. Were these guys responsible for what had happened to Danny? Had we already stumbled upon the answer to our questions, before we'd even hit the camp? I'd been about to shout that we were police officers, but Whitt's face made me hold my tongue. Maybe we could learn something here.

"Where are you two going?" Richie took hold of my head and turned me to face him. "What's your name, pretty?"

"Harriet Blue," someone said. They had my wallet. I heard my garbage bags of possessions being pulled from the backseat. "From Sydney."

"You're a long way from home, Bluebird," Richie said, leaning against the car beside me, his long arms folded. "What are you doing all the way out here? Is this chump your boyfriend?"

"Back off, loser," I snarled.

"Ooh," Richie said, smiling. "You're a nasty girl."

"If someone had told me there'd be wild pigs out here, I would have brought my bow and arrow."

"But, baby, you've already shot an arrow, right through my heart." Richie grinned and clutched his chest. There was a low moan of appreciation from the group. "Little Bluebird and her overdressed boyfriend all the way from Sydney. What a gift."

"I'm from Perth, actually," Whitt said.

"Well you can't come through here without paying the toll. We own these roads, and they're not free."

The men had found Whitt's suitcases in the boot. I heard them clunking onto the road.

"I can let the boys find payment in your stuff." Richie licked his bloody lip. "Or, you and me, we can settle the tab together."

"Urgh!" one of the boys in the car cried. "They've got pictures of dead feet!"

One of Richie's cronies came around the hood of the car with the file on Danny, and the Forensics photographs.

"Check this out!" someone said. He was holding up my service pistol—and police badge.

Suddenly, I was free.

"Uh-oh," Richie said.

"Yeah, uh-oh, motherfucker." I shoved my captor away.

I wanted to pound Richie's face in. But I knew that arresting this lot for roughhousing us in the middle of the desert wasn't going to get me any closer to finding out if they'd killed Danny Stanton. We needed to see them in their natural environment. Let them lead me to some evidence. Whitt took my gun back from the scumbag who'd found it. They were all backing toward their car.

"What was that you said about a toll?" I was advancing on Richie. He never stopped smiling.

"Well, look, you guys can have a government service discount tonight. Free entry. Access all areas."

"Mate, that's so nice of you."

"What can I say? I'm a gentleman."

"Get in your car and get the fuck out of here," I said. I slammed the hood of their car closed. "Run away, losers."

We watched them backing their car into a turn, our things strewn all over the road in the dark.

"What luck. First suspects," Whitt said cheerfully. "And we're not even there yet."

As they pulled away into the night, Richie made a gun shape with his fingers, and pointed it at my face.

CHAPTER 12

THE CAMP WAS a great steel monstrosity in the middle of a plateau of rocky earth. A dump of tall machinery lit up by sodium lamps reflecting on the low clouds. It was busy, with workers in fluorescent orange and navy-blue coveralls walking along the roadways even as midnight approached, some of them carrying paper cups of steaming coffee. Diggers rolled along slowly, their flashing lights rolling over a mess of demountable buildings labeled with cardboard signs.

I turned as a troop of young girls in plain clothes sauntered past, giggling.

"Who are they?" I asked Whitt.

"Bilbies." When I didn't answer, he said, "Australia's cutest desert animals."

"Prostitutes? Way out here?"

"Three weeks is a long time for some guys," Whitt

said. "It's good money. Better than they get in the cities."

I didn't want to know how much more the camp *girls* were making than me. Whitt stopped the car at a demountable by the border fence.

"This is our donga." He looked at the piece of paper we'd been given at the boom gates.

"Bilbies, dongas. It's all a bit R-rated out here, Whitt."

I was about to push at the door of the tin building when a great hairy man wrapped in a towel yanked it open from the inside. He passed me with a frown. Just inside the door I was met with a cork partition on wheels, the same kind Nigel Spader had been using to build a case against my brother. The partitions made a long hall, dividing the small building into three tiny rooms.

"Turn left," Whitt said from behind me.

My "room" was smaller than most prison cells. There were two camp beds a foot apart, taking up almost all of the available space.

"This is for the two of us? Together?" I said.

"I guess so." Whitt was chest to chest with me in the tiny hall outside our room. "Partners *and* roomies, hey?"

I felt sick. I'd been hoping I could get some space to myself to have a small, private cry about Sam. When I cried, which happened about once a year, it was only ever for a minute, and only in complete solitude. I'd really been looking forward to this one.

I foraged through my garbage bags for my cigarettes. Beyond the partition, someone rolled over in their bed, making the cork divider wobble on its uneven legs.

I took a walk around the camp to clear my head, located the nearest shower block and peeked inside, listening to the men singing in the steam. I saw more Bilbies sitting with some miners outside a donga, smoking, hands riding up short denim skirts. As I passed a fenced-off area filled with diggers I noticed a long-haired miner sitting inside the cabin of one. He tapped a substance from a small plastic tube onto the back of his hand, making a rough line, which he snorted. He blinked a few times and straightened his hard hat before turning the machine on and rolling it out of the lot.

I was on my third cigarette by the time I had completed a full circuit of the accommodation side of the mine. Despite the shifts being night and day, music played in almost every donga and there was plenty of loud laughter, phones ringing and the smell of marijuana drifting from windows. The eyes of the men that followed me as I walked by were dark, hardened by exhaustion and lonely nights in the middle of the desert, dreaming of home. In the morning, I planned to learn what I could about Richie and his crew. But if that lead failed, from what I could see, there was plenty of badness going around the camp to tap into.

CHAPTER 13

WARFARE OF THE mind was just as critical to success as warfare of the body. The Soldier knew this from his training days as he watched the weak fall around him, saw their minds crumble under the weight of their duty. A strong mind could outlast the yearnings of the body for food, comfort, relief from pain. It took a mechanical mentality to operate in a mechanical way.

Fear and anger were the worst diseases. In Afghanistan, crossing west through the tiny villages around Nangarhar province, he'd been ordered by his commander to go into the townships at night and take a young woman. Drag her out into the desert and let her go running back home barefoot, her clothes torn, her wailing waking the whole village. Hen-plucking, they called it. His unit never violated the girls they stole—there was no way any of them would risk the possibility of their own flesh and blood growing up in the filth these people lived in. But the crying girls served their purpose. Their abduction sent the village men into a fury, sent the men in surrounding villages into shared outrage. Angry soldiers make stupid soldiers. They are careless, heavy-handed. Blind with emotion.

The female detective seemed to have the mental strength of a worthy adversary, the Soldier thought. But he hadn't observed much of her yet. Fear was the most potent test, and from the moment he laid eyes on her he'd wanted to see her fear.

It was 0412 hours when she rose. The horizon beyond the wire fence was only just turning gray with the coming dawn. The Soldier watched her pad across the bare earth in her towel and flip-flops, a toiletries bag clutched to her chest.

In the bathroom block, she was alone. He let a good amount of steam cloud the demountable then slipped inside. The side of the cubicle rose to the top of her small breasts. She stood for a long time with her face in the jet stream, sighing hard, looking almost as if she were going to cry. *Trying* to cry, even. It seemed hard to let go. The Soldier knew how that felt, how dropping the mask could become so unnatural, so terrifying. He wondered what troubled the detective. Whether he could tap into it. Secrets were a magnificent tool.

He crept to the pile of things she had left on the bench and crouched down. He looked through her phone. The web pages she had visited. Her pictures, of which there were disappointingly few. He did an inventory of her personal care items. Vitamins, and a box of diclofenac. He turned the box over. For the treatment of joint inflammation. He tucked the box into his jacket.

She had put shampoo in her short, dark hair and stood facing him, her eyes closed as her fingers raked at her scalp. He watched her pouting lips, looked at her naked body. The soap running down her hard stomach and strong legs.

She turned and he reached out, ran a finger through the wet tail of hair at the nape of her neck.

She gasped, and he ducked behind the cubicle door. He heard her rinse the water from her eyes, spit. Nothing to see. His whole body was hard with excitement. He saw her hand through the gap in the cubicle door as she reached down for conditioner. He rose slowly as she blinded herself again.

He made a fist and slammed it into the door of her cubicle.

"Jesus!" she screamed, twisting. In the pause before she threw open the cubicle door, he backed away into the steam then retreated into the darkness beside the demountable. He listened to her turn the shower off inside. She pushed the door open and stumbled down the stairs onto the earth, her feet immediately caked in sand.

"Who was that? Who's there?" she roared. "Come out here, you fucking piece of shit!"

She had a dirty mouth on her.

The Soldier crouched in the dark, looked at the well-formed muscles moving in her shoulders, her lean neck. Was she shaking?

She'd be a good recruit, he decided. He would train her to die well.

CHAPTER 14

IT HAD BEEN a night full of noise. Snores and coughs from the other side of the cork divider. Music from the other dongas. I'd hoped a hot shower would send me to sleep, but the experience left me rattled and angry at whoever had messed with me in the dark. I'd watched the light move over the ceiling, where a huntsman spider the size of my palm sat still as a stone directly above my bed. Whitt slept with his back to me, the collar of his royal-blue pajamas showing above the blanket.

I rolled out of bed in nothing but my underpants at seven. He choked at the sight of me, covering his eyes.

"Whoa!"

"They're boobs. Get used to it, roomie," I said.

On the way to breakfast with our contact from the mine, Whitt edged around the subject of my troubles. Even by my standards, I'd been distinctly unfriendly to him. But what was happening in Sydney seemed to take up almost all the room in my mind now. It was an incredible effort to talk to Whitt at all. I'd lain on the bed in silence that morning, checking news websites on my phone for updates on Sam, as he re-ironed his shirts that the scumbags on the road had tossed around.

Two girls had come forward in separate incidents, accusing Sam of assaulting them on bike paths, not directly in the Georges River area but in surrounding suburbs. One of the girls said he jammed a stick into her spokes and dragged her into the brush, bleeding and screaming. She only felt comfortable coming forward now that they'd found her attacker. She was sixteen.

"Sounded like some real dramas on the phone yesterday," Whitt said as we walked to the chow hall. "Anything I can help with?"

"No."

"Is Sam a friend, or . . . ?"

I stopped walking. For the first time, it occurred to me that Whitt might be a plant sent by Nigel's team in Sydney to observe me, find out if I'd known all along about Sam's supposed crimes. After all, how could I miss it? I was supposed to know all the signs of a sexual predator. I was supposed to be an expert in picking men with dangerous tastes. Maybe they hoped I'd get close to Whitt, confess to him that I'd known but I couldn't give up the only family I had.

He was standing there looking at me. So considerate. So caring. It was a convincing performance.

"Where did you say you were based?" I asked. "Who's your regular partner?"

"Perth." He turned suddenly and continued walking.

"And your partner?"

"Ishmael... Carmody."

"What was your former department? Who's your chief?"

"OK, I get it," he sighed at me. "I was just curious."

"Do me a favor and keep your curiosities to yourself, Whitt. All right?"

"No problem." He saluted.

I followed him across the camp grounds, watching his feet move through the dirt ahead of me. The cheerfulness was just a ruse, I decided. As gentlemanly as Edward Whittacker seemed, I knew I couldn't trust him.

CHAPTER 15

THE CHOW HALL was three adjoining demountable buildings crammed with fold-out tables and chairs. Groups of miners sat here and there, hunched over cooked breakfasts served on plastic plates. I went straight to the coffee urns and grabbed a handful of sachets, dumping enough sugar and coffee into my cup to give me a good morning hit.

I was aware of a presence beside me as I peeled open a milk container. He was a short, wiry man with a hard face, small eyes set in a permanent squint from what looked like years in the desert sun. A weathered hand reached for the coffee tub and slammed it back into its place against the wall.

"Coffee rations are two sachets a day!" he growled.

"Excuse me?" I said. His name tag read "Linbacher."

His uniform was different to the miners in their dusty high-vis coveralls and boots. He was wearing a white shirt with pleats ironed into the chest. I guessed he was some kind of security guard.

"Coffee rations," he said slowly, as though talking to a child, "are two . . . sachets . . . a day. You dumb or something, are you?"

"No, I—"

"Mine personnel daily rations provide two sachets of coffee, two of sugar, two milk. You're a mine *visitor,* so you're not even counted in rations. You already leave us in deficit. Then here you are, just loading up whatever you want. This camp gets a food and beverage run every thirty days, on the mark. If everybody just goes around using up whatever resources they want, we run out of food. You want that? Huh?"

"Yes. I want that," I drawled. "I want us to run out of food."

"Don't be a smart-arse."

"Look, mate, we're not on Mars," I said. "Can't you just go to Bandya for coffee if you run out?"

"That's not the point!"

Veins had begun to rise at the man's temples, so I didn't argue further. If he were to have some sort of stroke on my account, I wasn't sure the camp would have the medical rations to deal with it. I slurped my coffee as loudly as I could and left him to his sputtering outrage.

The breakfast offerings were prison food. I recognized the powdered eggs and thin bread from visits to Long Bay Correctional Center inmates to drum up leads on rape cases. The roast tomatoes were swimming in lukewarm water, and stacked behind the buffets I could see bean tins as big as beer kegs. Linbacher watched me closely as I surveyed the options with my sad plastic plate.

I found Whitt at a table near the windows, peeling the lid off a tub of gourmet granola with dried figs. He even had his own long-life milk in a tiny box.

"You're some piece of work, aren't you, Whitt."

"Avoid desperation with preparation," he said.

"I'll bet you've got that tattooed on your butt."

A miner walked to the end of our long table and slapped a copy of a Perth newspaper onto the surface. Someone must have brought a stack in from town. The cover, from what I could see, was a picture of Sam at a work Christmas party. His shy smile. The headline was a single word: MONSTER.

Whitt's fingers began to dance on the tabletop. Before I could discover the source of his discomfort, a big burly man in a miner's uniform appeared beside me.

"Harriet and Edward?"

"That's us." I stood and offered the bearded man my hand. His smile was wide and kind. He might have been early forties, handsome in the way farmers and desert people can have a kind of earthy wholesomeness to them.

"I'm Gabe Carter," he said. "It's my kid you're looking for."

"Your kid?" Whitt asked.

"Oh, you know, sometimes it feels a bit like that," Gabe said. He took a seat beside me, setting a white hard hat on the tabletop. "I was Danny Stanton's divisional officer. I've got twenty young guys under my supervision at the mine. They work for me, and they bring me their problems, personal or otherwise. Whatever they need, I'm their go-to guy. And that's how it's going to have to be for you two while you're on the camp."

"Why's that?" I tipped my head.

"Well," he laughed, then looked more serious. "Because no one wants you here."

CHAPTER 16

"THE MINE BOSSES are in damage-control mode," Gabe said. "Two months ago an exposé aired on *60 Minutes* with a couple of ex-miners from this camp. The program was about fly-in fly-out mining and what a difficult life it is."

"Fly-in, fly-out?" I asked.

"FIFO, they call it," Gabe said. "Most shifts, or 'swings,' are three weeks on the camp, one week back home. There are almost no permanent workers on the camp. It's cheaper to set the mine up this way, with miners flying in and out from major cities, than it is to put roots down and establish a proper mining town. Everything here is temporary. When the resources dry up, the whole camp just moves on."

"So what did the program say that was so damaging?" Whitt asked.

"Well, *60 Minutes* focused really heavily on the dark side of the mining world. The drugs. The Bilbies. The suicides. I mean, it's tough out here. I'm sure you've had a look around and seen a few things. The mine bosses don't want any more bad press, and they're pretty sure you two will bring it, whether you find out what happened to Danny or not."

We nodded.

"What do *you* think happened to him?" I asked. Whitt had taken out a notepad and was jotting things down as Gabe spoke.

"I don't know. I haven't the faintest clue. A lot of people around here are trying to tell me it was suicide. But I don't see it." He shrugged. "He was a pretty happy-go-lucky guy."

"Are there many suicides on the camp?"

"The lifestyle lends itself to it," Gabe said. "The isolation. The loneliness. Some of my crew have told me over the years that the job becomes a cycle they can't find a way out of. Out here they get big money and a secure job, and they don't have to spend a dollar in the time they're away if they don't want to. Accommodation, food, uniforms and everything is paid for. Many of them turn up without any kind of experience. They're high school dropouts."

I looked around. He was right. Many of the miners sitting around us were still young enough for pimples. One sitting near us had a full set of braces.

Gabe went on. "Some of the miners have young families, and when they see their bank accounts after their first shift cycle they go crazy. They buy big houses and big cars and their girlfriends get nice and comfortable and start having babies. After a few months, the boys start to wear out. They get tired, and they want to quit, but their families need them. They have insane mortgages and car repayments. Their parents are so proud of them for being a success. If these guys leave here, they're looking at twice the work for a third of the pay."

"Lots of pressure," I said.

"Oh man, do they feel the pressure," Gabe agreed. "And they don't tell anyone they're feeling so lost, of course, because they don't want to look like pussies. Sometimes it all becomes too much for them."

Whitt seemed distracted by the newspaper at the end of the table. He reached out and flipped it over while Gabe was talking so that the back page showed; the sports page. The gesture was swift, meant to be overlooked. I didn't overlook it.

"The camp bosses didn't want an investigation into Danny at all," Gabe said. "I kept going to them with my concerns and they kept telling me that he must have walked off the job. Gone nuts and went out into the desert. Some of the guys around here, they do go a bit nutty sometimes. If they miss a few return trips home, they start to get cabin fever. The isolation messes with their minds."

"Did Danny miss any trips home?" Whitt asked.

"No."

"Did he seem to you like the isolation was getting to him?"

"No," he repeated. "Not to me. He seemed like a happy, normal kid. I'm like a father or a big brother to these guys. I can tell when something's up. I kept telling the bosses that we needed an investigation. But I couldn't get through to them."

"So what changed?"

"We lost two more miners," Gabe said.

CHAPTER 17

GABE WALKED US out of the chow hall into the morning light. The camp was busy; miners were walking past us toward the main entrance where a security brief was being given.

"Hon Lu actually went missing two months ago," Gabe said. "But I didn't know until now. Like Danny, he just disappeared one night."

He handed me a photocopied picture of a young Asian guy sitting at a table in what looked to be an outdoor café. He had a shy smile hidden beneath a bright Australian flag hat, the kind given out free with the newspaper on Australia Day.

"Where'd you get this?" I asked. "Do you have the original?"

"I copied it from a picture I found on the wall in Hon's room. I thought I should leave the room as it was." He shifted, uncomfortable. "You know. In case we eventually find out it's a, um..."

"A crime scene."

"Mmm." Gabe looked away.

"How did it take two months for you to discover him missing?" Whitt said. "Was he one of your guys?"

"Yes, he was one of mine. My main team are all construction guys, but I have a small group of stores personnel under my care. Hon was in charge of food storage. I asked around about Hon on the morning he should have shown up for work, and his mates on the camp just said he'd gone AWOL."

"Why would they say that if it wasn't true?" Whitt said.

"Rumors spread around this place faster than lightning. It's possible someone just assumed he'd taken off on his own and then it became public knowledge."

"When he didn't turn up for work, did you check that what the other guys were saying was true?"

"I sent alerts out to find him on the camp. The announcement system goes all through the place, even down into the mines. Sometimes these guys get drunk or high in each other's dongas and they just sleep on the floor, so I wondered if he was just lying somewhere waiting to be found."

"Was Hon like that? Had he ever been late to work for that reason before?"

"No. But there's always a first time, I guess."

"So what came of the alerts?"

"Nothing. No sign of him. Someone said they'd seen him go to town the night before. There are regular nightly trips there. Guys hitch rides with each other there and back."

"Did you check with the hotel in town to see if he'd stayed?" Whitt tried.

"I did. He wasn't there."

"Then what?" I asked.

"I just forgot about it. I know that's stupid, but I was so used to people taking off." Gabe squinted at the red desert, his hands in his pockets. "These young workers, they come to work for a couple of weeks or months and then they up and vanish."

"And there's no system for chasing them down?"

"It's just like any other job, the mine's duty of care for the workers ends when they leave the camp grounds. The bosses tell me all the time—if they're not on the mine, they're not our problem."

"Right," I said. "They sound like a cuddly bunch."

"Well I guess they're only concerned with time, and money, like most bosses." Gabe shrugged. "It eats up a lot of time, chasing the miners down. You ring their phones and they don't answer. You leave emails. You call their wives or girlfriends, and they don't know where they've gone. You start to panic. You call the police, their parents, their friends. Then, after you've been sweating your arse off about them for forty-eight hours, you finally find out that they're in Darwin or Fremantle or some bloody place. *Aww, I just got sick of the work, Boss. It's not for me. I met some old mates here in Freo and I've been hanging out here getting drunk and I'll be home soon.* The girl miners are even worse."

"How's that?" Whitt asked.

"The guys deal with their loneliness by drinking. The girls deal with it by finding a guy to hang on to. When they break up with their boyfriends here on the camp they just run home without saying a word to anybody."

"So when were you sure Hon was missing?" I asked.

"I believed the guys when they told me that he'd just had enough and gone home. I didn't call anyone to check up on that; I just took him off the payroll and reassigned his job and his bunk. Then all of a sudden two months later his parents ring me. They tell me he rings them every month, and he hasn't called. They haven't heard anything. I tried to call Hon again but the number was disconnected."

"And you're telling us there's a third one missing now?"

"Yeah." Gabe handed me another photo. A small, freckly young woman with bright orange hair. "Tori King. Nineteen. Her sister's here on the camp. Amy King's been hassling her divisional officer for three days about Tori. Says her sister wouldn't have left without telling her she was going. Tori's divisional officer did the same thing I did when she didn't turn up for work: he looked, couldn't find her, and he didn't think anything of it after that. I only found out about Tori being missing after I started asking around the other divisional officers."

"What's the story with this one?" Whitt held Tori's photograph in the shade of a donga.

"She disappeared from the camp. That's all I know. She'd been to town that day, but at four o'clock in the afternoon she returned to the camp, and none of the

CCTV cameras on any of the gates out of the mine caught her leaving again."

"Where on the camp was she last seen?"

"In the rec room. She told the others she was going to bed and walked out the door into the dark. That was it. That was the last anyone heard of her."

CHAPTER 18

GABE LEFT US outside Danny Stanton's donga, driving off in a van. I'd wanted to ask him more about the kind of people hanging around the camp who weren't miners—Richie and his crew, and the prostitutes—but he had a workday to get to, one the camp bosses wouldn't let him sacrifice to help us.

I watched as his van rolled away, its cracked rear window caked in dust. Whitt was already sweating in the dry heat, pulling his tight business shirt away from his chest.

"The Bermuda Triangle of miners," he said, looking at the red horizon, which was interrupted only by clumps of spiky desert plants. "I don't know where I'd like to die, but I know it's not out there."

"We don't know that Hon and Tori went out there," I said. "I'll get Sydney headquarters to run a search of their bank, phone and email accounts."

"Good plan. Might as well add Danny to that search. See who he was interacting with in the days before he disappeared," Whitt suggested. "He might have announced his intentions to somebody."

We went inside the donga and found it split into three, the same as our own. The right and middle sections were empty of men. The cork partitions beside the beds were pinned with photographs of families, work timetables and pictures of naked women. In the leftmost section we found a miner lying on his bunk with earphones in, reading a car magazine. Above his head hung a poster of a naked blond woman, her legs spread wide and fingers trailing just above her hairless sex.

"Nice!" I said.

The young miner sat up and yanked his earphones out.

"This your sister?" I asked, nodding at the poster.

"What? No. Who the fuck are you?"

"I'm Detective Inspector Harry Blue, Sex Crimes. This is Detective Inspector Whitt, Preparation and Orderliness."

Whitt sighed.

"Is this Danny Stanton's bunk?" I asked, pointing to the empty bed.

"It was."

Danny's bunk was exactly the same as mine, but it had been stripped bare to the canvas. There were some personal photographs on the walls, but a big hole was left where a poster had obviously been. A white plastic set of drawers, the same as was provided to every miner, sat at the end of his bed against the wall. When I pulled it open, I found it almost bare as well. There were bits and pieces left behind—a stack of safety training forms, a pencil, some elastic bands and an empty can of deodorant.

"Where's all Danny's stuff?" I asked his roommate.

"It was like this when I got here," the young man said. "I didn't touch nothing."

I waited for a second for the miner to change his tune. When he didn't, I strode over and grabbed a handful of his hair. I yanked him off the bed.

"Where. Is all. The stuff?"

"Harry!" Whitt grabbed at my arm.

"I swear it was all gone when I got here!" the young miner wailed. "People can take your shit when you go AWOL. Those are the rules. You leave it behind, it's up for grabs. When the news came down that Danny was dead they cleaned the place out."

"Who did?"

"Everyone!" He was twisting, trying to pull his head out of my grip. "Anyone! People are in and out of the mine all the time! They leave clothes and magazines and shit when they go home and people take it if it's any good."

"Did you take anything?"

"No! Yes! Fuck, yes! I took his iPod." He waved at the device on the bed. "And some wank mags. And a couple of T-shirts."

I pulled his hair backwards. "What else was there? What did the others take?"

"His phone and wallet were here," the miner panted. "Someone took those. There was some cash and some books."

"Who took the wallet and the phone?"

"I don't know."

I pushed my boot down on his foot.

"I don't know! Fuck!"

"Where did everything go that no one wanted?" Whitt asked from the doorway.

"If nobody wants it, it goes into Lost Property."

"Where's Lost Property?"

"In the admin building! Stop! That hurts!"

I shoved the miner onto the floor. There was nothing more I could gain from being in Danny's former room. I took down all the personal photographs left on Danny's wall and pocketed them.

"Get rid of that poster," I told the young miner, pointing up at the woman above his bed. "It's not good for you. Staring up some girl's love-tunnel all day long. Fucking creep."

Whitt caught the door to the donga as I tried to slam it closed.

"Love-tunnel?" He smiled.

"These people are animals." I waved an arm at the miners walking by. "A guy goes missing for a few days and they raid his stuff like hyenas. I'm assuming Tori's and Hon's rooms were picked over, too. Which means we've got three missing young people and no trace they were ever here."

CHAPTER 19

WE LOOKED AT Tori's and Hon's rooms and found the same signs of possessions ravaged. The drawers had been emptied onto the floor in Tori's room, which she had had to herself. All that was left of her was a small pile of odd objects, hairbrushes and some scraps of paper. I gathered up Hon's and Tori's photographs and put their stacks alongside Danny's.

On the way to the administration building I called Pops, letting Whittacker walk ahead of me between the rows of earthmovers and steamrollers in the transport yard. I paused as the phone rang in Sydney and watched two young miners embracing in the shadows between the tall digging machines. Their hard hats knocked together as they came in for a kiss.

"Blue," the Chief said when he answered.

"I don't know what kind of hellhole you've sent me to, Pops, but you've really outdone yourself here," I said.

"Hello to you, too."

"I can't decide if it's a zoo or a high school. No one's over the age of thirty. They play shit music all night long and they have zero interest in finding their mates. The victims' possessions have all been raided. All the men have got their heads stuck in porn or drugs and I'm sleeping so close to my partner I could high-five him from bed."

"Any other complaints?"

"The food sucks. And I'm seeing...I'm seeing weird shit on the news about Sam." My bravado faltered as my voice cracked over my brother's name. I turned away when Whitt glanced back at me.

I'd spent the early hours of the morning listening to Whitt breathe in his sleep and thinking about Sam. I fantasized about calling him, imagined what he would say when we finally made contact.

I didn't do this, Harry.

They've got it all wrong.

I couldn't wait to hear my brother say those words, to identify himself as someone completely apart from the monster plastered on the front pages.

Tell me you didn't attack these women, Sam. Tell me you didn't abduct them, torture them, rape them. Tell me you weren't out hunting them. That you're not what they say you are.

"We've got three young women who have made fresh claims against your brother," the Chief said. "They're saying they were afraid to come forward before now, but they saw him on the front page of the paper and they know he's the guy. The third woman just sat down to make her report. Some items of interest were confiscated from his apartment last night. DNA samples and the like have been taken, both from Sam and the women who have made the allegations. We're organizing our material to lay formal charges. Right now, he's still in processing. That's all I can tell you."

"Who are these women? What are they saying?"

"Blue, I said that's all I can tell you."

"I want to speak to him," I said. "I want to speak to his lawyer, and I want to see a brief from Nigel on the case. Who's representing Sam? I want his number."

"Harriet, when it comes to this case, you are a member of the accused's family."

"I'm his only family!"

"Listen to me. You are family, and that means you're not a cop," Pops said. "You can't go demanding to speak to people. You can't go demanding briefs. We have to preserve the integrity of this investigation, and that means you have to wait in line just like any other civilian."

"Wait in line? I'm waiting in the *dark*, Pops. I'm waiting in the dark in the middle of fucking nowhere."

"That's right. I'm glad you are. Because if you were here, you'd be kicking down doors and punching journalists," he said. He was right. His voice softened when he spoke again. "I will call you the moment any contact is allowed. Either with Sam, or the lawyer. I promise you that. OK?"

I requested the phone, email and bank account

records for Hon, Danny and Tori, and listened to the Chief writing my requests down. The familiar sounds of my old office were in the background. Phone calls and quiet voices. If I'd been in Sydney over the previous twenty-four hours, it would have been far from quiet. My skin was burning with rage. I'd chewed my nails to pieces.

Whittacker was standing on the steps of the administration building, admiring the giant crane that marked the center of the camp, a fourteen-story-tall structure that was capable of lifting whole demountable buildings from one side of the camp to the other.

"One more thing before I go," I said to the Chief. "Has Nigel got someone keeping an eye on me?"

"I gave Nigel full administrative clearance on this case, Blue," the Chief said. "His surveillance maneuvers have been completely up to him."

So that's a yes, I thought.

CHAPTER 20

IN A CUPBOARD in the administration building, Whitt and I discovered shelves of discarded objects labeled by the date they arrived. The oldest was the "six weeks" shelf, which held items about to be thrown out completely. None of the items would be Hon's. I started pulling things out of the more recent shelves and spreading them over the floor, categorizing them. There were patterns in the types of objects miners left behind. The women left underwear, T-shirts and beauty products. Men left magazines, sporting equipment, shoes. There were the odd exceptions—a Monopoly set that Whitt looked good and hard at, a trumpet and some origami paper.

I pulled a notebook from the "two weeks" shelf and opened it. There was no name on it, but I recognized Danny's awkward, square handwriting from the safety training forms he'd left behind in his donga.

"This is him," I said, and sat down. Whitt crouched on the dusty floor beside me so he didn't ruin the seat of his pants.

I felt the prickling in my fingertips that I get when I think I've discovered something important to a case. Adrenaline climbing up into my throat. All cops feel it at some point. They look the killer in the eye. They find the bloodied knife. And that rush sweeps through their veins, as dizzying as a drug.

The first few pages were notes on safety briefings from Danny's arrival at camp. Then there were lists of scores and initials in what looked like football rankings. There was a crudely drawn picture of a miner smoking a fat joint and the inevitable pages of sketched naked women you find in the diaries of schoolboys. I guess Danny's teenage years weren't all that long ago.

And then, on the very last page, a row of words.

Killer. Dark. Hunter. Vengeance.

CHAPTER 21

THE SOLDIER SAT in the rear compartment of the sedan, wedged behind the second row of seats, his legs out flat and his hands in his lap. It was easy to recall the strategies he'd relied upon in the grasslands outside Kabul, standing sentry for his camp in the sweltering nights. In television programs, sentries wandered back and forth, smoked and talked, but in reality a good guard was as hidden and as lethal as a snake. He would stand with his hands on his thighs and his head up, eyes scanning the horizon, watching for the tiniest flicker of movement. He didn't move his head unless he needed to. His arms remained still, his breath rhythmic. He was a man made out of stone.

Sweat rolled down his temples now as he listened to the sounds outside the car. The two detectives approached with heavy footsteps. The vehicle rocked as they climbed into the front seats a meter or so from where he sat.

They drove, and the Soldier closed his eyes and tried to pick out the woman detective's breathing against the rumble of the tires. His body twitched and tightened at the sound of her voice, but he didn't move. He remembered lying in the shade of a tree in the desert in Janda, picking off young men coming down the mountainside with his Barrett. Giant black ants had wandered over his fingers, up over the back of his neck. He'd never flinched.

The gift of stillness was good for close combat, too. His platoon had stalked the alleyways through Peshawar in the fragrant evenings on lone agent reconnaissance missions and he'd taken down henchmen with his hands. In close quarters, surrounded by rooftops guarded by enemy soldiers, guns were impossible. Only silent deaths sufficed. He'd been the one to introduce the zip-tie method to his platoon. The zip tie was simply looped over the enemy's head and yanked tight. Pulled hard and fast enough, the thick translucent band compressed the windpipe completely, trapping air inside the lungs before it was forced upward in a scream. Strangulation was usually such a loud and dramatic death, because of the weakness of human hands.

The only trouble was putting the enemy soldier down before they ran off, gripping madly at their throats. If you could get them on the ground quickly enough, he'd told his commanding officer, their focus would go to getting air before getting away.

The Soldier listened to the detectives talking and

thought about what might happen if he crept over the seat in front of him and looped a zip tie around Detective Whittacker's neck. What would be Detective Blue's priority? Saving her partner, or keeping the car on the road? To whose life was she loyal—her partner's, or her own?

Loyalties in times of war are so very interesting, the Soldier thought.

CHAPTER 22

WE TOOK A table in the corner of the crowded pub, placing two glasses of red wine between us. The pub, one of only three buildings comprising the town of Bandya, was well equipped, with huge television screens showing the football, comfortable couches and vending machines full of snacks not available on the mining site. The prices were horrifying. I had a hot rush of guilt spending as much on a glass of wine as I would have on a bottle in Sydney. But then I realized there had been a strangely troubled feeling lying over me that had nothing to do with the wine, an unsettled tension in my stomach. I felt like I was being watched, and decided it was my natural instincts warning me about the traitor in my midst, the stranger posing as my partner.

A packet of anti-inflammation drugs I kept on me at all times was missing from my toiletries bag. I knew I had the drugs when I arrived on the camp. As a long-time boxer with a couple of vicious bouts under my belt, I suffered the telltale aches and pains from shocked and torn joints. When it rained, my wrists and knuckles flared with burning pain, my elbows and knees ached and swelled. They could rebel against me at any time. The drug was prescription, so I was deeply annoyed at whoever had taken it. There'd be no replacing it out here in the middle of nowhere.

Gabe Carter arrived and was standing at the bar with some of his friends watching the football, a cold beer in his hand. His face spread with a kind smile at his friend's joke.

"All right, you," I told Whitt. "Let's break down these missing miners."

I laid the photographs of Danny, Hon and Tori on the table.

"What have we got?"

"Well, if we're looking for a pattern, we don't have much on face value," Whitt said. "Hon's Vietnamese but the other two aren't, so that dismisses a racial motive. There's no gender pattern. Or age bracket. Tori was nineteen, Danny twenty-one and Hon thirty-one. Their backgrounds have no similarities. Hon was very well-to-do. Danny was your average working-class boy, and Tori comes from a long line of welfare cheats."

"Did you get onto the families?" I asked.

"I called Danny's and Hon's families this afternoon," Whitt said. "They're devastated, of course. There was no stable number for Tori's parents. We'll have to catch her sister tomorrow and get the lowdown."

"Did either family mention anything about the guys' mental state the last time they spoke?"

"Hon's parents said he was a pretty stoic person, so if he'd had a problem he wouldn't have shared it with them. Danny's sister said he sounded edgy but she didn't know why. He didn't mention anything specific. I asked her what she thought the words in the notebook meant. She didn't have a clue."

Gabe wandered over to our table and sat down beside me, aligning the pictures of the missing miners before him. Through the windows beside us I spotted Richie standing further along the building with two of his crew members, smoking under the porch lights.

"What's the news, team?" Gabe said.

"The news is dismal," I said. "We don't know how Danny died, or if Hon and Tori are dead at all. We're waiting on a Forensics report, which we'll get from Perth, and phone, email and bank records for all three, which we'll get from Sydney. Right now we have no bodies, and no suspects."

"Oh dear," Gabe said.

"So let's talk suspects," I said. I turned and pointed through the window at Richie. "I want to know everything you know about that guy out there."

CHAPTER 23

GABE LOOKED OUT the windows at Richie.

"Richie? He's the camp drug dealer," he said.

"You actually have a designated camp drug dealer?"

"Well, there have been rivals in the past, I think," Gabe said. "But it's just nicer and neater if there's just one dealer servicing the entire camp. Things just get messy if there are multiple guys for that sort of thing."

"How are the big bosses all right with there being a drug dealer hanging around?"

"Hey, some guys are going to do drugs." Gabe shrugged. "That's a reality. If they don't have someone out here supplying them, they'll bring it back from Perth, or they'll fly it in from Sydney, and that raises the risks significantly of the camp losing miners to arrests and the mine getting more attention it doesn't need."

"So the bosses just endorse it?" Whitt asked.

"They don't *endorse* it, but they don't try to stamp it out. It just happens, and it's going to happen whether the camp bosses like it or not. You get a whole bunch of guys, and you isolate them and give them absolutely nothing to do in their downtime, and they'll do drugs. It happens in the military. It happens in prisons."

"Richie and his crew stopped us on the road outside Bandya," Whitt said.

"Oh yeah, they'll do that. The Bushranger's Outback Welcome. I've heard that if they catch travelers they'll rob them. If they catch people on the way to camp they generally leave them alone—but they send their message, that visitors are not to mess with them. Richie must have realized you were on your way to the mine?"

"No, he realized we were cops," I said.

Gabe laughed. "That must have been awkward."

"It was. Do you know the guy well?"

"No," Gabe said. "I don't have anything to do with him. I'm too old for that crap. I've got too much responsibility."

A news bulletin took over the television screens, replacing the green football field with the cool gray of a reporting desk. Whitt put his glass down and got up, heading directly for the bathroom.

The first story was about Sam. I was afraid to look. I closed my eyes and listened.

"Tonight we bring you a Network Ten exclusive as more information surfaces about Samuel Jacob Blue's dark past," the reporter said. "We talk to a long-term foster parent of Blue and his sister, and reveal the pair's traumatic childhood in state care."

I gave in and looked. There were pictures of my brother and me as children, playing in the yard of some foster family or other. I don't remember how many homes we were shuffled through after we were removed from the filthy drug den in which our mother kept us. A picture of her flashed over the screen. I tried to remember if the picture was true to her, but she'd always been a blur of thin arms and slurring lips to me. I was three when they took me away. Sam was seven. We didn't know our father.

I was frozen by the shocking detour into my past in the thirty-second news preview. All eyes in the bar were trained on my history, my private world. Luckily, there were no recent photographs of me, and no one seemed to make the connection with my surname. I knew it was only a matter of time before the dots were connected.

When I opened my eyes, I realized Gabe hadn't been paying attention to any of it. He was watching Richie and his men outside. The sunset streaming through the window lit the dark red in his hair. I felt gratitude sweep over me in an irrational wave as I looked at the big man before me.

Thank you for not knowing who I am, I thought.

CHAPTER 24

GABE SUGGESTED I talk to the camp Bilbies, who might have heard something about the disappearances in pillow talk with the miners. I got out of the bar quickly and onto the porch where the prostitutes were grouped, away from the exclusive prime-time special on my life.

"Good evening, ladies. Detective Harry Blue, Sex Crimes…and Missing Persons, at the moment. Homicide, maybe. I don't bloody know anymore."

"Ooh! Hello!" one of the girls cried, a redhead with pouty lips. "Homicide, did you say? How exciting! Who's dead?"

"*Danny Stanton,* Jaymee. Christ." One of the other girls slapped her own forehead. "Everybody on the camp's been talking about it. She lives under a fucking rock, this one."

"Who's Danny Stanton?" Jaymee frowned. "Was he cute?"

"He's *dead,* honey," I said. "Right now he's about as cute as a bag of maggots. I want to know who killed him, if anyone. Do you ladies mind if I ask you a few questions?"

"This is just about the only time I wouldn't!" Jaymee said. "This is great. I've never been a witness before. Ask us anything."

"Did you all know Danny well?"

"No," a tall, dark-haired girl said. She was wearing a silver necklace with "Beth" written in cursive letters at the throat. She was so broad-shouldered and chiseled about the face I wondered if she was trans. "Stanton was a straighty-one-eighty. Too young for our clientele. Not that we didn't try. We always try."

"Did he have any enemies that you know of?"

They shook their heads.

"What about these two? Hon Lu and Tori King." I showed them the photographs.

Jaymee gasped. "That's the bitch what stole my hair straightener!"

"*I'm* the bitch what stole your hair straightener, you moron," another girl said.

"Oh. Right."

"You know, you're hot for a lady cop." The tall one, Beth, ran the back of her fingers down the length of my arm. "You could make a lot of money out here. You got handcuffs?"

"I'm presently engaged in gainful employment, thank you. But please, feel free to alert me of any future opportunities," I said.

"Too bad." She continued to stroke me.

"Look, I'm fresh outta suspects on this case." I slapped her fingers away with the photographs. "Who else should I be looking at? Anyone on the camp who strikes you as violent?"

"Oh, there's plenty of violence around," Beth sighed. "Some of the guys are ex-soldiers. They're used to solving problems with their fists."

"The camp's a good place to get a job if you're just out of prison, too," one of the girls said. "They're pretty laid-back about criminal history checks, so some of these guys are ex-cons. The bad food don't bother them."

"They're a bit freaky, the ex-cons," Jaymee said. "They like to play games. I'll be the inmate, you be the guard. Urgh! Weird!"

"Anyone around who particularly bothers you?" I asked. "Ex-cons or otherwise?"

"Well, there's Linebacker. What he did to the dingo . . ." one of them said. They all paused, remembering, their faces dark.

"What?" I asked.

"Aaron Linbacher," Beth said. "Everybody calls him Linebacker, which is funny because he's such a weedy little troll. He's head of security here."

"I think I've had an encounter with the man myself," I admitted.

"Yeah, he's a creep," Jaymee said.

"He's responsible for keeping the dingo population down around the camp," Beth explained. "His duty is to kill them quickly and humanely if they become a nuisance. Sometimes the miners feed them and the dogs get the idea that they belong, and Linebacker has to dispose of them. We were all sitting around one day and we heard a gunshot, and the next thing you know this dingo comes crawling around the side of the toilet block with its back legs shot off."

Jaymee cringed. "They were *off*. Like, completely off."

"I think I get it. That's a big caliber weapon," I said.

"I don't know much about that. But we were all pretty grossed out. Then Linebacker appears carrying his huge gun and laughing, and he just lets it crawl and howl for its life," Beth said. "We told him to finish it off but he wouldn't. He thought it was funny."

I looked around, excited to tell Whitt about the lead, and realized he was still gone. Through the window I could see the news on the television screens had moved away from Sam. The next story was local news, a bulky, mustachioed man in a police uniform receiving an award on a stage. The headline bar beneath the images read "Detective Ishmael Carmody and partner of fifteen years Detective Matt Horner receive bravery awards."

As I watched my new partner's cover story being obliterated on the television, the liar walked out of the bathroom and smiled at me through the windows.

CHAPTER 25

OUTSIDE THE PUB, a group of young people was huddled. They were a very different crew to the miners; many were dreadlocked and tattooed, their skin deeply browned. They might have passed for gypsies in their colorful clothing, but for their high-tech four-wheel drive. The vehicle's top was cluttered with satellite and solar equipment, huge fog lamps sitting atop custom scaffolding. Along the side of the truck someone had skillfully airbrushed the name "EarthSoldiers."

I decided to keep my knowledge about Ishmael Carmody to myself, to use it at the right moment to catch Whitt out. I stood beside him, watching the EarthSoldiers.

"Who do you reckon these jokers are?" I asked.

"Those are the activists," Richie said. His crew had materialized out of nowhere by our car. He leaned against the driver's door, arms folded. "Don't you go messing around with them, Bluebird. They're weirdos."

The activists unfurled a huge banner on the side of the truck that read "Money means nothing in a nuclear holocaust." Black-and-white pictures from Chernobyl.

When I turned back around Richie was closer to me, his shoulder almost touching mine. His men had surrounded Whitt. "Thanks for the tip, Robin Hood. But if you're going to answer any more questions, you're going to need a mint." I waved my hand in front of my nose.

"Your mama never teach you any manners, police lady?" Richie said.

"She was a prostitute and a junkie. Manners were thin on the ground."

"See, this is what I want to hear," Richie said. "My mother was a pro, too. We got stuff in common! Tell me more."

"Actually, if you want to chat, I'm up for a chat," Whitt said. I was surprised at his sudden assertiveness. He strode over and slipped between Richie and me.

Richie smiled widely. Two of his bottom teeth were solid gold. He jerked a thumb at Whitt. "Get a load of this pussy, would you?" The smile disappeared. "Mate, you're funny, but you need to back the fuck up out of my space."

Richie shoved first. Whitt shoved second, harder. I backed out of their circle and let them scuffle.

"Richie, I really hope you don't hurt that fucking guy," I said. "He's with me."

"You've got some big talk, Bluebird." Richie turned to

me. "Lady cops get like that. You manhandle a few city slickers and suddenly you think you're the big bitch in town. Well, what if I do this?" He grabbed the back of Whitt's neck.

The two twisted into each other, then Whitt took a solid punch to the stomach. He sank to the ground, coughing.

Richie was advancing on me now, sweeping his lanky hair back. He moved into the imaginary boxing ring I had drawn around myself. I loosened my shoulders and cracked my neck on the left side, where it was always tight.

Hands up, head down. Breathe, Tiger. Remember to breathe.

I put my hands up, ducked my head low behind them and slid into a fighting stance.

"Look at this, would you," Richie said, laughing. "It's Rocky."

Singing the *Rocky* theme, he came toward me, making all the big mistakes at once—face unshielded, body tall, feet set wide apart. His hands were open, ready to slap me. The underestimation was his worst mistake.

I stepped in, reached up under his arms and cracked him hard in the jaw with my right fist, my left clenched tight at my eye and my chin tucked against my chest. I stepped back again and bounced. He felt the pain before he saw me move.

"What the fu—"

His words were cut off as I stepped in for a couple of left jabs to the nose. I stepped out and bounced as he stumbled backwards.

There was blood in his nose, clogging it. I sidestepped and whacked him hard in the ribs.

Just play, I told myself. *Keep cool, and don't hurt him. He's just an idiot.*

I could kill this man with a single punch. I needed to hold back. His crew was cheering him on. He swung wildly at me, a full arm throw that, if it had connected, would have sent me flying onto the ground.

I ducked, shifted right, came up and love-tapped him on the chin. I heard his teeth crunch. I was back in the ring. I was losing my sense of time and place. I drifted, the way I did when I fought Pops, my movements becoming mechanical. He swung. I ducked. He jabbed. I leaned. I was hitting harder and harder all the time. I knew I needed to hold back, but my mind was elsewhere.

I was thinking about Sam.

Please tell me you didn't do it, Sam. Please say those words.

There was shouting, and I was jolted back into the present by people wrenching at my shoulders. The activists had stepped in, and so had Richie's people, dragging us apart. Richie was on the ground, blood running into his eyes and sand in his mouth.

"Fucking bitch!" he was howling. "Someone get that fucking bitch!"

The windows of the pub were full of eyes. I fought through the crowd and got to Whitt.

"Might be time to call it a night," I said. His face was dark with the disappointment of a man shown up by a woman. I'd seen it plenty of times in my career. He climbed into the driver's seat and I piled in beside him as Richie's people started kicking the doors and beating on the windows.

As we pulled away, I saw a light flashing out in the desert, a tiny pinprick in the blackness. I tried to judge how far away it was, but we were traveling too fast. The light blinked and disappeared as we drove off into the night.

CHAPTER 26

THE SOLDIER OPENED the door to the detectives' donga and stepped into the darkness. The moon was high. He'd stood outside the demountable building at 2234 hours and listened to the noises within for a couple of hours, learning the individual creaks of the two bunks in the far left section, the rhythms of their breathing. His body remained still as a stone in the shadows beneath the open window, until the whispers inside gave him cause to smile.

"So your mother was a junkie, then?"

"Shut up, Whitt. I'm tired."

"It's just a weird thing to volunteer to such a bad guy. Kind of... personal."

"Who knows who the bad guys are anymore?"

"What?"

"Forget it."

"People like that could use your secrets against you."

"He probably will. They all will."

"What do you mean?"

"I mean if you don't shut up I'm going to smother you with your own pillow. I'm tired. Go to sleep."

The Soldier knew what she meant. He'd watched her striding across the bar, her eyes flicking briefly to the television screens, her face set as her personal heartache was served up for the hungry mob.

Humiliation was an excellent tool for personal growth, a sort of ritual that could harden even the weakest soldier. There were countless opportunities for the young recruit to let their team down, whether it was by arriving last to the checkpoint on deployment, or by being discovered with an unsatisfactory bunk on the base. His squad had participated in the ritual humiliation of repeat offenders, of weaklings who couldn't fall into line. The soldier who couldn't keep his uniform straight was dragged naked into the accommodation square and beaten. The soldier who didn't keep himself clean was doused in disinfectant chemicals and scrubbed with a broom. The soldier who couldn't arrive on time was branded with a cigarette burn for every minute he was late. If he was of sufficient character, the humiliated soldier took his punishment with the pride of a man who had been taught something and who would never forget it.

What would her brother's sins teach Detective Blue? What would she do when her ritual was complete?

It was now 0227 hours. The Soldier stepped carefully into the section belonging to the two detectives and stood in the dark between the bunks, looking at them. Harriet slept the deathly slumber of the new recruit, dreamlessly, her lean body twisted in the sheets and one hand tangled in her short, dark hair. He leaned in close to her, breathed in her scent, making a memory of the smell of her that he would recognize on the desert winds. Already she wore the scent of her new environment, adapting as a true warrior would. Her hair carried the charred smell of the mine, the burning oils and ground steel, and her skin smelled of the land, baked sands and rains long gone. She'd be difficult to hunt, when the time came.

"Sam," she whispered, a frown forming then receding as she returned to her dream. The Soldier smiled again, a secret stolen.

He saw a huntsman spider wander up the cork wall beside the sleeping detective, pausing in the dim moonlight. The Soldier reached out and plucked the spider up, set it carefully on her naked skin. He watched the delicate creature walking over the bare landscape of her neck.

CHAPTER 27

THE MOUTH OF the main mine was the epicenter of activity on the camp. In the bowels of a huge pit, the sides rippled with rock steps as wide as a four-lane highway, a tunnel had been cut deep into the earth. The tunnel was high and wide enough to accommodate a Boeing 747. Miners in hard hats walked in and out of the tunnel in groups of two and three, moving to the side now and then to allow orange trucks with tires as tall as me to rumble through.

On our way to meet Tori King's sister we spied a group of EarthSoldier activists beyond the main gates, brandishing their gruesome banner. Whitt and I stood and watched as they harassed individual miners walking along the fence line.

"Excuse me? Excuse me! I was just wondering what you'll be doing four billion years from now?" one of them asked, following a pair of miners along the wire. "Because when they activate the uranium you're digging up, that's how long it'll take to become safe again!" As she followed the miners she held a placard that read "Fukushima: Never Again." She was a petite girl with a head of long, thick, purple dreadlocks. "What are you doing to compensate the Indigenous peoples this mine has displaced? How much money is their lost cultural heritage worth? Hey! I'm talking to you!"

Another miner arrived and the activists dropped their hateful faces and gathered around to speak to him. When he carried on through the gate, I stopped him.

"What's the deal there, mate? Are you friends with them?"

"Friends?" he said. "Aww, nah. Not really. I just borrowed a lighter from Shamma last time I saw her and I was giving it back."

"I thought the miners and the activists were supposed to hate each other," I said. "Aren't you guys 'the enemy' to them?"

The miner squinted back at the EarthSoldiers, who had resumed their yelling.

"It's not like that," he said. "I mean, we're all in this together, aren't we? We're all stuck out here. They don't like what we're doing but we help each other out sometimes for weed or cigarettes or whatever. They yell a lot but they're just angry at us about our jobs. They don't mind us as people."

"Do the mine bosses know you have such an easy relationship with them?" Whitt asked.

"I guess not," the miner said. "We try to keep a lid on it. They do cause us a lot of trouble."

"What kind of trouble?"

"Well, they're a pretty sneaky lot. They have raiding nights, when they get in and steal stuff. Like, they'll steal parts from the big trucks, usually something that'll take weeks to replace. Sometimes they lock bits of equipment together with massive chains. You'll wake up in the morning and half the mine is chained together, and some of those chains take hours to grind off. If they've had a really good raid the activists can get the whole mine shut down for the day."

"Right," I said. "How irritating."

"Well, to be honest, we kind of like that, you know? Secretly, I mean. Us miners get paid no matter what, so when the mine shuts down we all just go down to the pub." He laughed. "It's the bosses who get cranky about it."

"So the fact that you're friends with the activists is sort of a secret between the miners?"

"I wouldn't even put it like that, you know?" The miner glanced off toward the EarthSoldiers. "I mean, they're all right sometimes but their leader woman is batshit crazy. They're kind of like the dingoes. You can interact with them a little bit, but they're wild, mate. You can't trust 'em."

"Where do these people live?" Whitt asked. "Surely they're not on the camp?"

"Nah, mate," the miner said. He swept a hand over the desert. "They live out there, in the Never Never."

"Out there," I murmured, and looked at the horizon.

In the daylight it was fairly harmless, but I knew that as soon as darkness fell, a landscape that could hide an entire community of people was somewhere a lost or wounded young miner would face a real fight for survival.

CHAPTER 28

AMY KING WAS carrying a wooden crate into a narrow mine tunnel. The tunnels spread deep into the ground, becoming less and less well constructed as Whitt and I followed directions to find her.

She was the spitting image of her sister. Freckled and orange-haired, she looked like a child in her oversized high-visibility shirt and helmet.

"Amy King?"

"That's me."

"I'm Detective Edward Whittacker, and this is Detective Harriet Blue."

"Oh, finally!" Amy set the heavy crate on the ground. "Took you long enough. Tori's probably halfway to bloody Mexico by now! I been asking them to get some cops out here for days."

"Why would Tori be halfway to Mexico?" I asked.

"I don't bloody know!" Amy sighed. "You're the police. You tell me. She's got to be somewhere."

"Right." Whitt drew his notepad and pen from his pocket. "Why don't you tell us all about it?"

"Last time I seen her was in the rec room. That's the last time anyone seen her," Amy said. "She was *fine*, mate. Bloody *fine*. People keep telling me she must have gone and thrown herself into some hole, or shipped off to Sydney, or whatever the hell. She ain't done nothin' like that. So you can cross that right off your list."

We followed the girl as she took lightbulbs from the crate and began replacing those lining the ceiling with the new bulbs. Every few meters she unscrewed a bulb and gave it to me. When my hands were full I walked them back to the crate.

"Gabe Carter told us she just walked out and went off to bed?" I said.

"That was it."

"Did she say anything?"

"She said 'Fuck you' to me. I was wearing one of her favorite tops. No big deal. Certainly nothing to go wandering off into the desert about like some people reckon."

"Where are all of Tori's things?" I asked. "Surely you got in there and saved them from being raided by the other miners?"

"Surely!" Amy snapped. "Like I didn't try! Tori worked over on the west side. I didn't know she was missing all the next day and night. I'd had the fight with her about the shirt the night she disappeared—the Friday. So the next night, when I couldn't find her, I thought she was probably just avoiding me. Playing hide-and-seek so I couldn't apologize for nicking her shirt. Sunday morning, I still hadn't seen her. I asked around, and no one had! She'd been gone all that day. Without anybody telling me, they raided her stuff like she wasn't coming back."

"Everybody seems like they're just itching to get at other people's things out here." I threw my hands up. "Why, when they have so much money on their hands?"

"Because this place is a bloody island, mate," Amy said. "If you forget to pack your socks when you leave home back in Sydney or Darwin or wherever the hell you come from, that's it—you've got no socks for three weeks. You can't just go off the camp and buy more! If you want a fucking pack of cigarettes you've got to drive half an hour into town and half an hour back."

"But, wait a minute, I saw a vending machine at the admin office," Whitt said. "Wouldn't there be cigarettes in there?"

"Nope. If you leave cigarettes in the vending machine Richie's crew buy every pack and mark them up fifty percent. So whenever the catering companies come out to restock the machines, everybody goes and buys them. The point is, stuff is precious here. You should see how much these girls sell tampons for when someone has forgotten their supply. I've seen them go for ten bucks apiece."

"It's madness," Whitt said.

"Do you know what stuff of Tori's went missing? Was her wallet and phone still here?" I asked.

"I don't know, but I've seen a phone that looks a hell of

a lot like Tori's around. One of those Bilby bitches has got it. But she's probably taken Tori's SIM card out. There'd be no proving it's hers."

Whitt went to the heavy wooden crate at the end of the tunnel and lifted it, saving me my third trip with blown bulbs. He carried it to where Amy was. *So much for that back injury,* I thought.

"If I was you guys, I'd be keeping an eye on those whores," Amy said. "They're nasty pieces of work."

"I found them pretty helpful," I said.

"Yeah," Amy snorted, "they're pretty good at making you feel like they're doing you a favor. If they were talking to you at all, it would have been to find out what you know."

"Why would they care what we're up to?" Whitt said.

Amy stopped and pointed a lightbulb at us.

"Three or four months ago a guy from the engineering department screwed one of those girls and didn't pay the bill. I heard the Bilbies got together and drove him out into the desert, dropped him off at sunrise in his boxer shorts. No shoes, nothin'. Guy gets back into camp five hours later with second-degree sunburn and heatstroke." Amy shook her head, disgusted. "Not so helpful that time, were they?"

CHAPTER 29

WHITT ENGAGED AMY in some general chitchat while I jotted down in Whitt's notepad a list of inquiries I would make. I needed to know the full names of the Bilbies and their criminal histories, and whether the story about the miner who hadn't paid his bill was true. The medical center could tell me that. If Tori had left her wallet and phone behind when she disappeared, that was a bad sign. But a possible sighting of the phone in the possession of one of the camp prostitutes wasn't solid enough to pursue.

I followed slowly behind Amy and Whitt, writing in the dim light of the new bulbs.

"So this is what you do all day?" Whitt asked. "You replace lightbulbs?"

"Yeah. Pretty mind-numbing, right? It's the power surges. They happen all the time. Surge hits a particular line and it blows the lot of them." Sweat was running down Amy's neck as she reached for the bulbs. "Cheaper to just replace the bulbs than reconfigure the electricals."

"This mine does a lot of things the cheap way," Whitt commented.

"You're not wrong."

Halfway along the isolated tunnel, we came upon another tunnel blocked off with a wooden barricade.

"What's down there?" I pointed into the dark.

"Nothing," Amy said. "That's an exploratory tunnel. The miners went down that way looking for uranium ore, and didn't find any."

"Looks dangerous." Whitt squinted into the blackness. "It's not even lit."

"Lit? They should be destroyed. But that costs time and money, mate, which the bosses don't like to waste. Instead of filling them in, the miners just block off the unused tunnels."

"Do people go into them?"

"Oh, I've seen people go into them," Amy smirked. "Good place for a secret snuggle. But most people know not to go too far in. It's dangerous. Trip over and knock yourself out in one of those tunnels? Ain't no one gonna find you."

"How many of these tunnels are there?" I asked.

"Who knows? I'd say dozens. I heard some of them come up in the desert. But that might be bullshit."

"Wait. So you're telling us that if you could find an entrance to these tunnels, you could get into the mine from the desert?" I stopped in my tracks. "Just about *anyone* could?"

"You could, but you wouldn't." Amy walked on. "No one would want to get in here that bad. The exploratory tunnels aren't braced. The chances of collapse are pretty high. There are also black holes—tunnels that stop going horizontal and drop straight down. Some of those holes are kilometers deep."

Amy stopped, looking at the bulbs in her hands. I saw what might have been a wave of hurt and loss sweep over her. She was a tough girl, but for a moment her lips pursed. I could tell she was trying to hold back what were obviously terrifying thoughts.

"I hope she's not down one of those holes," Amy said finally. She lifted her eyes to me. "Tell me she's not down one of those holes."

CHAPTER 30

EMERGING INTO THE stark light of day was painful. I slapped Whitt's notebook against his chest, feeling dejected. Amy saw us to the mine entrance, where a drawn and tired-looking Richie was making a deal with a young miner. Richie glared at me through the eye that wasn't swollen shut with bruises, and then turned that glare on Amy as she went back to work.

"The more people we talk to out here, the lower my mood gets," I told Whitt, cracking my worn knuckles. My joints were already starting to ache from the pub brawl the night before. Soon the pain would spread to my wrists, if I didn't find those pills. It felt like nothing was going right.

"Our potential crime scene just increased pretty dramatically," Whitt sighed. "The search parties looking for

Danny went out over the desert. But they didn't go underground. Is it possible the dingo that brought his foot back to camp found it in one of the tunnels?"

"I don't know. I don't want to think about it. It sounds like an awful way to die," I said. "Let's not get distracted, Whitt, because at this point there's no evidence that the tunnels have anything to do with our case."

"I wouldn't dismiss them so quickly," Whitt said. "I mean, where did Tori go that night when she left the rec room? We know she didn't leave the mine by any of the official entrances, or the security team would have caught her on CCTV. What if someone took her out of the camp through the tunnels?"

"Amy said the exploratory tunnels are dark and dangerous," I said. "If someone was using them to come back and forth from the camp, they'd have to know them very well."

"And who does that sound like?" Whitt said, nodding at something over my shoulder. I turned and saw the EarthSoldier activists. They rattled the fences as a group of miners walked by, their fingers hooked in the diamond wire and eyes wide with anger.

CHAPTER 31

LUNCH WAS JUST as appetizing-looking as breakfast had been the morning we arrived at the camp. I stood gazing at the sausages swimming in oily, translucent juice, slowly baking in the overhead lamps of the steel buffet.

"What's the standard allocated portion of these . . . meat sticks?" I asked the caterer.

"You can have two of those snags, if you want," she drawled.

"What about this potato-scented glue?"

The lady put a hairy arm on the counter.

"You think that's the first joke anybody ever cracked about the food here, honey?"

"What joke?"

She narrowed her eyes at me.

At our table, Whitt peeled the lid off another of his

Boy Scout Cuisine delights. It was butter chicken with basmati rice. Butter chicken was a down-and-out favorite of mine back in Sydney; my treat whenever I lost a case, or my perp got away, or my victim failed to testify against her attacker. The smell of it made something in my stomach twist. I munched on my dry sausage.

"Sitting there staring at me like that won't make this meal taste any less amazing," Whitt said, stirring his rice.

"Maybe it'll do something for the flavor of mine," I said.

He leaned over and scraped some of his butter chicken onto my plate. I had to remind myself that he was a spy and a liar, and not my friend, as I gratefully accepted the food.

"How's the case?" Gabe Carter said as he dropped into the seat beside me. His plate was full of camp food and his helmet was caked in dust.

"Two words. Blake Korby," I said.

"I know that name." Gabe frowned.

"Miner. Engineering department. The medical center staff just confirmed that he was treated for severe blisters, sunburn and heatstroke a few months ago. A little birdie told us it was because he tried to rip off the Bilbies, so they dragged him out into the desert and made him walk back."

"Ah, yes, I heard that." Gabe nodded. "I was on leave at the time, so I wasn't here to see it, but I heard it was bad. I don't think it was over money, though. I think he got a bit rough with one of their girls and they wanted to send a message."

"Maybe we should be taking a closer look at them," I said.

"I don't know." Gabe shifted uncomfortably. "I don't know if that helps you guys at all. Those girls are not what they're cracked up to be."

"What do you mean?"

"I mean they're good people. Some of them come from some very rough circumstances, and when they act out it's because that's how they were taught. I don't think they'd ever kill anyone. None of them are that vindictive."

I'd got to know plenty of prostitutes in my work back in Sydney, and Gabe was right—half of the working girls I knew were gentle people caught up in the wrong life. But the other half, I'd learned, were like anyone else living on the edge of society. Dangerous and desperate, the kind of people who would do anything to survive.

"How do you know so much about these ladies?" I asked. I was surprised by my sharp tone. "You use their services?"

"No!" Gabe laughed. "Not me. No thanks. I know it from chatting to them. That Beth, she likes a glass of wine and a good gossip just like anybody else."

A smile crept over my face. I quickly dropped it as soon as I felt it form.

"Tell us about those activists, then," Whitt said.

Gabe's face darkened. "Now there's a bunch of proper suspects," he said.

CHAPTER 32

"I'VE ALWAYS BEEN very wary of the EarthSoldiers," Gabe went on. "I think they're smarter than people give them credit for."

"Why do you say that?"

"Well, firstly, they've been out there for eight months." Gabe pointed to the desert. "Sure, OK, some of their people have been swapped out for new people, but their overall presence hasn't let up. If you ask me, anybody with the money and resources to survive out there for that long shouldn't be underestimated."

"Why don't the camp bosses just send a security detail to shoo them away?" Whitt said.

"They've tried. But the activists keep their camp mobile, so whenever Linebacker gets a security detail together to go and chase them down they're not where they were last time. They know the desert. They know how to get in and out of this mine. They know which pieces of equipment to take down, and when they're going to be left unguarded."

"They sound like a wily bunch," I said.

"You don't know the half of it." He leaned forward. "Linebacker got a team onto them once and pinned them down in a cave out there. His guys come bursting in with guns and torches, and sure, maybe they were a bit heavy-handed. They'd been hunting the activists for weeks. They got excited. Well, disaster strikes when Linebacker's team realizes the activists are running a live blog."

"A live blog?"

"It's called Operation Desert Storm. Cute, right? They run cameras in their camp 24/7. These cameras feed video to the EarthSoldiers' website. The website counts how many days they've been out here, fighting the cause against the mine. People all around the world can tune in at any moment and see what they're up to, whether they're sleeping in the sand or protesting at the gate or whatever."

"Pretty powerful fund-raiser, I imagine," Whitt commented.

"I don't know." Gabe shrugged. "All I know is there was plenty of upset after footage of Linebacker's team storming the activists' camp hit YouTube. One of the girls got pushed to the ground and hurt her ankle. Even CNN picked up the video. They threatened to shut down the mine. The orders now from the bosses are that no one touches the activists. They're red-hot."

The door to the chow hall slammed and Linebacker

himself came creeping in, the wiry security guard going straight to the coffee station to survey the dwindling supply. While Whitt and I watched the man with apprehension, Gabe smiled and raised an arm in a friendly salute.

"Aaron!" he called. "Aaron! Borrow you for a minute?"

Linebacker shuffled over, his hard hands brushing uncomfortably at the front of his immaculate uniform.

"Aaron Linbacher, you've met Detectives Blue and Whittacker?"

"Meh," Linebacker grunted.

"The detectives are interested in hearing about the EarthSoldiers."

"The EarthSoldiers?" Linebacker looked away, disgusted. "Terrorists. Insurgents, the lot of them."

"That's a bit of a heavy accusation," Whitt said. "Can you really call what they're doing 'terrorism'?"

The older man glared at Whitt and folded his arms across his chest. "Terrorism is ideologically motivated violence or threat of violence," he said. "It is cowardly behavior designed to intimidate."

"I know what terrorism is," Whitt said, smiling. "I just don't see the violence or threat of violence in what they're doing."

Linebacker bristled. "On 5 April this year a three-ton steamroller over in the E7 quadrant malfunctioned while it was being used to surface one of the equipment roads," Linebacker said. "Our engineers inspected the machine and found that the brake cable had been sabotaged."

"The brake cable and the accelerator cable in those

things look sort of the same," Gabe said. "It's possible the activists got their wires crossed."

"That's not the point!" Linebacker snapped. "Doing something that recklessly endangers the lives of others for an ideological cause is terrorism! I talked to the fence group after the incident and told them what they'd done. Told them someone could have been killed. You know what they said? Huh?"

"What?" I asked.

"They said, 'Close the mine, and no one gets killed.'"

CHAPTER 33

THE HUNTSMAN SPIDER had taken up residence on the wall above my pillow, a hairy brown star hanging in a cork sky. When I turned on my phone, I found it full of messages about Sam. I'd been keeping the device on silent so that no one would hear the almost ceaseless bleeps that had started with the first news reports. I had sixty-two missed calls. The message list was full of phone numbers I didn't recognize, journalists from every paper in the country. I lay on my bunk and read them as Whitt talked with Forensics in Perth about Danny's foot.

Some of the messages were kind, careful inquiries. Some were not.

How does it feel to know your brother is a serial killer?

Harriet, can you comment on Minister Boyd's call re bringing back the death penalty for Sam?

Detective Blue, were you/Sam sexually abused in foster care system? Possible motive for killings? Please reply!

There was one number I did recognize. Julius Dean's mother had been a foster carer who had taken Sam and me on for a short period when I was eight years old. Julius had been eight as well, and very understanding of our strange ways—the anxiety about food I developed from being lumped in with hordes of hungry, unwanted kids in homes all across Australia. The plans my brother and I were constantly making to run away.

Julius, Sam and I had been friends until we had been moved on to another family. He'd come to visit me as I'd lain awake some nights in the fold-out bed in the back room, a bad sleeper himself as a kid. We'd talked about his mother. I'd lain awake after he was gone, imagining what it might have been like to have one of my own. I recognized now, as an adult, that the boy Julius had probably had a crush on me. Without knowing how long I'd be in his life, the boy'd probably been taken with the new and interesting little girl who'd come to live with him, with her stories of families and schools far away. I'd either ignored it, or been oblivious to it at the time. I'd never had childhood crushes. I knew I'd never be anywhere for long.

They brought Sam in here for a medical exam, Julius's text read.

I sat up. How could I have forgotten? Julius was an outpatient doctor at the Prince of Wales Hospital! They would have brought Sam in to the hospital to be physically processed. They'd have photographed him, taken samples of his fingernails, blood, skin, urine. If an insanity plea was on the table, an MRI and CT scan, as well as a physiological exam, had probably been ordered by Sam's lawyer. I texted Julius right back.

What should I know? How was he?

Julius replied almost instantly. *Big scratch on neck. Many small scratches on forearms. Consistent with fingernails. Old enough to fit with death of last victim. I'm sorry, Harry.*

My hands were shaking as I wrote back.

How was he? I repeated.

Cold, Julius wrote.

I put the phone away and sat cracking my aching knuckles.

CHAPTER 34

WHITT ENDED HIS phone call.

"All right," he said, looking at his notes. "Danny's foot tells us a bunch of things that might be very useful. Firstly, blood and tissue samples had a normal isotonic intracellular level."

"English, please." I stretched out on the bunk, my face in my pillow.

"His blood plasma levels were normal. When you suffer dehydration, your plasma levels drop. His didn't. He also had normal electrolyte levels—the sodium in Danny's blood when he died was steady."

"Uh-huh."

"So it's reasonable to conclude he wasn't out there, wandering around the desert, lost, for any significant period of time."

"What if he was, and had water with him?"

"I thought about that. If he had water, that accounts for his normal electrolyte levels. But listen to this: The team took samples from the mine sand when they collected the foot. The sand in and around the mine has high concentrations of the airborne chemicals produced by the mining equipment. Carbon. Petroleum. Ethanol. The sand in the desert is chemical-free. So if Danny was out there for any major length of time, the sand in his boot would have been mostly chemical-free. Deep-desert sand."

"And it wasn't?" I said into my pillow.

"No, it wasn't. There was a thin layer of deep-desert sand, enough to suggest he walked around a little. But not enough to suggest he walked all the way out there. Or that he was there for hours and hours."

I turned slightly. "So if he didn't walk from the mine, he got into the desert by other means. And he was only there briefly before he died. Not long enough for his boots to fill up with deep-desert sand."

"That's what it looks like."

"So what did he go there for? If he didn't walk, he must have driven. Why drive out into the middle of the desert?"

"No idea," Whitt said.

"If he did drive, why didn't the search teams find the car?" I said.

"Which car?"

"*Any* car. Say Danny drove into the desert alone, and died somehow. Why isn't the car still there?"

"Good point." Whitt made some notes.

"If he drove with someone, and that someone drove

the car back, who the hell was that someone and what did they do to Danny?"

"Exactly." Whitt nodded.

The darkness and softness of my pillow felt deliciously safe. Even straightening up again, opening my eyes to the room, seemed too much of a threat to my psyche. If I could just hide in the pillow, I might not think about Sam. Cold, callous Sam, covered in the defensive scratches of women he had abducted and...

"What's wrong with you, then?"

"Nothing," I said. "I'm tired."

"Well there's no time for being tired. Let's go grab you a coffee at the chow hall, and then we'll..."

Whitt's words trailed off. On the radio in the next room, the chatter and advertising had broken and the theme song of the six o'clock news sprang to life. I heard Whitt's bunk creak, and when I looked up, he was gone.

CHAPTER 35

I LEAPT UP and ran out of the donga after him. Half of me was driven by Whitt's strange behavior, and the other half was snatching gratefully at a distraction, any distraction, from my thoughts about Sam.

"Hey!" I called. Whitt was already halfway across the accommodation yard when I caught up to him. "Hey, what are you doing?"

"Oh, I just thought I'd get you that coffee." He laughed uneasily. "I thought we should go, and then I thought I'd just go myself and—"

"Cut the bullshit, Whitt." I shoved at his shoulder. "You think I haven't noticed you disappearing like a fucking ninja every time the news comes on? What the hell are you up to?"

"Up to?" he scoffed. "I'm not up to anything!"

"You disappeared last night just in time to miss a cute little news report on your former partner, Detective Carmody." I poked him in the chest this time. "He got an award. Strange thing though, some other guy got an award, too. *His partner of fifteen years.*"

"Cops can have two partners, Blue."

"Not in my department they don't."

"You're being very nosy." Whitt straightened. "I don't think it's fair. There's no reason for it."

"Oh, I just want to get to know you better, Whitt," I said. "Why don't you tell me more about that back injury?"

"Actually, that's a good idea. Why don't you tell me why *you're* out here?" he said. "We never got to that, did we? Let's get into it. Let's get into a long, deep discussion about *Sam,* whoever he is, and why you're having such a difficult time getting to talk to him on the phone. Let's have a discussion about why your phone was lighting up all night long. Why are you getting so many calls? Who's calling you?"

"You're an arsehole."

"*I'm* an arsehole?"

"Yes," I said. "And a liar."

"That's hardly an answer to my questions, Harriet."

"I'll answer your questions when you answer mine."

We stared at each other in the fading afternoon light. Some miners had stopped nearby to watch the fray, and as we fell into angry silence they shuffled on, disappointed we hadn't come to blows.

CHAPTER 36

I TOOK SOME time off from Whitt at the very edge of the mine, watching as the great red sun sank below the horizon. Though only three days, it felt like a month since we had arrived at the camp, and my heart was heavy with guilt that I'd made so little progress on finding out what had happened to Danny, Tori and Hon. Amy's eyes as she finally let the concern for her sister overwhelm her tortured me. They were the eyes of someone facing a future maybe completely free of answers.

Tell me she's not down one of those holes.

All I knew was that Danny's death felt sinister. And I didn't believe that Tori and Hon had taken off on their own account. The meagre physical evidence we had so far on Danny pointed not to a young man who'd got cabin fever and wandered out into the desert on his own. Someone had *taken* him out there.

And from his message in the notebook, it seemed to me like he hadn't wanted to go. Had the others met the same fate?

I sat on the stairs of an empty donga and browsed around the internet on my phone, testing the theory of the EarthSoldier activists and their apparent "terrorism."

As it turned out, there *was* such a thing as "ecoterrorism": violence threatened or carried out in the name of saving the environment. I glanced at cases of "tree-spikers" in the Amazon during the 1960s and '70s, who secretly hammered iron nails into the trunks of trees that tore apart the chainsaws of loggers. In some cases, this had caused the loggers serious injury, and tree-clearing programs had been stopped out of fear of deaths. There were plenty of groups accused of ecoterrorism for setting fire to mills, power plants and animal testing facilities without care for who might be inside. I searched for convictions, and there were plenty.

Marie Mason, twenty-two years in prison for burning down a research facility working on genetically modified crops.

Daniel Gerard McGowan, seven years in prison for burning down a lumber mill.

The FBI website described how members of two organizations in the US, the Earth Liberation Front and the Animal Liberation Front, liked to threaten and stalk individual employees of companies they opposed. They'd send letters to company officials threatening the families of the men they employed.

The EarthSoldiers themselves were an organization with environmental and political protesters across the globe. There were EarthSoldiers chaining themselves to logging equipment in Tasmania and more of them chasing down Japanese whaling ships in the Indian Ocean. There were EarthSoldier activists camped out in the desert in African countries, trying to disrupt bands of poachers. The pride of their website was their "live" protest coverage. Visitors to the website needed only to click and they could view real-time footage of several EarthSoldier protest sites.

I tried to view the webcam coverage under the title "Operation Desert Storm: Western Australia." A text message from a journalist interrupted the loading of the stream.

Detective Blue, 60 Minutes *producer Tony Gardener here. I'd like to offer you $400,000 for an exclusive interview on Sam. Let's talk!*

I pocketed the phone in disgust.

CHAPTER 37

OUT IN THE desert, I saw a light.

It glistened just once in the dark, a flash of something circular, like a lens in a pair of glasses sparkling at just the right angle in the moonlight. I stood staring at the spot where I'd seen it until my vision blurred, but I didn't see it again. It must be the activists, wandering back to their camp from the fence. I glanced back toward our donga in the distance and decided I didn't need Lieutenant Liar's help on this lead. I walked along the fence to the gate, glancing up at the CCTV cameras as I headed out into the dark.

I'd been a night wanderer as a kid. I was as moody and acid-tongued as most people my age when I was a teenager, but I was also exhausted with the game—the foster-system cycle that put my brother and me with young parents with big dreams. Couples in their twenties, looking to do something "different" and "daring" by adopting a pair of troubled teens, would take us both on for a few months' trial period. Sweet-hearted Sharon and Dashing Dave from Mosman, their eyes gleaming with hope that one day Sam would call Dave "Dad" and I'd break down in gratitude to Sharon for saving me from my destructive self.

The placements always went the same way. Badly.

Sam would give Daddy Dave one too many hateful stares over the top of his paperback novel, headphones screaming in his ears, and Sharon would become uncomfortable with a certain look Dave gave me as I lounged poolside in my bikini, and our new happy family would crumble.

So I'd walked at night to escape the pretending. If they locked me in, I climbed out the windows to tour the streets. I liked to know I could escape, physically, if I needed to. That they could shuffle me around, but they couldn't cage me.

The desert wind whipped my hair as I rose out of my memories and back into the present. I hadn't realized how far from the camp I'd strayed. I looked back in the direction I thought the mine was, but saw only blackness. I must have been walking downhill, I decided, and lost the mine over the rise of rocky land. I turned and walked back the way I'd come, but in what felt like ten minutes there was still no sight of the lights of the mine.

I must have been turned around somehow. I stopped in the dark and listened to the howling of the wind.

The wind had been coming from the east when I left the camp.

Hadn't it?

The sky was mottled with fast-moving clouds. My mouth was bone-dry. Where were the activists? If I called, would they hear me? Did I *want* them to hear me?

I'd tucked my gun into the back of my jeans as I'd left to be away from Whitt, a habitual thing I did when I was feeling like the world was against me. I was glad to have it. My gratitude swelled when I heard footsteps nearby, the sole of a boot crunching over slippery rocks.

"Who's there?" I yelled, drawing my weapon.

"I can see you," a voice whispered.

CHAPTER 38

"STOP WHERE YOU are!" I yelled.

"I give up," Gabe Carter laughed. "Don't shoot."

The moon peered out from beneath the clouds, and I recognized his burly figure in the dark.

"Oh, Jesus. What the fuck is wrong with you?" I pushed him hard so that he stumbled backwards.

"Sorry. I couldn't resist. I saw you when you came over that rise there."

"I'm lost," I admitted. "Hopelessly lost."

"I thought that might be the case. Luckily, I'm willing to assist. I'll show you the way back for . . . " He looked at the sky. "Oh . . . a hundred bucks?"

"I'll give you a hundred stitches if you don't shut up and take me home."

"Come on." He took my arm. "This way."

We walked in the darkness, up over rises and down

into valleys. I'd followed a gentle slope and gone around a curve, he told me, probably letting the stars lead me as they shifted across the sky.

"What the hell are you doing out here?" I asked.

"I like to walk at night. See the stars. It makes me feel . . . free, I guess. Do you know what I mean?"

"I think I do."

I had no idea I'd traveled so far. It was frightening to have been so lost in my own thoughts, creeping further and further into danger like a swimmer being pulled out to sea by a smooth current.

"It's like an ocean out here," Gabe said, as though he'd read my thoughts. "Can't tell the distances in the dark. No landmarks. Well, not unless you're trained to see them."

"What do you mean?"

"Over there," he said. "That's Venus. The yellow one by the horizon. If you head that way, you know you're going west."

"I can't see where you're pointing." I blinked. "It's pitch-black out here."

His warm hands fell on my shoulders, traveled down my arm, and I smiled secretly as he lifted my hand straight out. His big, hard fingers encased mine, taking my index finger and guiding it toward the distant planet.

"That way," he said. "The yellow one."

"Ah, right."

"That's Venus. That one's Saturn. If you follow that one, you're going southwest. The Square of Pegasus is to the north, there. That lot over there is the Southern Cross."

"I know what the Southern Cross looks like. It's on the bloody flag." I elbowed him in the stomach.

"All right, genius. So now you should be right to find your way home, then."

"No, no, no," I said, smiling. "You can lead on. I hate to interrupt a guy when he's doing a good job."

I followed the big shadow before me, strangely happy. Was I actually laughing with this man in the middle of the desert, even with all that was going on back home? Was I really thinking about his warm hands on mine, when all around me my life lay in ruins?

Over a rocky rise, the orange lights of the mine rose bright and inviting. My mood plummeted when Linebacker emerged from his guard station as we arrived back at the gates.

"You two." He pointed at us, and then the ground. "Here, now."

As we approached his office, I noticed Gabe's outfit. He was wearing a black tracksuit and heavy black boots.

"You were out-of-bounds," Linebacker snapped. "Do you have any explanation for it?"

"Well, I was just taking a walk," Gabe said, "and I happened to run into Detect—"

"You have no official explanation for your infringement. No special approval," Linebacker said.

"Infringement?" I scoffed. "Mate, don't get your utility belt in a twist. We were only going for a walk."

"Aren't you only here on the camp because one of our miners went for an unapproved walk into the wilderness?" Linebacker sneered.

"No," I said. "As a matter of fact, I'm not."

"He didn't walk out there?" Gabe asked.

"No. He drove. Or he was driven. It's unlikely but nonetheless possible that he flew. But he did not walk."

Linebacker stomped back into his tiny office block, slamming open the door and muttering to himself. I noticed a huge black rifle with a gigantic scope leaning upright in an electronic case bolted to the floor by his desk. An iron bar slid through the trigger, and a ring around the gun's barrel meant it couldn't be released from the case without a code. It must have been the thing he used to hunt the dingoes.

"I'm writing both of you up," Linebacker said, reappearing with a large blue notepad.

"Writing us up! For what, a detention? Give me a break." I turned and started walking. Gabe followed.

"This is going in the incident log. I'm compiling an official report!" Linebacker yelled after us. "A detailed summary of the type and regularity of security breaches!"

"Loser," I told Gabe. "Complete loser."

"Aw, come on. It makes him feel important," Gabe said. "He thinks he's at the forefront of everyone's safety. He's the thin blue line between us and the black abyss."

CHAPTER 39

THE SOLDIER STOOD nearby and waited in the pitch-dark of the tunnel while the traitor came to her senses. The walls of the tight space were illuminated within his night-vision goggles, the poorly braced walls and roof of an exploratory tunnel a long way from the main vein of the mine.

As she came to from the dull blow to the back of her head, Amy groped in the dark before her. She even swiped at her own eyes with the back of her hand, terrified she was blind. Soon enough the rich, damp smell of the earth hit her, and she realized she was deep in the mine. From the sheer heat she had to know she was far from the moonlit surface.

The Soldier shifted, and Amy twitched at the sound of rocks crumbling beneath his boots. Her mouth was open and her chest heaving with terror. The Soldier took no joy in seeing her terrified. For the sake of the code, he needed to give her the same chance he gave the others. He was a fair man—a man with principles.

As she was a woman, his duty would be particularly difficult tonight. Crossing through Torkham, it was the two women he'd encountered there who had haunted his dreams in the early months of his deployment, not the dozens and dozens of faceless men and boys whose beards and bright smiles made them all blend into one.

It had been a good trick. The younger of the women had been standing outside the crude house on the side of the road with what must have been her mother, holding armfuls of cheap plastic flowers and bags full of *sheer pira*. The two were waiting for the rabble inside the house to get into the cars and leave for the wedding. The young woman was garbed in traditional royal-blue and fuchsia robes trimmed with gold. She'd smiled so sweetly as the first of the convoy units stopped to watch the peasant family emerging in all their finery.

The young bride had taken out six soldiers herself with the bomb vest, getting right up close to the first vehicle's driver's window by offering the sweets. The mother had killed two more and disabled a tank traveling second in the line. The women always came up with the best ruses. They'd fake helplessness as their donkey lay by the side of the road, luring good men to their deaths. They'd run screaming from packs of men, robes torn, pretending they'd been raped and escaping into the arms of the enemy. They'd send their young sons and daughters forward to beg for water, strapped with dynamite.

The Soldier's detachment had slaughtered the phony wedding family. But the justice they served was too late.

He shook those bloody memories away now and tossed the mining helmet at Amy's feet. He came to attention and cast his eyes away from her as he prepared to give his instructions.

"Who's there?" she wailed.

"If you reach the surface before me, I'll let you live," he began.

"What the fuck?"

"The tunnel in which you stand runs east-west on bearings of zero-seven-zero and two-five-zero respectively," he reported, his voice filling the small space. "At its shallowest, the tunnel is one-point-five-six kilometers below sea level, and at its deepest is one-point-nine-nine kilometers below sea level."

"What the fuck is this?" Amy staggered, clutching at the walls in the dark. "What the fuck!"

"Four hundred and eighty-one meters along the tunnel running east, your weapon is waiting." He swiveled, and pointed down the tunnel behind him as though she could see him. "Four hundred and eighty-one meters along the tunnel running west, my weapon is waiting. We're green-lighted, soldier."

"Fuck!" Amy shivered. She bent and groped at the helmet at her feet, fingers wandering blindly until she found the light strapped to its front. "Fuck, fuck, fuck!"

"Move out!" the Soldier barked. He turned and began jogging.

CHAPTER 40

"OH MY GOD." Amy's hands were numb, her blood rushing through her head, loud between her ears. "Oh my God. Oh my God."

Her own words from earlier that day came back to her.

Tell me she's not down one of those holes.

Her throat was tight, but she wouldn't let the tears overwhelm her now. Whatever had happened to Tori down here, it wasn't going to happen to her.

She twisted the light on the helmet and threw it on her head. The tunnel before her sank into blackness as the light trembled on the walls. Thoughts flew through her mind, visions of what it would be like if one of the braces slipped and mud slid through the tunnel in a great wall, knocking her down, filling her lungs, burying her forever.

She ran, now and then skidding to a halt as she thought she spied a hole in her path. Without warning the blackness in front of her split and she was faced with a fork. He'd said nothing about a fork.

"Prick," she seethed. "Fucking prick."

The anger pulsed in her, and she turned, looking back into the nothingness from which she'd come.

"I'll kill you! I'll fucking kill you!"

Nothing there. No sound but her own frantic breath.

Amy sprinted into the left tunnel. The earth rose here. Inch by inch, she was moving toward the surface, toward safety.

She heard a *pop,* and her arm flew out. There was no pain, only a hard tug, and the last two fingers of her hand were gone. She glanced at the place where they had been and ran on, focused. Another *pop,* and she was knocked sideways as a bullet nicked her hip. She looked back, saw a flash, and heard the bullet sail past her.

In the tunnel up ahead, a shape. A milk crate, a large rifle resting on its surface. An offering. She leapt forward.

CHAPTER 41

HE FOLLOWED CALMLY as she seized the weapon. She'd used one before. She knelt and actioned the rifle, turned and fired a spray of bullets into the dark.

The Soldier ducked, smiled at the effort. Far too high. Amy threw herself into the opening to the right. He turned the corner in time to see her looking up the muddy rise. Light from the main entrance to the mine was dancing on the roof of the tunnel as people moved back and forth across it.

The Soldier felt his features set, his eyes narrow in a frown. He dropped a knee, aimed and fired. Amy stumbled and fell as the bullet smashed her left knee.

"Help! Someone help!"

He walked forward and grabbed her ankle, not ready

for the moment she twisted in his grip. She swung the butt of her rifle and cracked it into the side of his head, bringing red lights at the corners of his vision. It wasn't enough. He dragged her backwards into the dark as her scream rose up around the tunnel walls.

CHAPTER 42

I FOUND WHITT in the rec room, sitting down to one of the flavored lattes he had brought to the camp in little sachets. I'd left him sleeping and taken a long walk around the mine that morning, seeing it from all sides, the huge center crane seeming to follow me like the eyes of a portrait.

The rec room consisted of two demountable buildings that had been joined together to create a wide space that featured a gym with plenty of free weights, and a couch area for relaxing and reading. Some miners were working out on the gym equipment, while a healthy crowd was gathered around a huge television set in the couch area where a video game was being played. The crowd cheered as one of the pair on the couches scored, but I couldn't see the game over the shoulders of the miners.

There was a boxing bag hanging in the corner. I felt a little zing of excitement at the familiar cracks and creases in the red leather.

"Morning," Whitt said carefully as I sat down beside him.

"Morning, partner. Ready to catch this guy today?"

"I'm certainly going to give it my best," he said. "I've just got off the phone with Hon's parents. They want to fly out here, but I told them it wasn't a good idea. They're not going to do anything but get in the way."

"They're going to learn that their son made no mark here," I said. "That there's not so much as an odd sock left over to say he ever visited this place."

"Ah," he said. "Your cheerfulness has returned."

"I'm bothered by that, Whitt. I'm bothered that there's nothing left of these people. It's like they were erased."

"This whole mine's going to be erased when the ore runs out," he said. "They'll pick the place up and move the entire thing on to the next spot. The winds will blow in and cover the tunnels and fill in the holes and bury the equipment they leave behind. They're like gypsies."

"I hate it," I said. I really did—all the uncertainty, the ticking clock running down to pack-up time. It reminded me of my childhood.

"What do we know about Amy and Tori's parents?" he asked.

"I made some calls this morning chasing that up. Amy and Tori's father is a widower. The two girls took him to court and got an Apprehended Violence Order in 2011 when he tried to mow Amy down with his car. They've been on the run from him since then."

"He's not a possible suspect, is he? Does he know where they are?"

"By all accounts, no," I said. "He's on a fishing boat in Cairns. He's still next of kin, so Queensland police informed him that Tori's missing. He had nothing to offer that would help."

A silence fell between us, and the tension that had risen the evening before seemed to swell. Words unsaid played on my lips. Whitt was looking at his phone.

"Hon's parents said the last time they spoke to him was on his monthly call," he explained. "Hon always calls on the first of the month. I'm the same. Only it's weekly. My mother's always waiting for the phone to ring Monday night at six."

He looked sad. A rare moment of vulnerability. I watched him carefully.

"My brother is Samuel Jacob Blue," I blurted out.

CHAPTER 43

I LOOKED FOR that sparkle of recognition in his eyes, an instant flash before he suppressed and disguised his knowledge. There wasn't one. For a moment, I could believe he knew nothing at all about my brother.

"I'm sorry, I don't . . ." He shrugged.

"The Georges River Killer."

Whitt's frown deepened.

"Well, that's what the papers are calling him, anyway." I sipped his latte. "If you ask me, he's got nothing to do with it."

I let the fact that Whitt ran from any form of news remain unspoken and unexplained between us. Instead, I told him about the morning in Sydney that I'd learned Sam was going to be hauled in as one of the nation's most savage serial killers. Once I had begun, the words seemed to fall out of me. I gave up everything, hardly looking at him as I spoke. If Whitt was spying on me for my colleagues back in Sydney, he was now hearing direct from my mouth that I was shocked and appalled by what they were saying. The accusation was as much a surprise to me as anyone.

"We had rough childhoods," I said. "We bounced around foster homes until Sam was old enough to be my legal guardian. The media is making a feast of that now to try to explain what went wrong with him."

"What *they think* went wrong with him, you mean," Whitt said. "There's nothing wrong with him by your account."

"Well," I began. I stopped. The momentum of my confession had been so strong now new thoughts were coming up, and I could hardly tell what they would be before they were out.

"Well, what?"

"I saw some stuff on the case wall in Sydney," I said. "Photographs of the inside of his apartment. The stuff they found. Things keep coming back to me, too, about our lives. There were foster fathers who were tough on him. Beat him, sometimes. I don't know what else. He's always had a quick temper. He's always been . . . secretive. We were a great team, you know?"

He nodded.

"We needed to be a team, to survive. But there has always been a small part of him locked away from me. I could tell. There was *something* there, some part of him I could never get to. But isn't that the same with everyone?"

Whitt was listening intently. Half of me couldn't

believe I was being this honest with him. The other half felt such awesome release at saying the words out loud, seeing where they went.

"How can I think like this?" I asked.

"You're thinking like anyone in your situation would," Whitt said after a time. "You're confused. Anyone would be confused."

We looked at each other, and inevitably my old wall started to come up again. Alerts were ringing in my brain. Opening up was dangerous. I'd done too much damage already, and now my instincts were kicking in.

"All right," I said, standing up sharply. "We don't have time for deep-and-meaningfuls. Get up, and let's go see Amy again. See if she remembers anything, now that she's had some time to think."

I left without waiting for Whitt to follow.

CHAPTER 44

WHITT AND I TURNED the corner outside Amy's donga and almost ran right into Richie and a decidedly unhappy-looking young miner, who were standing there in the morning light. Richie's black eye was very dark, rimmed in the sick yellow of a healing bruise. His miner friend stiffened at the sight of us and shuffled off, seeming to take the opportunity to get out of a sticky situation.

"That didn't look like a very friendly exchange." I nodded at the retreating miner. "Bad debts?"

"Why don't you mind your business, Bluebird, and I'll mind mine."

"Must be a rough gig. You can't rely on those junkies."

"What?" Richie snorted. "Is this where I go rattling off about my drug clients and the ins and outs of my work so you can snap it all up on tape? Sounds like you're the one who needs schooling."

"We're not taping you," Whitt said.

"This whole operation has been very sloppy," Richie sneered at me. "The cover story about the missing miners. Obvious bullshit. You've been right on my tail since the moment you arrived. Well, here I am, sweetheart. Check me out all you want; I'm not a drug dealer."

I laughed, hard.

"I'm not." Richie shrugged his narrow shoulders. "You can believe the rumors, if you want. You'll be wasting your time. I'm a freelance goods trader, and I specialize in entertainment."

He whipped a catalogue out of his back pocket and thrust it at my chest. I browsed hundreds of titles of DVDs.

"Movies, games, consoles, books, magazines," he counted on his fingers. "I can get you foreign titles, rare titles and adults-only titles within twenty-four hours. I've got prepaid internet cards, phone cards, credit cards, mobile phones. I also have contacts in adults-only live action entertainment."

"It's a great cover story." Whitt patted him on the shoulder.

"It's not a cover story. I can show you pay slips."

I ran a finger over the catalogue and examined a fine white dust in the sunlight. The two men watched me.

"Is this cocaine?" I asked. Richie swallowed. I dabbed the powder on my tongue and rubbed some onto my gums. "Sure tastes like cocaine."

"It was a commendable effort." Whitt patted Richie again.

"Since you're such a magnificent mover and shaker

in the merchandise trade on the mine, maybe you can tell us if anyone has been shuffling these items around." I took my notebook from my back pocket. "A black iPhone in a blue case, belonging to Danny Stanton. A white iPhone in a pink case, belonging to Tori King. A tablet, silver, possibly an iPad, belonging to Hon—"

"I wouldn't know about any of that stuff." Richie waved a dismissive hand. "I missed the pickings on all of those. That's why I'm here bright and early today to get Amy's stuff. Someone said she's got a new laptop."

"Amy?" I glanced at Whitt. "Amy King?"

"Yes, Amy King." Richie gestured to the donga beside us. "I got the lowdown. She missed her shift last night, and no one's seen her. Missed roll call this morning, too. My contact's about to turn up and tell me if she checked in at her shift this morning. I heard she's taken off to Darwin to find her sister, so if that damn laptop's there, it's mine."

I shoved Richie out of the way and ran up the steps into the demountable. Amy's section was messy, except for the bed, which was tightly made. A plastic bag by the windowsill caught my attention, and I went there, lifted two takeaway boxes out into the light. Pub food. The lid was off the top box, and a plastic fork lay on the floor. The receipt at the bottom of the bag read a purchase time of 1837. She'd bought dinner to keep her going through her night shift. She'd come home, opened the first box…and something had happened to her.

Someone had been lying in wait.

CHAPTER 45

WHITT FOLLOWED ME into the chow hall, his phone pressed to his ear as he reported Amy missing to his boss in Perth.

I found Gabe Carter putting on his hard hat and gathering his empty plate and cutlery.

"Amy's gone," I said breathlessly. "I want a full search of the mine. All the miners need to be called out and accounted for. How do I get one of those alerts going?"

"Wait—what?" Gabe shook his head. "Amy King, you mean?"

"She's gone!"

"How do you know?"

"Just fucking trust me," I snapped. "Who do I see about a search party out in the desert?"

My face was flushed, my neck burned—the familiar

sensation of extreme guilt. Had talking to Amy out in the open put her in danger? Whoever the killer was, had he seen her walking us out of the mine? Had he deemed Amy a threat?

Who had been there in those moments? There had been dozens of miners walking in and out, driving trucks, working in the tunnels that ran off the sides of the main vein. I couldn't remember anyone specific, anyone who had already piqued my curiosity.

I realized I was cracking my aching knuckles, staring into space.

"OK. Perth headquarters know she's missing now." Whitt hung up his phone. "They're going to see what her phone and accounts are doing and put out a BOLO in and around Perth. But they won't send a chopper until we get confirmation she's not on the mine. Failing that, they'll take a request from the mine bosses."

"Good luck with that," Gabe said. "You're not going to get the bosses to empty the mine or send out a search party. This place shuts down, you're talking tens of thousands of dollars in losses per hour."

"Let's just keep our heads," I told Whitt, talking more to myself than to him. "She could still be here."

"Those King girls, they were out at the EarthSoldier camp now and then, as I recall," Gabe said. "When the camp weed was low a few people used to go out there. Made friends with them, sort of. I know Tori used to go. Maybe Amy went to question them."

"Right," I said, turning to Whitt. "We've got to go see them. If she's not on the camp, I want to know she's not nearby either."

"I'll go into town, see if anyone's seen her there," Gabe offered. "I'll get someone to cover my shift. If you guys go into the desert, don't be stupid." Gabe pointed at me. "Take a satellite phone, and a hat, sunscreen and water. Lots of water. The EarthSoldiers' camp won't be far, but it's serious out there. We don't need anyone else getting lost."

CHAPTER 46

I JOGGED BACK to the demountable to change my boots and grab sunscreen, my heart still hammering in my chest. I needed to get a hold of myself. It was entirely possible Amy was still on the mine somewhere, that we'd meet her on the way back from the EarthSoldiers' camp, a sudden urge to speak to them having overtaken her the night before in the midst of unpacking her dinner. It didn't make any sense. But all I could do was look for her, and if I didn't find her, I'd panic then.

As I entered our donga, a loudspeaker announcement sounded somewhere nearby, preceded by shrill musical tones.

"Amy King, please report to the administration office immediately. Amy King, please report to the administration office immediately."

I stopped just inside the doorway to my and Whitt's

section. On the window, the huntsman spider had been smashed to death, its hairy legs adhered to the glass by the sticky yellow of its innards. I felt revulsion swell up in me.

"Whitt!" I whirled around, hearing him walking up the stairs of the donga.

"Yes?"

"You killed the fucking spider?" I could hear the horror in my own voice. There was a pause as he tried to understand what I was saying. He rounded the corner, his brow furrowed.

"Huh?"

"The spider, you arsehole." I gestured to the mess on the window. "What'd you do that for? You know they're harmless, right?"

"Oh no." He balked at the sight of it on the glass. "Yes, I've seen it getting around the room. It was on the ceiling last night. I've rather been getting to enjoy its company. It was like a weird little pet."

"So why the fuck did you kill it?"

"I didn't! I didn't do this, are you crazy?"

"What, so someone else came in here and smashed it all over the window and just left it for us to find?"

"It seems so." He shrugged.

I went to my bed and started unlacing my boots while he stared at the spider. It was so strange for him to talk about the thing in exactly the sense I'd been thinking about it—a mild enjoyment in a hard world, a quirky little pet. But I didn't believe anyone else would have come into our room and hung around long enough to notice the thing and hunt it down. Why would anyone come into our room at all? There was nothing here of value or interest.

I was trying to decide why Whitt would lie about something so strange and cruel when I spied the corner of a familiar box poking out from beneath his pillow. I stood and slapped the pillow off the bed, snatching up my packet of diclofenac.

"What the fuck?" I said slowly.

Whitt was standing in the doorway, watching me. "Wh—"

"Don't," I said, putting up a finger. "Don't play dumb. You knew I've been looking for these. I told you to keep an eye out for them. You knew that I needed them."

"Harriet," Whitt said, "I did not put those there."

I found that my fists were clenched, the box squashed, the pill packet crackling. Through the throbbing fury, the blood rushing through my head, the alert for Amy sounded again in the distance.

"We're going to go and look for Amy," I said. "And then we're going to talk about you fucking off back to Perth and leaving me here to handle this myself. I don't trust you. And if we can't trust each other, we're wasting our time out here."

"Harriet, I—"

"Shut it." I pulled my hiking boots on. "Just shut it, Whitt. You can only make it worse."

I glanced at the wreckage of the spider as I walked past him out of the demountable, letting my eyes flick to his for the briefest of seconds. He looked mortified. He was a great liar.

CHAPTER 47

OK, I REASONED. *So it's possible your partner is not only a spy for Homicide back in Sydney, but also some kind of mind game–playing weirdo.*

I trudged through the desert, Whitt a few meters behind me, sweat rolling down my temples and along my jawline.

Weirdos, I could handle. It was weirdos who liked games of power, brutality and submission that made up most of my caseload back in the Sex Crimes department. The controlled, buttoned-up type like Whitt who liked to mess around with a woman's confidence was admittedly in the more dangerous category. They were the husbands who put GPS sensors on the bottom of their wives' cars. The boyfriends who turned a woman against her friends with complex secrets and lies, who cut her off from her support network. The ones who took and hid her personal items so she'd wonder if she was going crazy, so she'd be on edge, so she'd be easier to control.

They were the ones who hurt animals, to demonstrate to her what might happen if she crossed the line.

A squished spider was a very subtle message. But it meant something, or he wouldn't have left it there for me to find.

The dry desert heat seared in my throat. I stopped and let Whitt catch up, looking at the rough map Gabe had drawn me. As we were leaving the camp, the alert for Amy was sounding. She'd not responded in the twenty minutes it had been active. I knew the message was echoing in the sound system deep underground, over handheld radios and through speakers on the ceilings in the rec room, the admin building, the chow hall. It was playing across the truck yards and throughout the sun-scorched pumping stations.

She wasn't answering.

I swallowed hard and wiped my brow.

"It's pretty serious out here." I took off my cap and fanned my face. "It's not even midday yet."

"Look at the heat haze." He squinted into the horizon. Great mirages had opened up on the desert flats, looking like wide black lakes. Sweat was running into my eyes. I crouched on my burning legs.

"They get camels out here, you know," he said. "There is something like half a million feral camels in the Outback. The British brought them over during colonization."

"I'm sure they fit right in." I folded the map. "This way. We've got to cut through a valley up ahead."

A massive gorge swelled before us, sloping sides covered in crumbling yellow rock. We descended carefully, dropping down cliffs sometimes taller than ourselves.

"Fossils!" Whitt paused ahead of me as we hit the bottom, pointing with his water bottle. "There must have been a river through here at one time."

"Hurry up." I walked past. "This is a missing persons hunt, not National Geographic."

Whitt's water bottle flew out of his hand with a loud *pop,* smacking against the flat rock behind him.

The sound of the gunshot came second, thundering around the valley in a series of echoing claps.

We both stopped, Whitt with his hand still extended, trying to decide what had happened. More gunshots hit the dry clay around us, sending up great puffs of smoke.

"Get down!" Whitt dove toward the nearest rock, leaving me to scramble behind him. The shots pattered the ground at my heels, the whole valley now filled with deafening blasts overlapping, shuddering in my eardrums.

"Jesus!" I panted. "Where is he? Can you see anything?"

Whitt peered through a crack in the boulders, looking at the upper edge of the valley. There was no telling what direction the gunshots were coming from. I huddled close to the warm rock, my hands and knees aching, scraped raw as I had clambered along the ground to safety. I looked behind me and saw that all that was left of Whitt's water bottle was a cap and a fragment of charred plastic. Big caliber weapon, with a pretty serious scope. The gunshots ended, leaving only the painful ringing of our traumatized eardrums in their wake.

We were pinned in direct sunlight.

My hands were shaking as I gripped at the rock.

CHAPTER 48

THE TREMBLING IN my limbs wore off after fifteen minutes, but tension remained, making my muscles ache. We were crouched behind a rock that was merely waist-high, but when we tried to shift sideways to a bigger shelter the gunshots started up again, sending shards of clay flying.

"It's not the activists, surely," Whitt said.

"Only Gabe Carter knows we're out here," I said. "Unless someone has been watching us this whole time."

"Maybe the same someone who stole your pills," he said.

I snorted sand and dust from my nose. I wanted to snap at him, but I couldn't fight with Whitt now, not while both our lives were on the line. If we were going to get out of this alive, it was going to have to be a team effort.

The sun crept overhead, baking my uncovered forearms and the back of my neck. We sipped from the remaining water bottle and reapplied sunscreen, but we were in direct light, and our body temperatures would send us into heatstroke if they kept rising. In twenty minutes, we were both breathing through our mouths in short inhalations, our clothes drenched with sweat.

I slid back against the rock and Whitt followed.

"Well, this is pretty shit," he said suddenly. I couldn't help but laugh. It was so out of character for him. I couldn't stop for a minute or so. When I looked up, there was a sort of relief in his face that the strain between us had eased again, if only briefly.

"I'm not a threat to you," Whitt said.

"Whatever."

"No, really. My coming out here to the mine has nothing to do with you."

"So why lie about it?"

He wiped his face on his T-shirt, hid there for a while in the dark folds. When I'd decided no answer was coming, he lifted his head and spoke.

"I wasn't in Drug squad in Perth," he said. "I was in Homicide."

I watched as he struggled, looking at his hands in his lap.

"Couple of years ago I was on the case of a murdered kid. Seven years old. Some long-haul trucker found her body in a ditch. All the leads in the case pointed to these three brothers who had child pornography links. It was grim, the whole thing. It just ruined me for a while there.

I went through two partners. No one could take it. The nightmares."

"I'll bet," I said.

"I had nothing on these guys. They were slippery as eels. Every time I thought I had something to pin them with, they just seemed to wriggle out of my hands. Their father was a lawyer. A very imaginative one. I chased them for a year, totally obsessed. I used to pick one and follow them around on my days off, just hoping they would lead me to something. They were all I talked about, the Cattair brothers. A few months of that and my friends started turning away from me. I got lonely. And, you know," he said, smirking bitterly, "there's one friend who'll never leave you."

"The bottle," I said.

"That's right."

"What a mess." I found myself smiling sadly.

"It gets messier," he said. "My whole life was collapsing. My apartment was a wreck. I wasn't showering or eating for days at a time. It felt like my whole success or failure as a human being was tied up with these three guys. So I just... I went for it. I planted evidence."

I couldn't believe he was telling me this. I'd almost forgotten all about the valley around us, the gunman. The heat was making everything surreal. White lights flashed at the corners of my eyes and my head pounded.

"It didn't work, of course," Whitt said. "It was such a colossal disaster, in fact, that the Feds came in and threatened to lock me up for it. There was a giant cover-up, which is the only reason I was able to keep my job.

But the Cattair brothers are well beyond our reach now. They'll never be tried for what they did."

He chewed his lip, searched the huge blue sky.

"I'm very particular now," he said. "The obsession is almost reversed. If my life isn't totally organized, totally prepared, I feel like everything is falling apart. Something as small as an unironed shirt can set me off, make me feel like I'm coming off the rails. When I planted that evidence, Blue, I let go of everything. My morals. My self. My grip on reality. What if I do something like that again? What if I do something *worse?*"

I understood what he was saying about having a firm grip on the steering wheel of life. I'd felt, for days, like I was losing mine. Maybe my suspicions about Whitt had been that obsession he was talking about—that desperate need to hold on tight.

"I don't watch the news because I don't want to see anything about them," he said. "The Cattair brothers. They'll kill again. I know they will. And when they do, it'll be my fault. They're out there in the world right now because of me."

"You were trying to do the right thing." I reached for his hand.

"I'm a cop." He shifted away. "There are no excuses."

Whitt was thumped forward suddenly, and I heard the telltale crack of the gun. He gasped and scrambled up into a crouch, gripping his arm. He fondled the torn fabric. A graze.

"He's circled around," Whitt said, looking up at the valley wall. "We've got to get out of here."

CHAPTER 49

WE MOVED, MAKING a run for a group of rocks that blocked us from where we guessed the shooter was. Only a few gunshots split the air. The rocks were bigger, and I felt instant relief as their shade fell over me. Every muscle in my legs throbbed. Whitt peered over the top and a bullet popped into the rocks behind us, spraying dust.

"This almost feels like a game," I said. "He could easily have taken us out on that run."

"I've heard about stuff like this from a colleague who served in Afghanistan," Whitt panted. "He'd seen Black Ops snipers training in the desert using the villagers as game pieces. You wait until they wander out into the plains, then you see if you can drive them where you want them to go. He saw guys force some teenagers off a cliff, herding them with gunshots."

"So we won't move," I said. "We'll refuse to play. When it gets dark we'll make a run for it. Unless..."

"What?"

"Unless he has night vision." I'd started shaking again. "We've got to get out of here, Whitt. If Gabe sends someone out to find us we'll be leading them right into a trap."

"Then we'll have to keep moving." He glanced up toward the valley wall. "We might find a tunnel or something. Those rocks over there. You ready? Let's go."

As brave as he sounded, Whitt hesitated for a second, rocking on his heels, before sprinting across the distance to the next pile of rocks. I ran after him, and it was only when I had cleared the shade of my hideout that the shooting began.

I slid in the gravel as the gunshots hammered the ground before me. There was no choice but to dive into a shallow depression, flat on my face. I tucked my body up against the side of the tiny ridge. A golden scorpion, driven up through the sand by my landing, scuttled away from me, its tail curled.

Whitt was crouched behind the rocks we'd been aiming for, his eyes wild. Now that the shooter had split us up, we couldn't collaborate. Whitt covered his face for a few seconds, thinking. The sun burned on the back of my neck, searing already scorched skin.

When I looked up, Whitt was tapping his chest and pointing down the valley, mouthing words.

I'll draw him away.

He pointed to the lip of the valley above us, the slope leading to the sky. He pointed to his own eyes.

You run up there. Try to get a look at the shooter.

I raised my middle finger. *Fuck you. I'll draw him away. You run up the ridge.*

I knew I was the better runner, and with my background in the ring, I'd be the more sure-footed of the two of us on the loose rocks. Yes, making myself the target was the more dangerous job. But I didn't have time for any of Whitt's outdated, chivalrous bullshit. I wanted to get out of the valley alive.

Whitt sighed. When he looked again, I smacked a fist into my palm.

I'll hurt you.

Whitt bit his lip, weighing his options. Before I could offer more threats, he ran.

"Arsehole," I snarled.

I turned and sprinted up the valley wall, my thigh muscles locking on, screaming in pain as I dashed up the rocky stairs. My feet slid in the sand but I gained height quickly, the lip of the valley within my reach.

I could hear gunshots peppering the valley below.

I grabbed the last ridge and slid onto the earth, flattening beside a group of rocks. I could see Whitt bolting along a row of rocks, shots smashing through the gaps in the boulders, sickeningly close to his head.

I searched for the ridgeline and caught a glimpse of a man's shoulder as the shooter shifted his aim, a long arm covered in desert-camouflage fatigues. His face was hidden in the shadow of a large rock.

There was a pause, and then a single shot echoed through the valley. I heard Whitt yell and he seemed to slide, disappearing from my view.

"Whitt!" I screamed. The ridgeline before me exploded

as the shooter sprayed bullets my way. I could only lie with my face in my hands, waiting for the noise to stop.

It did. When I looked up, the arm and the shape in the shadow were gone.

I started clambering down toward the bottom of the valley. There was no sound from where I'd last seen Whitt. No gunshots pocked the earth before me.

"Whitt!"

I ran hard through the sand. The ground beneath me sloped down, and I skidded to a halt before a huge crack in the desert.

Whitt was dragging himself up from where he'd fallen on a narrow shelf right beside a colossal drop. Wind rushed past me from the black depths. My partner was grazed or banged up on every inch of skin I could see. Blood ran down his cheek.

"You all right?"

Whitt examined the torn shoulder of his shirt, the missing left cuff. His grazed palms left bloody prints in the dirty fabric.

"Ruined." He threw up his hands, a smile in his eyes as he looked up at me. "Fucking ruined."

CHAPTER 50

OUR ENTRY TO the EarthSoldier camp was announced long before it occurred. A piercing whistle sounded. People were standing about in groups, watching us. In the struggle in the valley I'd twisted my ankle, and Whitt looked like he'd been in a car accident. But none of the bedraggled group came to help us.

There was silence until a tall woman with long gray braids stepped forward.

"I'm Ocean Devine of the EarthSoldiers International Collective," she said. "We're on Indigenous land, and we have the permission of the elders to be here."

"Calm down, Gandalf," I said. "We haven't come here to challenge you. We're state police detectives investigating some disappearances connected to the mine."

"What happened to you?" Shamma, the girl with the

purple dreadlocks, piped up. A big guy wearing only tattered jeans pushed her back.

"Someone shot at us," Whitt said. "We need your equipment to report the incident to the authorities. If you've got any of your people in the area, I'm going to need you to call them in. It's not safe."

"And we need medical attention," I said. I snatched a bottle of water out of the hands of the nearest hippie. "Jesus Christ, I thought you people were all about helping out your fellow man."

"We'll grant you entry to our camp if you surrender to a search," Ocean said.

"Knock yourself out. Whitt's clothes are about to fall off his bones anyway." I trudged to the mouth of the great cave where they'd formed their camp and flopped onto one of the blankets on the sand. I spread my arms and legs out on the cool, soft wool. "Everything hurts. You'll have to search me from here. I'm not moving."

While I lay quietly dying on the rug, some men searched Whitt and a couple of girls came over and gave me a halfhearted pat-down. Whitt sat nearby and Shamma opened a medical pack.

It didn't escape me that one of these people might have been the shooter. I observed them carefully as another girl knelt beside me and started fiddling with my grazed hands. The outfit was not amateur. Three of the high-tech four-wheel drives ringed the face of the cave, and similarly expensive equipment was spread out everywhere—hard-cased laptops and satellite phones, radar equipment and power generators. For a bunch of environmentalists, they were packing some serious gear.

I came back to my senses when the girl who was seeing to my hands snapped a twig in front of me and started rubbing it into a bowl.

"What the hell is that?"

"It's tea-tree stem," the girl said. "I've got some aloe vera for the sunburn. This is goatsfoot." She showed me a plastic tub of brown paste.

"Goatsfoot!"

"The plant is called goatsfoot. It's from the north of the state."

"Haven't you people got any real medicine?" I rummaged through the box beside her.

"We're committed to cruelty-free medical intervention," Ocean said. She crouched beside me. "We don't use any pharmaceuticals that are wholly or in part derived from the unethical treatment of animals, or from animals themselves. So that leaves us with little choice but to rely on what we can gather from nature."

The girl smeared some of her concoction onto my palms. The pain was gone almost immediately, but I wasn't about to shout it from the rooftops.

"Has Amy King been out here in the past twenty-four hours?" I asked.

"Your people are constantly in and out of here." Ocean's lip curled in distaste. "For a group who's so careless about the environment, they'll sure trudge through it to get weed. They toss their waste along the way. Water bottles that take billions of years to biodegrade. Let me ask you, what'll you be—"

"—doing in a billion years?" I asked. "Nothing. I'll be dead in the cold ground, *not* listening to lectures about the environment."

"That'd be right," she sneered. "It's all about you. It's all about now."

"It's all about Amy King," I said. "You seen her?"

"Detective Blue doesn't mean to disrespect your cause," Whitt said from nearby. "But the girl's been missing since last night, and we think her disappearance might be connected to the disappearance of three other miners, including her sister, Tori."

Some of the girls near Whitt exchanged meaningful looks with Shamma.

"We haven't seen anyone in the past twenty-four hours," Ocean said. She tucked her hair behind her ear, and I noticed a plastic tag poking out from the silver strands. The tongue of the tag was threaded through the cartilage at the top of her ear.

"What the hell is that?"

"This?" she asked. Her face hardened. "This ear tag was worn by an eight-month-old Australian lamb. His name was B211349. He was stunned with electricity, and then slaughtered. His throat was slit, and his body was consumed."

I breathed long and deep through my nose. "And you wear his ear tag?"

"Some of us have their names tattooed on us," one of the girls nearby said. She showed me the inside of her forearm. "We mourn them."

I didn't know whether to laugh or cry, and I couldn't help some sign of that emotional struggle showing in my face. Ocean noticed. The tall, sun-bronzed woman got to her feet, and as I watched her go to the group of men by the cars, three more men came in from the desert, barefoot and covered in dust. One of them was wearing desert-camouflage pants, but no shirt. Ocean tossed a mean glance back at us as we sheltered in the cave, the kind of look I'd seen plenty of times. It was the gaze of someone measuring up an opponent for a fight.

CHAPTER 51

I TRIED TO hurry along the guys who were giving us a ride back to the camp, though the EarthSoldiers didn't strike me as people who did anything quickly. I used one of their satellite phones to call the mine. Gabe Carter was not yet back from town. In the background of the call, I could hear the alerts for Amy still going out.

"I don't know what's worse," I said, "mourning dead lambs, or the blatant hypocrisy going on here. How long's it going to take for all of these gadgets to biodegrade?" I asked Whitt, kicking a generator as we wandered restlessly through the EarthSoldier camp. "That Shamma girl's got makeup on, I swear."

"Maybe it's cruelty-free makeup," he said. "I wouldn't go trying to argue with these lot. They sound pretty practiced. They'll just tell you they need all the tech for their cause. A minor sacrifice for a greater good."

"Yeah, well, if they're so big on making sacrifices, maybe they'll stretch to a human sacrifice." We paused at the edge of the EarthSoldiers' camp, beyond the overhanging rock. "The way Ocean spoke about that lamb; they must see the person who killed it as...something else. A murderer. This is a real war to them. And remember what Linebacker told us. They nearly killed someone with the steamroller stunt. I don't see them wearing that miner's helmet in mourning had the guy been squished."

"Maybe we should get some background checks," Whitt said.

"I agree. The shooter was wearing a desert-camo shirt. There's plenty of that pattern getting around." I gestured at some girls sitting in a circle at the back of the cave, two of them wearing the army-style pants.

We wandered out of the camp and stood in the shade of the ridge, eyeing the drivers. I only hoped Gabe had found Amy in the town. Every second that Amy was missing, she was in danger. I couldn't understand why no one else saw that. I was about to launch into a tirade at the men near the trucks when the girl, Shamma, approached me.

"Are you guys here about Danny?" she asked.

"Yes." I focused on her. "And others. Did you know him?"

She ducked her head and scratched at her mass of messy locks. "We were friends, I guess. I was sad to hear what happened. Are you guys sure he's dead? I mean, you don't know he's not out there somewhere just...just missing a foot?"

"He's dead," I said. "The animal predation was post-mortem."

"And we're really sorry for your loss," Whitt chimed in, elbowing me.

"Thanks." Shamma shrugged. She turned to go then hesitated. "Can I show you guys something?"

"We don't have ti—"

"Sure," Whitt said.

We followed the girl around the side of the ridge, into a narrow strip of shade. I was itching to get back to the camp and trailed behind. When I caught up, Shamma was kneeling in the sand by a little mound of stones.

"The boys found a kangaroo a couple of weeks back." She drew a finger through the sand, tracking a neat concentric circle out from the stones. "It was badly injured. The wound had stopped bleeding, but it seemed to have been wandering a long time. It was exhausted. It died here, on the camp."

Whitt crouched down to look more carefully at the stones, the mound of earth where they had buried the creature.

"Its leg had been blown off," Shamma said. "What kind of person would do that?"

CHAPTER 52

WE RETURNED TO the mine, and Whitt went off to the medical center to have his cuts and scrapes seen to. The sun was already casting afternoon shadows. When I rounded the corner to my donga, I found Gabe there. He came forward, his mouth falling open.

"What the hell happened? You look terrible!"

"We were shot at." I sat on the steps, exhausted. "Someone hunted us in the valley like dogs."

"Oh my God." Gabe looked around. "Where's your partner?"

"He's gone to the medical center. He fell down a crevasse. I'm going to sit here for a minute, because I'm fucking tired. And then we're going straight to the bosses. There's a shooter on the loose. No one is safe."

"You won't find any of the top administration here," Gabe said. "I've already tried to approach them about

Amy. There's a meeting on at a mine to the north, and all the brass have gone there."

"I'll get police approval if I have to," I said. "We're shutting down this camp pending further investigation."

I stood and stumbled. Gabe caught the arm I threw out.

"I want a phone, an aspirin and a glass of wine," I said.

"You want a glass of water, it sounds like," he said. "You've probably got heatstroke. Your arms are absolutely fried."

He turned my arm over. The skin was fever red, right to my fingertips. I could already feel the burned back of my neck beginning to itch beneath my collar. I sat back on the steps and the big man sat beside me.

"So there was no sign of her?"

"No," he said. "Couple of people saw her in the town, buying dinner. She got a ride here, and someone else saw her on her way to her donga. That was it."

I tried to breathe deep. Since I'd been told about Sam, my stomach had been teetering on the knife-edge of nausea. The heatstroke, and my concern for Amy, didn't help.

"I can't believe I lost her," I said. "From right under my nose. Why didn't I recognize her as a possible target? I lost her, and I lost the killer out there in the valley. I should have run right at him. I should have done what I could to get a better look."

"Harry, are you absolutely certain it was the guy you're looking for?"

I looked at him, and my look must have been frightening because he put both his hands up.

"I'm just playing devil's advocate. Is it possible it was some Outback dickhead out there trying to run you off their land? Or one of the EarthSoldiers warding you off?"

"He wasn't trying to get rid of us, Gabe," I snarled. "He was trying to *kill* us. Bullets were hitting the ground at my fucking feet. Whitt fell down a fucking hole in the earth."

"I'm sorry," he said. "I had to ask. The bosses are going to ask you the very same tomorrow. They're going to suggest, the way they have with Hon, Danny and Tori, that the whole thing is an overreaction."

"And I'll wring their fat fucking necks."

"That's not going to get you anywhere," he laughed.

"I feel like I'm losing it." I rubbed my eyes. They ached with exhaustion. "If anything happens to Amy, it's all on me."

"Do you always blame yourself for everything?" Gabe grabbed my hand. I hardly noticed. "Or is it just this case?"

"I don't know. I just feel cursed right now," I said. "Everyone who has anything to do with me is in danger."

"It's probably worth the risk." I realized his fingers were around mine and resisted the sudden and all-consuming urge to snatch them away. All my life I've had the impulse to retreat from kindness.

There was so much risk in getting involved with Harriet Blue. The foster parents who cared for me. The boyfriends who loved me, who I routinely dumped without explanation when things got serious; the mere sight of a man's toothbrush in my bathroom too much commitment. The bosses who took me on, the wildcard, the girl with the temper. Part of me was sure Sam was innocent and something to do with me had caused this hellish thing to come into his life. It had to be me. I stained people. I brought the danger to their doors.

CHAPTER 53

DESPITE KNOWING THE hassle Gabe and I faced if Linebacker caught us, we snuck out of the camp and into the desert. The sky was cloudless, huge and pricked with stars. It was a hot night—almost none of the heat of the blinding day had dissipated yet. We walked for a while in silence, and just as naturally as he had when we were back on my doorstep, Gabe took my hand again. I felt that old familiar tingling up my neck, excitement, crashing against a heaviness in my stomach brought on by memories of the last time someone had walked with me this way. All my feelings for past lovers were distant and painful. I felt my body rebelling. On the horizon, the purple of the sunset lingered like mist.

We found a large, flat rock and sat side by side on the warm surface, watching the moonrise.

"If he meant to kill you," Gabe said suddenly, "why aren't you dead?"

I had to think for a moment. My near-death experience that day was the furthest thing from my mind. Someone had tried to kill me, and it was a stranger's hand in mine that had me consumed with terror.

"Oh, you know. My incredible speed and agility saved the day," I said.

He laughed. "Is Whitt incredibly fast and agile too?"

"No, he's just lucky." I remembered his story while we sheltered in the rocks, and I looked toward the camp, wondering how he was going at the medical center. I'd left him in their care, the nurses stripping off his jeans, peeling a sweat-wet shirt off his shoulders. Gabe followed my glance, catching sight of my gun poking from the back of my jeans.

"You wear that thing everywhere?"

"I will be from now on," I said, flipping my T-shirt down over the weapon.

"I bet a few men have copped a shock going for a handful of your arse and finding a police-issue Glock."

"Where I come from, a sudden arse-grab is not the generally accepted greeting."

"Well, you're in the Outback now." He smiled.

"Maybe you should get the word out. No grabbing Harry's arse. No grabbing Whitt's arse, either—he'll be wearing a gun, too."

"I'll try to contain myself."

"I think he's all right, that guy," I said, glancing toward the camp again. "But I'm not sure. It's so hard to trust people when there's so much at stake."

"It's so hard to trust people when there's *nothing* at stake," Gabe said. "If you've been burned good enough once, you'll always be scarred. Your instincts change."

"You sound like you're speaking from experience," I said.

He smiled sheepishly. "How personal do you want to get?"

"*You* can get as personal as you like." I shrugged. "Me? I admit nothing."

He looked at the horizon. The wind tossed the hair over his brow.

"I came out here to ruin my marriage," he said.

CHAPTER 54

HE LET THE words hang in the air. The unease in my stomach was growing, my body telling me that I was too close to this guy, that I was too vulnerable. That if I let him draw me in with his secrets, I might have to offer some secrets in return.

"Our story was a great story, you know?" he said, stretching out his legs. "When I heard my father tell it in the toast at the wedding, it sounded made-up. She and her girlfriends were heading out to an art gallery one night, dressed to the nines. Ball gowns and stuff. Some charity thing.

"As I'm driving on my way to work I see their group looking like they've come out of a photo shoot and I almost put my car up the back of a truck. Then the sky opens up and it pours. Straight down."

He threw his hands down.

"Oh no." I laughed.

"So I shout, 'Get in! Get in!' while they're all panicking. Looked like a bunch of wet chickens. There isn't a strip of shelter anywhere. They didn't even think about it. They just threw themselves in the car."

"Not at all concerned that you might be some kind of axe murderer?"

"Well, I was wearing a McDonald's uniform."

I laughed hard. "What? How old were you?"

"Nineteen."

The pain in my stomach was easing.

"Michelle got in the front seat," he said. "When we got to the front doors of the gallery I asked her if she wanted to go get some ice cream instead. She actually said yes. I blew off work and we drove off together."

"That story does sound made-up."

"Doesn't it? The craziest part is, a year later I married her."

A silence fell between us, in which a real sadness lingered.

"She was out of my league. It was obvious that first night we met, and it stayed obvious, through the engagement, the marriage. She'd decided to settle down in a suburban home with some lug-head construction guy when she could have been sipping champagne with movie stars, the way her family was.

"It was when we had our second daughter that she changed," he sighed. "She was going out a lot. We used to have these roaring fights. She just hated me, you know?"

"Wow," I said.

"I felt like it would be easier for her if I left."

"So you came out here," I said.

"Yeah. And after a while I stopped going back. I'd do back-to-back shifts and I wouldn't call. I gave her a ticket out. She used it."

"Do you see your kids now?"

"Whenever I can," he said. "It might be better for them, this way. And Michelle, too. She's going to law school."

"Law school won't keep you warm at night," I said.

A smile spread over his face. "No. No it won't. And she must be freezing." He wiped sweat from his brow, flicked it away. "Because I'm pretty hot."

I laughed, a great honking sound, the kind I do rarely in the company of people I don't know. It made him laugh too. He put an arm around my shoulders, held me close. I squeezed my eyes shut as my stomach fell again, excitement and terror as our lips met.

Alert. Alarm. Panic stations. A rush of images before my eyes.

Sam. The dead girls. The strange room in the photos on the case wall. Danny. Hon. Tori. Amy. Whitt. The dark tunnels beneath the earth, falling down and down into nothingness.

Just let go, I told myself. *Just fucking let go.*

I slipped into his lap, raked my fingers through his sweat-damp hair. He pulled me down against him, crushed me.

"Oh God," he whispered, his forehead pressed against mine.

I wound my arms around his neck.

CHAPTER 55

WHAT. THE FUCK. Did you do?

I walked through the camp, keeping to the alleyways between the accommodation buildings, going nowhere, hiding more from my own mind than from any real threat. I was so frazzled by what Gabe and I had done in the desert that I stopped now and then and looked up at the stars.

What. The. Fuck.

I slept with a guy on a case.

I slept with a guy I hardly know, on a case.

I slept with a guy, here, now, while I'm stuck in the middle of fucking nowhere and Sam is facing life in prison and someone is picking off young miners like ducks, while someone is hunting Whitt and me, toying with us like game pieces.

By the time I came to my senses, I was standing outside the mine. A truck rumbling past me threw orange light up against the huge rock walls. I had vague memories of passing Linebacker along my journey, watching him smoking a cigarette on the first platform of the huge crane. I'd seen him but not really seen him, my head was in such a mess.

But I knew what had drawn me here. This was the last place I'd seen Amy. I decided that I wasn't going to sleep, not with my mind in this kind of turmoil. I needed to look here, even if I was stopped eventually and told to get my arse out of the working section of the mine before I got myself killed. If it looked like I knew where I was going, surely they'd ignore me. I took a hard hat from the rack, signed in casually at the safety station and started walking through the upper tunnels of the mine.

I searched every face that passed me in the dark, nodding grimly. *Just off to meet a witness. Nothing to see here.* They were all so young. I found myself wondering how so many parents felt about their young sons and daughters going off for such dangerous work, so far away. But maybe I was projecting my youthful fantasies about parents and their concern for their children onto these kids. After all, I had no idea what it was like to be someone's girl on the cusp of adulthood. Calling Mum to tell her I'd made it home after a big night out. Letting her buy me things for my first apartment.

Maybe real parents weren't that needy. I didn't know. If we'd had real parents, what would they be going through now with Sam locked up, men and women in my own police force putting together evidence for his first committal hearing? My fantasy parents, when I envisioned them, were older than they should have been.

Wide-eyed, frightened, pulling back the lace curtains as journalists banged at the door.

I imagined protecting them from the press. Telling them to keep the door closed, not to listen to the terrible things they were saying on the news. Me being their hero in this terrible time.

But, no. I was alone. There was only me to decide how to handle this, and so far I hadn't made any clear decisions at all. Pops had forced me out into the middle of nowhere, where I'd quickly almost got myself and my partner killed, before jumping into the lap of the first guy to make a half-decent joke in my presence.

The miserable criticism trailing through my mind was interrupted by the sound of a yelp. A high-pitched wail of surprise, a pause, and then a scream.

I stopped dead in my tracks. I was deep inside the mine now, alone in one of the major veins coming off the entrance cavern. A long row of gold lightbulbs hung at my side. Their glow barely penetrated a narrow exploratory tunnel blocked with a wooden barrier that read "NO ENTRY."

I stared into the emptiness, trying to pick out anything beyond the barricade. Had I really heard a scream, or was I just stressed out of my mind?

I grabbed at the torch on top of my helmet, clicked it on. It didn't work. I must have grabbed a helmet from the rack waiting to have their lamps recharged. I glanced back the way I'd come, wondering if I'd be able to find my way back here if I went to the main tunnel to call for help.

The scream came again. I drew my gun.

CHAPTER 56

I'LL KILL YOU! I'll fucking kill you!

The words rang through the tiny tunnel, bouncing off the dark walls. The Soldier watched Detective Blue's silhouette in the entrance to the exploratory tunnel, actioning her gun and flicking the safety off.

He pressed play on the small recorder in his hand. Amy's scream was shrill.

Help! Someone help!

"Who's there?" Blue called.

The Soldier crept backwards slowly, around the curve of the tunnel. When he was sealed in darkness, he pulled his night-vision goggles down and switched them on. A soft whirr, followed by a gray cloud floating just before his eyes.

Then she emerged there before him, creeping forward

in the soft earth, one foot before the other, her hip leading and gun out straight, double grip, ready to go. The slow, deliberate movements of a spider. The Soldier liked to see her like this, in attack mode. He walked backwards, taking bigger strides until he was at a good distance. With the recorder in his pocket, muffling the scrabbling sounds of the rewind, he went back and pressed play again.

Help! Someone help!

He stopped, pressed himself against the wall of the tunnel and watched her creeping toward him, blind. One of her hands left the gun and reached out, and as it did he noticed the minor tremor, the only part of her body that wasn't taut like a wire, ready to snap. He could even see the muscles in her neck flexing, a single vein bulging at the side of her sweaty brow. She edged closer, was almost on top of him, her eyes white hollows in the light of the night vision. It was torturous to watch her pass without reaching out. Giving her a little flick. A sharp little pinch.

He must have breathed too hard, because she turned swiftly, grabbed blindly in the dark.

"Where are you?" she said.

"Right here," he answered.

The Soldier kicked at her shin and sent her tipping forward, followed up with a smack across the face. Her gun flew into the tunnel. She sprawled in the dirt, but like a good boxer she wasn't down for long. She lunged at his legs, and he couldn't help but let a laugh slip from him as he fell into the dirt with her.

Funny little tiger. She couldn't resist a good old brawl.

But this was not her game.

The Soldier pulled his torch from his belt and cracked her over the head with it.

She went out like a light.

CHAPTER 57

WAR WAS A complex thing. Not many people understood it as well as the Soldier did. He walked along the tunnel slowly, dragging the unconscious Detective Harriet Blue by her ankles. He glanced back at her, as though he could talk to her, as though he could teach her with his thoughts. Her arms and hands trailed over rocks and bumps behind her head.

There were scientific aspects to war, he thought. Strategic calculations. Risk versus reward. Probability, expectation, information management. You could measure war in its millions of variables, pitting optimal environment against available technology, levels of training and quality of leadership. But it was the moral variations within war that interested the Soldier. How the battlefield could develop or destroy loyalty. It created heroes. It created traitors.

The world needed war.

As he dragged her toward the hole, the Soldier had many important decisions to make. He'd made them on the battlefield plenty of times. *Should this man die?* That was a question he must have asked hundreds of times. He'd stormed through trenches and underground bunkers, spraying bullets, being sprayed himself, dust in his eyes and blood on his jacket and men screaming all around him.

They'd cleared rooms in hot houses one at a time, massacring the enemy inside their bases. As he'd moved from room to room with his team, he'd sometimes looked down upon an enemy soldier struggling on the ground with a bullet in his guts.

Should this man die?

Sometimes he'd pulled the trigger. Sometimes he'd let them suffer, let the kill credit go to someone else. Sometimes, if he'd admired something, like the cut of their clothes, how they handled the pain, how they'd thrown themselves in front of the women as the shooting began, he'd move on, the trigger un-pulled.

He stood and watched Detective Harriet Blue coming to her senses, rolling onto her side, gripping at her bloody head. Watched her grope in the dark, remember where she was, rise suddenly to her feet, hands out, trying to decide what had happened.

Should she die? he wondered.

He did admire her very much. She was a good adversary. He was enjoying playing with her.

Before he could decide, she seemed to hear him there and ran at him. He grabbed her hair and slammed her into the ground, fell on top of her, dragged his torch back out of his belt.

He held her head steady by a chunk of her hair and clicked the torch on. Made sure she got a good look at the hole in front of her, the endless depths, the dark.

That's where you're going, bitch.

He picked her up, stepped back, and threw her.

CHAPTER 58

I SLID ON the earth and grabbed out. My hands gathered dirt until they locked onto a wooden plank marking the very edge of the hole. My eyes were clouded by purple explosions of light, the torch burning through my night vision like wildfire. I held on tight. My legs kicked at nothing.

"Coward!" I snarled. "Cowardly piece of shit!"

My arms were shaking. I knew he was still there in the dark. If he kicked my hands I was gone. I'd fall down there into the abyss.

There are also black holes. Amy's voice was in my head. *Some of those holes are kilometers deep.*

I could hear my own cries echoing down through the depths. I hung on and waited for him to finish me.

But the sound of him walking away cut through my own panicked breathing. His footsteps gave me the strength to find a foothold, to claw my way up onto my belly. I lay on the ground and breathed, still clenching handfuls of dirt as though I'd fall if I let go. I knew if I screamed, the tunnel would carry my voice to him.

"I'll find you!" I howled, my voice trembling. "I'm coming for you, arsehole!"

CHAPTER 59

I PUSHED AWAY the horrified men and women who tried to crowd around me at the entrance to the mine. I must have looked pretty bad, because phones were picked up and directions were given. I didn't care. I marched straight back to our donga. Whitt had obviously been called, because he came out in only his stripy pajama pants, his bullet-grazed arm sporting a thick white bandage.

"Jesus," he said as I came toward him. "Blue, are you—"

"No. I'm not. He's here. He just—I was—in the mine." I couldn't catch my breath. My chest felt tight. I knew this was shock. I'd seen it plenty of times in my line of work. If I just pushed through it, it would go. I thumped my chest with my fist, tried to get the air moving. "There's a hole. The killer."

Shock is unique to each individual. Some people go into hiccups. Some people's teeth start to chatter. Some people collapse, go catatonic. The body can't handle the total terror overload, the adrenaline dumped into the veins. I coughed and straightened up.

"Blue, sit down."

"No. No. The killer. He's here."

"Sit down!"

"I want—a radio!"

Whitt grabbed both my shoulders and looked at my eyes. He spoke very slowly.

"You have a hole in your head the length of my index finger."

I looked at him. He held up a finger in front of my nose.

"Oh."

I sat down on the front steps of our donga. Whitt ran inside and brought me a hand towel, which I pressed into my forehead on the right-hand side. I couldn't feel the wound at all. My pain sensors were switching off all over my body. I felt cold.

"What'll I do?" he asked.

"Evacuate the mine. Put the camp—into lockdown. Get the bosses back here. Call me a medic. Get my phone. Find Gabe. He'll help."

Whitt ran up the stairs and into the donga to find his phone. News of the attack had spread, and miners were steadily creeping from their dongas to glance over at me. I saw two of the Bilbies in the window across from me. I waved, unable to decide if I was more embarrassed or infuriated. When I bowed my head, I saw my shirt and pants were soaked with blood.

CHAPTER 60

I REMAINED ON the steps of the donga, letting the medic come to me. I wanted to send a message to the miners. Yes, there's a killer out here. The danger is real. Everything is not business as usual.

My clothes were covered in dirt and half my face seemed to be a bloody mask. When the medic finished wiping my cheeks and neck, the sterilized cloth was saturated with red.

"Number one," she said as she threaded a stitch through my scalp. "I think it's dumb that you won't come back to the med block with me. There's dust and shit getting into this wound."

"I'll be fine," I said, my eyes closed. "I've never seen 'Death by Dust' on the front page of any paper."

"It's not only that." She pulled the stitch tight, the base

of her gloved palms resting on my brow. "I think you should be in a chopper to Perth. You need an MRI. You could have a skull fracture."

"I don't have a skull fracture."

"How do you know that, genius?"

"I've had my skull fractured three times in the ring. I know what it feels like."

"So you're a boxer, then? That explains a bit."

Footsteps, and Gabe appeared in my field of vision. He took in the wound on my head.

"Holy shit!"

"It's fine."

I'd taken a few blows over the years, so I wasn't particularly worried about my head. However, Gabe's expression took me back to those early years. A good beating looks worse on a woman. Depending on the family you come from, most of the time it's a shocking sight.

The nurse let me go and I cracked my neck. When I looked up, Whitt and a man in slacks and an immaculate white shirt had joined Gabe before me.

"Harry, this is David Burns. He's the operational officer on duty."

I offered my bloody hand. He stared at it in horror.

"Well"— I let my hand drop—"I suppose I should have expected you to be just as welcoming as you were when we arrived."

"I apologize, Ms. Blue. The management team has been particularly busy this month."

"It's Detective Blue."

"I'm appalled at this," Burns said, his eyes wandering

over my head wound. "Am I correct in saying you were somehow accidentally unaccompanied in one of our operational areas?"

"Oh, I was intentionally unaccompanied," I said. "I asked for help finding Amy King a good nine or ten hours ago. I haven't seen a single man on search detail. I assume that wasn't an accident?"

Burns puffed out his chest. "I didn't send out a search detail, Ms. Blue, because there's no evidence to suggest—"

"There is now," I said. "I saw Hon's hat."

Gabe and Whitt looked at each other.

"Before the killer threw me into the hole," I said, "he was kind enough to turn on his torch and show me where I was going to end up. I looked down the hole and saw an Australian flag hat hanging on the side of the shaft. Caught on a root or a rock or something. The same dorky flag hat Hon Lu is wearing in a photograph I collected from his crime scene."

Burns scoffed, looking away. "You mean his bedroom?"

"Yes, when someone's been murdered, we generally call the last place they were sighted a *crime scene*." I smiled. "Because we think it's the *scene* where a *crime* occurred."

"All right." Whitt stepped forward nervously. "Play nice. The least we can do is shut down the mine, ensure that everyone's safe and take a look down the hole."

"The least we can do is nothing, Mr. Whittacker," Burns said, his hands in his pockets. "This investigation has, from the outset, been a farce. Everyone *is* safe.

And running an excavation mission in search of—what, clues?—is a ridiculous suggestion."

"*Bodies,* you idiot." I stood up, possibly too fast. "We're looking for bodies. I think Hon and Tori are down there. Maybe Amy too. If you don't approve a search I'll climb down there my fucking self."

"Ms. Blue," Burns said, "you've suffered a serious head injury. I don't know what you think you saw—"

"It's *Detective* Blue, you dickless ape!"

The medic snorted loudly then tried to cover her smile.

"Your stories don't make sense," Burns continued. "You've wandered without authority and without escort into a restricted area of the mine, endangering both yourself and my staff, and you've concocted this story about being... attacked? You've not seen this alleged attacker, and yet you claim to have seen a hat in a hole which you think is evidence of—"

"I'm going to kill this guy," I told Whitt calmly. "If you don't get him away from me, right now, I'm going to strangle him with his tie."

"OK." Whitt took Burns by the shoulder. "Mr. Burns, why don't we have a chat over here..."

When Gabe touched my shoulder I recoiled in shock. My skin felt electrified.

"The rest of the leadership team are supposed to fly in tomorrow morning," he said. "Why don't we just leave it for tonight?"

"Leave it?" I said. "Leave it! Yeah, sure, we just leave someone's missing kid down a dark hole in the middle of the—"

"I know." He nodded, rubbing my shoulder. "You don't have to convince me. I'm with you all the way, Harry."

"At least someone is," I said. "This place is... It's heartless. Fucking heartless. If the management don't get on board, Gabe, more people are going to die. I guarantee it."

CHAPTER 61

MY FISTS HIT the bag in the rec room with a satisfying *whap,* the impact sending shock waves up my forearms, toward my shoulders, through my chest. I twisted and gave the bag a couple of deep hooks to the side, bounced back and punched my imaginary foe's face square-on. It was pretty easy to lose myself in the workout. I had plenty of sparring partners to imagine. I was knocking Nigel upside the head for arresting my brother. I was giving Linebacker a sucker punch to the gut for chastising me like a child. I was slamming my fist into Burns's kidneys, imagining the man doubling over, sinking to the mat as the pain ripped through him.

When I turned around, three miners were hanging in the doorway to the rec room, staring at me. I spat on the floor and reached for my water bottle.

"Want to take a picture?" I snapped.

The men disappeared.

As I walked back to my donga I spotted Shamma and another EarthSoldier girl by the fence line, hidden from view behind a huge forklift. They were crouching, using binoculars to look across the ground between the machine's tires toward the transport yard. I followed their line of sight, but couldn't see anything. When I popped out from behind one of the forklift's huge tires, both girls yelped in surprise.

"Ladies."

"Holy crap, you scared the shit out of us," Shamma said. "What happened to your head?"

"I got a bonk on the brain from our suspect," I said, feeling the stitches. "None of your people were on the camp last night, were they?"

The girls looked at each other. Shamma opened her mouth to speak, and her friend cut her off.

"Ocean says we're not to assist in the investigation," she said.

"What?"

"We've got to go." She pulled at Shamma. The purple-haired girl stood fast, staring at her sandals in the dirt.

"Whoever it was, they killed Danny," Shamma murmured.

"Were you and Danny a couple?" I asked.

"Shamma, we gotta go." The friend was backing off.

"Sort of," Shamma said, her eyes finding mine. She clung to the diamond wire between us, and when she finally spoke, her words were low and fast.

"Ocean and a couple of the guys were out looping last night," she said. "They also have stuff on the camera system. You know, for the blog? Stuff that might help. But I don't know if they'll give it to you. They think you're after them."

CHAPTER 62

I SAT OUTSIDE the leadership team meeting room beside Whitt, browsing the internet on my phone.

"Looping," I read. "Environmental activist term describing the practice of looping heavy chains around equipment deemed detrimental to the cause, and attaching industrial padlocks. Activists will sometimes chain large pieces of operational equipment together, or chain essential buildings closed in an effort to slow production."

"They're a crafty bunch, aren't they?" Whitt said.

I couldn't help wandering further through the internet, looking for signs of Sam. I knew that, for a few days, information about the evidence gathered should shut down as the prosecutors prepared for the committal hearing. There'd be no point showing all their cards at this early stage. But some information would always leak.

I flashed my eyes across a few headlines, unable to take in more.

BLUE CRYING IN CUSTODY, GUARDS SAY.

"HE TOLD ME HE WAS GOING TO KILL ME": BLUE BIKE PATH VICTIM TELLS ALL.

TORTURED ANIMALS, WET BED UNTIL LATE TEENS—BLUE FOSTER PARENT REVEALS.

I clicked on the last link, then stopped myself. I couldn't focus on that now. It would drive me into a rage, and if I was going to convince the leadership team to support us in finding the missing miners, I needed to maintain my cool.

"What are we doing sitting here like a couple of schoolkids waiting for the principal?" I said. I stood and shoved open the meeting-room door.

Twelve men and women in suits were sitting around a long pine table. Burns was the only man standing.

"...a work of pure fiction," he was saying. He almost choked when he saw me.

Gabe jogged to a stop in the hall beside Whitt. "I miss anything?" he asked.

"No," Whitt sighed. "You're right on time for the show."

"Good morning! Well, isn't this a sight? Look at you

all." I swept an arm around the table. "You look immaculate. Nice earrings there, miss. Very stylish. I'm glad you all spent so much time getting dressed for this meeting while the bodies of four of your employees lay rotting in the ground, waiting to be discovered."

"My God." The woman with the earrings clutched at her chest, looked to Burns. "Is she serious?"

"This is exactly what I'm talking about." Burns rolled his eyes.

"Twenty minutes we waited out there." I pointed to the doorway. "That's twenty more minutes their families waited to hear what's happened to them. Would you pompous morons stop messing around and approve a search, please?"

"We'd just like to get our heads around the situation, Ms. Blue," an older man said, his hands open reasonably. "Mr. Burns was just briefing us. We understand so far that this is all connected to the disappearance of Daniel Stanton?"

"It's *Detective*." I felt my jaw click. "And yes. Daniel Stanton. Hon Lu. Tori and Amy King."

"You see, I was given the impression by the Perth police that there was no suggestion any harm had come to these miners." He looked around the table. "We were told that Hon Lu, for example, was deeply distressed that the food storage block was raided by the activists, and may have left the camp in embarrassment for not having stopped it. We're told Tori King left because she was having relationship problems, and that her sister went in search of her. Now, although some of Daniel's remains were recovered, so far there's no sign in any of these cases, including his, of—"

"Of foul play?" I pointed to my head. "This isn't foul enough for you?"

"Ah, yes. David has relayed your...claims of having been attacked by a man you believe was responsible for the whereabouts of the missing miners. Ms. Blue, really, I must ask—"

"If one more person calls me Ms. Blue I'm going to lose it," I said.

"You haven't lost it already?" Burns said, smiling.

"Oh, sweetheart." I smiled back. "I haven't even begun."

"Without further corroboration of your story, *Detective* Blue, I'm afraid I can't approve such an expensive and time-consuming use of our resources." The older man clasped his hands on the table. "The mine was shut down for five hours last night after your...accident. This cost in the ballpark of seventy-five thousand dollars. Alongside difficulties we've had in the early hours of this morning with local activists disabling some of our equipment, our focus for the present has to be getting this place up and running again. There's no evidence to suggest Daniel Stanton or any of the other young people you mentioned have been deliberately targeted by anyone, on or off the mine. And that's that."

"That's that, huh?"

They all stared at me, a human wall of defiance clad in silk and expensive wool. There was one young man, obviously the junior in the leadership team, who looked decidedly guilty. I took his quiet shame as a small triumph, a big enough win to get me out of the room without punching something.

I stood outside the boardroom and listened to them lock the doors behind me.

I wasn't even out there long enough for Gabe and Whitt to figure out what to say to me. I looked at them, and then I turned and kicked the boardroom doors back open.

CHAPTER 63

THE WOMAN WITH the nice earrings screamed. Four or five people stood. Eyes and mouths were agape. I don't think anyone in the room had seen an act of violence in a very long time. I was gambling on the idea that it was exactly what they needed.

"That's *not* that," I said, nudging aside the lock that had smashed out of the door and bounced on the carpet. The leadership junior looked secretly impressed. Whitt rushed in and started babbling, trying to apologize, to calm the situation, but I silenced him with a look.

"Samuel Jacob Blue is my brother," I said.

The room was silent, all eyes fixed on me. Burns rose sharply from his chair, his face purple with rage.

"What the hell are you talking about?"

"Holy shit," the leadership junior said. "Samuel Jacob Blue? He's the Georges River Killer!" He threw looks around the room, but none of his colleagues knew what he meant. "It's all over the news. He's just been arrested in Sydney."

"I'm out here in this godforsaken craphole you call a mine because my commanding chief wanted to keep me away from the media frenzy about my brother's arrest," I said. "He was arrested five days ago on three counts of aggravated sexual assault and murder. There are more charges to come. So far, I've been holding off the dozens of journalists who are trying to get a comment out of me. They're at my police station. They're at my house. They're cramming my phone with calls, messages and emails. Right now, I'm the most sought-after interviewee in the country."

I caught Gabe's eyes. His mouth was hanging open. I couldn't think about what I was sacrificing as my words spilled forth. I couldn't think about what this would mean once the miners got hold of it, once the likes of Richie and his crew and any number of other menacing characters wandering around the mine discovered who I was. Right now, I needed to find those missing miners, and it was sheer desperation pushing me on.

"If you don't conduct a search of the mine for those young people," I said, "I'm going to start taking calls from journalists. I'm going to tell them where I am. They're going to come out here looking for me, and before you know it you're going to have the entire nation, possibly the world, with their eyes trained on this very spot. If you think they're interested in me, they're gonna *love* the case I'm working on."

A heavy silence fell again, and it was only in the quiet and the stillness that I realized my whole body was shaking with anger.

I'd given up everything now, and whether my threat worked or not, there'd be nowhere to hide.

CHAPTER 64

I WAS AWARE of Gabe somewhere in the huddle of people around the desk outside the entrance to the mine, but I didn't acknowledge him, and he didn't come near me. I didn't know when we'd talk, but he'd probably insist on it. I was embarrassed at having jumped him in the middle of the desert, used him to sate my desperate, primal need to be held, distracted from my life. There was also the humiliation of Sam's situation, of how as a Sex Crimes detective I'd managed to do exactly nothing about my brother either committing, or at least being arrested for, some of the most horrific deeds in the country's history. I stole a glance over my shoulder at Gabe as he loitered at the back of the crowd around the computer table. He was looking at something on his phone. Was he scanning the headlines with this new understanding? Was he reading about my past?

At the fold-out table before us, two large laptops had been set up to display the video feed from a GoPro that was being lowered into the hole in the mine. I'd identified the exploratory tunnel the killer had lured me into, telling Burns and his crew, as well as the workmen he'd detailed, about the screams I'd heard coming from within. There were two sets of footprints in the sand and dirt leading to the hole, and clear signs of where I'd been struck, where I'd wrestled with the man who attacked me. A smear of my blood on the wall. But when I tried to show Burns these, his torch beam wandered off. The man was too stubborn to take me seriously even now.

Whitt and I watched the laptop screens as the GoPro was fed into the hole. Its torch showed only a black circle, rocky walls receding as the camera plunged deep into the earth. The hat I'd seen a mere three or four meters down the hole was gone.

"How deep is it?" I asked.

"This one's probably about a kilometer deep," a young miner said. "That's how far we went on each hole on that side of the mine before we moved on."

"If it's not collapsed," another said. "There's nothing bracing them."

We all stood and watched the black hole. Miners going in and out of the mine stopped now and then to ask people at the back of the crowd what was happening. Before long, a shape began to emerge. The circular bottom of the hole. The blue, red and white hat.

"There's the hat!" I cried.

"And there's the bottom of the hole," Burns said, barely

able to contain the triumph in his voice. "No bodies. Just as I predicted."

I stood staring deep down in the earth, at the sand and dirt and tiny rock chips lying on the surface. Burns radioed back to the leadership team that we'd found nothing. There was a distinct loosening of the tension in the people around me. Two or three walked off.

"Wait," I said. "What's that?"

I tapped the screen. There was a long, white object lying beside the hat. The men inside were radioed, and they lowered the camera slightly. The object wouldn't come into focus. Burns came over to the laptop screen and bent so that his nose was inches from it.

"It's a rock," he said.

"A single bright white rock at the bottom of a tunnel of mostly gray, black and brown rocks?"

Burns looked at me, grinding his back teeth. He swung quickly toward the ground and picked up a pale stone.

"See this?" he snapped. "This is a white rock. This, too, this is a white rock!" He swooped a couple more times, angrily gathering up a handful of dirt and rocks. "There must be a thousand fucking colors of rock here."

"Hey," Whitt snapped. "How about you talk to my colleague with a bit more respect."

"Respect?"

"Yeah, some fucking respect." Whitt moved forward, forcing Burns to back up. "I don't like your tone. We can play nice, or we can start making further problems for you. You're bordering on hindering a police investigation here, mate."

"You're hindering my *business*. You're on my property, without a warrant." Burns threw his hands up. "Since when does the curiosity of an individual police officer come before... before logic! Evidence! Fucking *reality!*"

"Put me down the hole," I said.

Whitt and Burns both turned to look at me.

"What?"

"I said, 'Put me. Down. The hole.'"

CHAPTER 65

GOING DOWN HEADFIRST seemed like a good idea until I'd been lowered about a hundred meters. The circumference of the hole was such that I could reach out and touch the walls as they slid by me, my fingers trailing over the grooves the huge drill had left in the clay and mud. The blood swirled to my head. I hung there listening to my heartbeat pound in my ears, my stitches throbbing along the wound in my head.

This is where I would have fallen, I mused. *This is where I would have died.*

"You all right, Harriet?" Whitt's voice asked.

I pressed the button for the radio at my waist. "It's hot down here."

"Adjust your camera a little bit, could you?" he replied. "We can only see dirt."

I straightened the camera on the front of my hard hat. The chin strap cut into my jaw, where sweat had begun to slide toward my nose. Whitt's radio crackled on and off between transmissions. I could hear Burns in the background, still whining about safety and money and time, the ludicrousness of the decision to let me go down into the hole.

"You're at about three hundred meters," Whitt said.

As the winch lowered me smoothly into oblivion, I wondered what death would be like if the shaft suddenly collapsed. A sudden crunch. The breath squeezed out of me. Dirt in my eyes and mouth. My eternal grave, deeper than I'd ever have imagined. I breathed slowly as I descended, watching the shadows bouncing off the walls.

"Six hundred meters."

The harness was bruising my shoulders. I didn't dare wriggle to gain comfort. If I slipped, I'd plummet four hundred meters to the bottom, deep into the darkness.

"Nine hundred and twenty."

"I think I can see the bottom," I wheezed. The heat was incredible. Sweat rolled along my forearms and off the tips of my fingers. "I see the hat."

The winch kept lowering. I was coming up on the bottom of the shaft too fast.

"Stop! Stop!"

The wire holding me ground to a stop, clanging and singing as it trembled in the faraway machine. I picked up Hon's hat and tucked it into my harness.

"Where's your white rock?" Whitt asked.

I turned my head and found it. A long, thin stone lying

on the surface of the dirt floor. I reached out, only inches from it.

"Lower me down a bit."

Two large clanks, and I shunted downward a foot. I grabbed the rock and pulled.

The finger snapped off in my hand.

CHAPTER 66

I BEGAN DIGGING down furiously, pulling the sand and dirt away from the hand, the arm, the shoulder buried there. Hon had flopped to the bottom of the hole with an arm raised over a mound of dirt, just the knuckle of one of his fingers showing above the surface of the dirt, looking like a pale, thin stone. The extreme heat in the hole and the rich soils had begun to degrade his corpse, loosening the skin and tendons around his finger, making him like dough.

I cleared the sand from around Hon's face, his dead, gaping mouth vomiting a steady stream of it from his black lips. My camera relayed images to the desk up top crowded with people.

"Oh Jesus, it's them," I could hear Whitt saying via the radio. "Get back. All of you get back. Get these people out of here."

I heard cries of horror on the radio. I stopped clearing away the sand and hung there, looking at the half-submerged body.

"Pull me up, will you?"

Now I stood, still harnessed, at the entrance to the mine, grateful for the sun on my face. I bagged Hon Lu's finger and handed it to Whitt. Perth was sending a proper crime-scene crew to go down the hole and excavate whatever was there, making sure to bag all the dirt and sand around the corpses in case there were fibers or hairs that would help identify the killer. There was nothing I could do now but wait to see what they would find.

The crowd around the table with the laptops had thinned, mainly, I suspected, because the people had rushed off to tell their friends what they'd seen. Already the news was spreading like wildfire. I looked up toward the fence line and saw a couple of miners talking to some EarthSoldiers through the diamond wire, pointing down the high mine walls at me. David Burns had disappeared completely. I was glad. I didn't know what I'd have done if I'd seen him, having just climbed out of the hole in which we'd almost been forced to leave the bodies.

"How many do you think are down there?" Whitt asked.

"I don't know." I cleared my throat. "At least two. When I pulled back the sand around Hon's shoulder I saw a foot that wasn't his, wedged alongside him. The sand was too loose though. Kept falling in."

Whitt gave me a pat on the shoulder and went to make some calls to Perth. I didn't know Gabe was approaching me until his feet came to a stop in front of mine.

"Hi."

"Hi." I looked up at his eyes, trying to gauge his emotions. There was no clue. He stuffed his hands in his pockets.

"Well. Looks like we'll have a circus on our hands," he said. "How many people are they sending out?"

"Oh, there'll be a coroner, an extraction team, couple of photographers. Most likely they'll get the bodies out of there quick smart and chuck them on a chopper back to Perth. It'll all be very quiet. They won't want to scare the rest of the camp."

"I think I'll get back to work," he sighed. "I don't want to be anywhere near here when they start bringing them out. Do you think there'll be journalists?"

"I don't know. They might not have reason to come, if the team gets the bodies back to Perth quick enough."

I wasn't sure the Forensics team would be able to get out and back and beat the press. Already miners were standing nearby, taking pictures of us on their phones. They'd alert the press for the sheer fun of it. Looking to give interviews, have their ten seconds on camera. Boredom with life will do that to you. Make you a reality TV star in waiting.

Gabe was examining my expression. I knew what he wanted to talk about, but I wasn't sure I could go there at that very second.

"I'm sorry about your brother," he said. "If the press come—"

"Thanks," I said. "I'll be fine."

I wandered away from him, too confused by what we'd done, and too terrified by what I'd seen down there in the earth, to speak to him anymore.

CHAPTER 67

IT WAS NIGHTFALL by the time the extraction team arrived. Whitt and I spent the afternoon by the desk at the mine entrance, reviewing our notes and watching who entered the area. The leadership team had approved a complete shutdown of the north mine, but that didn't stop people milling about, some pretending to check equipment or working on the trucks nearby. I saw Richie briefly among their number, and Linebacker. News of the discovery did a fast circuit of the mine and came back around to us, greatly distorted. Someone had brought us coffee and lunch. While I sat there trying to eat I listened to a small knot of miners halfway up the hill, voices traveling across the dusty earth bowl toward us.

"...said she found like ten bodies down there."

"No, no, *she* fell down there. While they were

rescuing her they found an *arm*. But that's it, there are no bodies."

"Davo heard from Richie... bits and pieces, like, fingers and stuff. And a rope and some duct tape."

I gave the miners a dark look and they withdrew. But by the time the mine had been lit with orange sodium lamps and the sun had fallen below the horizon, dozens more had returned, standing on the hill in groups. When the chopper came, they pointed and took pictures.

No one from the leadership team came to watch the extraction.

"You'd think they'd at least have one guy down here looking mournful," I told Whitt. "In case the press show up."

"They'll say they were up in the offices consoling the families," he said. "If they're down here when the press come they'll have to answer difficult questions about it."

I recognized one of the women who hopped down from the helicopter. Taylor Fink, orange-haired and cream-skinned, set her heavy bag down and shook my hand. For such a beautiful woman, she had a terrible nickname, "Finkles," which followed her everywhere. It reminded me of wrinkles and freckles, which was unfair, as she didn't have many of either.

"Detective Blue," she said. "What horrors have you got in store for me now?"

I'd worked with Taylor on a couple of bad human trafficking cases in Sydney. We'd raided a brothel in Campbelltown together and found two dead sex slaves in the basement. We hugged. I might have held her a little too long.

"What are you doing here?" I asked. "You've left Sydney?"

"Yeah, I'm in Perth now." She grinned. "The only thing that'd make me move that far would be money or a man."

"Should I guess from that smile which one it was?"

She winked.

I led the pathologist and her team to the hole and left them there.

When the moon was high, and the curiosity of most of the camp's population had worn away, three of the male Forensics officers emerged from the mine entrance with a stretcher covered by a sheet. The shape beneath was not flat, but lay scrunched on its side, arm up. It was Hon.

Taylor walked toward me wearing a white paper suit and blue gloves, her camera around her neck. Neither of us really wanted to hear what she had to say.

"There were three of them down there," she said. "Two young females and a tall Asian male."

"Fuck." I sighed.

"One of the females is very recent," she said. "Twenty-four to forty-eight hours. Her rigor mortis broke easily. From the lividity on all three bodies, it looks like they were chucked down there within two hours of death."

She sat on the edge of the desk and showed us a sketch she'd drawn of the bodies as they lay in the hole. One of the girls was on her side in a sort of fetal position, her legs bent. Hon had fallen on his knees in the curve of her body, one arm raised on a protruding rock. Another of the girls had fallen between these two bodies, flopped on her front across Hon's knees. Tori must have gone first, then Hon. The girl on the top of the pile was Amy. In the sketch, they were faceless, featureless people, their hands and feet rounded and limbs bent at odd angles. I watched as the team shifted another stretcher to the chopper.

"Any signs of what killed them?"

"Plenty," Taylor said. "One of the girls has got a chest wound like that." She made a circle with her hands the circumference of a tennis ball.

"If I were you," Taylor said, tucking her notebook under her arm, "I'd start rattling the cages to see which one of these guys has got a big, powerful gun."

CHAPTER 68

THE SOLDIER WATCHED Detective Blue as the chopper sailed away into the night. He saw the red landing lights reflected off her high cheekbones, making the whites of her tired eyes a glossy pink. As the aircraft disappeared, her face became a hard mask of determination. He stood in the shadow of a nearby digger and chewed his lips.

Yes, Detective Blue. Harden again. Feel the hollowness pulse in you. You are a soldier. You will avenge your fallen.

Every death became a hardening. A slow concentration of the muscles and bones, the same petrification that turned wood into stone. At the same time, the insides were worn away, until the Soldier became a shell that could not carry the useless cargo of love, terror, desire. There was no room for pity inside. When gunshots sounded, they echoed around his inner walls so that there was never any quiet.

When her eyes lifted to her partner, they sparkled in the dark with hate.

"We're going to start searching the accommodation areas," she said. "We'll confiscate Linebacker's weapon and have it checked. Call Perth. We need more men. A team to go out and search the EarthSoldier camp. A team to search the mines."

She was the mad king. The commander so ruined by battle that she refused to see the limits of her power. The leadership team was going to refuse all her directions. But that wasn't what mattered. What mattered now was the call of war.

As her partner jogged off into the night, the Soldier followed Detective Blue around the side of the digger, down a gap between two trucks and into the shadows behind the mine entrance. There he watched her standing in the dark, her fists clenched by her sides.

That desire to cry was in her again, he could see. She hadn't had a spare moment to let her guard down since she arrived. He'd enjoyed watching her feelings about her brother's situation play on her face whenever she stole a spare second to look at the headlines on her phone. He enjoyed seeing the strain in the taut muscles of her throat, her troubled swallow when each piece of dark news was presented to her.

Oh, to cry. What a guilty pleasure that would be. To let go, and let the hurt wash over her.

Detective Blue cleared her throat, set her jaw, and turned back around. Not a single tear fell.

CHAPTER 69

I SLEPT IN fits and starts, trading nightmares with myself. I dreamed I was calling out from the bottom of the hole in the mine, howling up toward the tiny gray circle of light far above, my legs trapped beneath Amy's body. When I wasn't in the hole I was in my bed, but my body was paralyzed with terror. A dark figure moved about the room, touching my things, standing over Whitt as he slept. I tore myself out of my dreams as a hard knock came on the side of the demountable. Whitt was gone.

I got out of bed and flung the door open in my underpants and singlet. Shamma with the purple hair was there, a cap pulled low over her face.

"I could get in deep shit for this," she said, glancing toward the end of the accommodation yard. She thrust some papers into my hands.

"Come inside," I said.

"No." She bounced impatiently on the balls of her feet. "I've got to split before Ocean finds out I'm on the camp. She's pulled everyone in. We're not to talk to anyone from the mine until further notice."

"Why is she trying to hold you all back?" I asked. "Doesn't she want us to catch whoever's doing this?"

"I don't know, man," Shamma sighed. "I never know what's going on. I'm only out here in the desert because I want to stop the mine. I'm trying to follow my dream, you know? I don't want to get mixed up in fucking murders and shit."

"Shamma." I grabbed her shirt before she could take off. "Do you think there's anyone out there on your camp who's dangerous enough to be responsible for this?"

The girl squirmed. "Look, mate, the mine's where the dangerous people are," she said. "I was here looping maybe a month ago and some guy caught me and threw me on the ground. Like, threw me hard, man. The guy spat on me."

"He spat on you?"

"On my face." She glanced toward the fence again. "Called me a harshee."

"What's a harshee?"

"I don't know. But I never been handled like that before, you know? Like I was worse than scum. I been in a few protests in my time, and they're always rough, but not that rough. This guy, he would have really hurt me if we weren't in the middle of the mine, I reckon. It was like he took it personally."

"Did you see his face?" I asked. "Can you tell me anything about him?"

Shamma twisted out of my grip and ran off.

I looked down at the papers the young woman had thrust into my hands. They were low-quality printouts from two of the EarthSoldier camp cameras. One of the cameras was angled out from the back of the cave, looking over a group of EarthSoldiers sleeping on mats on the ground, some grouped together, some splayed on their own. At first I couldn't tell what the purpose of the image was, until I discerned a shape from the cliffs visible through the mouth of the cave. It was the dark figure of a man walking across the camp between the trucks, carrying a large gun by his side.

CHAPTER 70

AS IS THE way with big corporations in times of crisis, most of the mine bosses had disappeared. A grave-faced David Burns walked the camp grounds with us, simultaneously wanting to look like he was cooperating with us and wanting to keep me away from the offices so I couldn't break down any more doors. He'd brought us cappuccinos in immaculate paper cups. I wondered what the coffee rations were for the elite.

Within minutes it was clear that the long walk and the boutique coffees were all the friendly gestures we were going to get.

"We'll start with checkpoints for entry into and out of the mine," I said. "Shut off all the smaller exits, restricting the flow of people and trucks to the two main gates. I'll need some of your people to do searches."

Burns listened quietly, staring at the ground.

"Whitt and I will conduct a search of the accommodation blocks today. I have some targeted interviews to conduct, as well. We're going to need to confiscate Aaron Linbacher's weapon and have it sent away for ballistics tests, along with any other weapons we uncover."

"We'll need to see your police history checks for all your personnel," Whitt added. "Weapons offenses, violent assaults..."

"I'll need you to surrender all the mine's CCTV from the past couple of weeks," I continued.

We came to a stop by the administration building.

"Well." Burns straightened his tie. "Unfortunately, you've only named one direct action that I agree with."

I opened my mouth, but found I had no words.

"The interviews." He nodded. "You can conduct the interviews."

"What?"

"I'll take your plans to the leadership team, obviously, but I can tell you now, their response will be the same. Your proposal breaches a number of our core principles here at the mine." He shrugged helplessly. "We cannot restrict the movement of people on and off the mine. Slowing down vehicles as they pass in and out of the gates for exhaustive searches is going to bring this place to a grinding halt. It's just not practical. That's not to mention safety. We need to ensure we can get emergency vehicles to different parts of the mine at a moment's notice."

I looked at Whitt. His face was impassive.

"The background checks? Well, I'll have to go to the

global franchise team for that. And the accommodation block searches? No way. There are activities that go on around the mine that are hardly legal." He put his palms out. "These are hardworking family men and women who live in a high-stress environment. I can't let you go through and arrest a good portion of the mine population for minor drug offenses in the search for someone—"

"We're not looking for drugs! We're looking for guns!"

"—someone that we're not even sure is on the mine at all."

"We understand that there are drugs on the mine," Whitt said gently. "We'd turn a blind eye."

"I'm not just talking about drugs. We know there are prostitutes here. There are likely pirated DVDs and pornography. And what if you do find guns? We're in the Outback. There are staff here who like to go out wild pig shooting and roo shooting. The place is probably riddled with guns."

"We're looking for a very specific weapon," Whitt explained. "It's not some pig-hunting peashooter."

Burns waved dismissively.

I struggled for words. "Do you grasp that there's a maniac on the camp? There's a fucking maniacal serial killer *on this camp*. He's here, somewhere. I have pictorial evidence of him stalking the EarthSoldier camp not two kilometers away. We pulled the bodies of three young people out of your mine. They'd been shot from a distance. They'd been . . . *hunted* . . . like *animals*."

Burns stared at me. "You're not telling me anything I don't know, Detective Blue."

"You're actually hindering our search," I said. "I mean...I can't believe you're not doing everything you possibly can to find the person who's done this."

"I guess the difference between you and me, Detective Blue, is that I'm a Big Picture man." He stood square-on to me, waved his arms out wide. "I'm managing over five thousand personnel here. I'm...I'm like a father to them. I'm in charge of their safety. Their happiness. Their productivity. Try to imagine that. The big picture. Try to imagine what it's like to have five *thousand* children who all need you very much."

He moved his palms together so that they were only an inch apart.

"You've got a very specific job to do. It's an important job, I understand that. But it's a Small Picture job. Now, I can't sacrifice my care of the Big Picture to meet the needs of the Small Picture."

Heat was creeping up my neck. My knuckles cracked as my fingernails bit into my palms. Whitt instinctively moved, putting one foot into the space between Burns and me, in case I lashed out. But for once I was so angry I couldn't move.

Burns shrugged for a third time, physically off-loading the burden I'd tried to put on his shoulders. It slipped off. He was a man nothing could stick to, not even the deaths that I was sure would come from his refusal to act.

CHAPTER 71

I BURST INTO the rec room, Whitt following. The men at the gaming spot paused and turned around. The crowd gathered around the couches began whispering. I found the Bilbies right where the miners I'd asked had said they would be—working out on the gym machines. The little blonde, Jaymee, was sprawled on a mat on the floor, doing halfhearted crunches, while tall and dark Beth was bench-pressing a good sixty kilos. She was being spotted by a nervous-looking girl in sparkly leggings. I went over and slid in front of the girl spotting Beth, taking the weight bar from her and putting it in the rack.

"Hey!"

"I need you," I said, leaning over the bar, upside down to Beth.

"I knew you'd come around eventually." Beth smiled

and chewed her bottom lip. "But generally I take appointments."

"I need all of you. Outside. Now."

Whitt met me in the yard. "What are you doing?" he asked.

"Bending the rules," I said, waiting as the prostitutes assembled around me.

"What's going on, sugarplum?" Beth brushed some desert dust off my shoulder. She looked at the stitches in my forehead. "Someone need an arse-kicking?"

"Not yet," I said. "I'm deputizing all of you. Unofficially. I need help in this murder investigation and I'm just not getting it from the top brass. I should have guessed that and gone to the underdogs first. But here we are."

"Oh, deputies!" Jaymee cried, clapping her sweaty palms. "Murder deputies!"

"I want you to put the story out that you've been robbed," I told Beth. "Tell the miners you're looking for a big bundle of cash, and go door-to-door searching for it. The guys should be happy to let you look through their things if you lay on the charm a little bit, right? Just be quick, casual and friendly, and get a look in as many dongas as you can."

"What are we really looking for?" Beth asked.

"Guns." I took out my phone and opened up the web page I'd found. I showed the phone around slowly. "We're looking for the sort you see in the top row here. See the big scope? You'll probably come across these ones here." I scrolled down the screen. "These are basic hunting rifles. Easy to get. We're looking for the more complicated ones. The big, expensive ones. When you see guns like these, I want you to snap a picture with your phone and bring it back to me."

"What if it's in some sort of case?" a young redhead said. "We can't just ask them to open it."

"Get a picture of the case," I said. "It might help. I also want one of you to get into the administration office and get me a list of all the personnel on the mine. The rolls. They should be in plain sight; they're checked every day. Just the names, nothing else. I'll send the names back to my station and get police history checks."

"I'll go to the admin office," Jaymee said, smiling. "I know Terry who works on the front desk. Now *that* guy's a creeper."

"We all stand to lose quite a bit of income if we're going to spend the next twenty-four hours on this," Beth said. "My appointment book's full."

"I'll cover your costs," I said gravely.

"We'll both cover your costs," Whitt said.

The girls smiled in appreciation and set off, leaving us alone in the yard.

"We've just got to hope whoever he is, he's keeping the weapon near him," I told Whitt. "This might be a total waste of our time if it's on one of the trucks, or he's got it stashed in the desert somewhere. But it's the best I can think of."

"It's a solid plan. It might turn up something. What are we going to do about Linbacher's gun?"

"That's my next trick," I said.

CHAPTER 72

LENNY XAVIER HAD his dream job. As a kid, he'd had one obsession: playing with skill-tester machines. His mother had taken to rerouting trips to the shopping center, because when Lenny spied skill-testers he would rush to the glass and stare at the treasures inside. Those closest to the chute were always the easiest bet, but they were often dumb—packs of cards or pink teddies. The real prizes were in the furthest corner—water pistols and bow-and-arrow kits. The risk was that he would finally snag a prize with the slick chrome arm and half-way back to the chute the arm would wobble, the prize falling free.

The tension of watching those steel fingers plunge into the pile of treasures was often more gratifying than win-ning. Somehow, when the prize flopped down the chute, it was less exciting than when it lay encased in glass, calling to him.

In the cabin of the 250-ton crane on the edge of the crevasse, Lenny felt the same quiet, electric thrill he'd felt as a child directing the arm of the skill-tester around the machine. He could see for hundreds of meters down into the great crack in the earth. The hot desert wind ruffled his hair as he sat in the operator's seat, the window open at his side. Right now he was lifting an old piece of a digger up from a shelf eighty meters below the surface.

Lenny's hands moved naturally over the controls, guiding the glossy joysticks with minuscule movements. The hook on the end of his line slid down into the crack easily, and Lenny rose up in his seat as he brought it within inches of the hunk of metal.

Mick, a plump figure standing outside, just in front of Lenny's crane, lifted the radio to his mouth. The speaker at Lenny's side crackled to life.

"About another two feet down, Len. Then bring it back tight. Over."

"Copy that, Boss. Over."

The radio blipped and died down. He lowered the line another two feet and then brought the joystick back toward himself, hearing the clunk of the hook sliding up under the digger's arm.

The radio crackled again. Static. He adjusted the dial, shifting from one of the mine's common frequencies to another, trying to find his boss. Between the frequencies, he came upon a voice.

"If you can reach the camp, I'll let you live."

Lenny looked down at Mick, who wasn't using the radio. His boss's hand was rising and falling gently, signaling Lenny to bring the line up. Lenny wondered if he had come across a radio station, or a UHF signal from truckers on some distant highway. But it was a good four hours to the nearest highway. And he'd never heard a non-mine station out here.

"Caller, can you repeat that? Over."

"If you can reach the camp, I'll let you live."

Lenny stared at the radio. The hairs on the back of his neck stood up, but only briefly. He shook the feeling off. He grabbed the radio and flicked the switch to retract the hook and line.

"Whoever's on this channel, you're coming through to the mine. You need to choose another frequency, mate."

There was no answer. Lenny realized he was sweating. He wiped his brow on the back of his wrist.

A sudden noise, a *crack* from one of the steel struts seemingly right outside the open window. Lenny stopped the line retraction and got up, pushed the window open further. Another sharp *crack,* and Lenny saw a bright burst of sparks spray off the steel just above the windowsill. On the ground, Mick turned and stared up at him, his eyes wide.

A *whizz,* and then a *crack,* and the window beside him shattered.

"Shit!" He sat back in his chair. He'd been trained to know when the crane was under pressure; when the wind was too high, and when static electricity in the air was causing the machinery to spark. But this was different. He grabbed the radio.

"Mick? Oi, Mick!" he called. He switched back to the previous channel. "Mate, something's— "

A second window exploded in the front of the crane bridge. Mick ducked, and Lenny rushed out of the bridge and onto the truck bed. He jumped from the vehicle and stood with his boss, looking up at the crane.

As the two men waited, both panting in the desert sun, the radio in Mick's hand crackled.

"If you reach the camp, I'll let you live."

CHAPTER 73

I STOOD AT the corner of Linebacker's cabin, watching Whitt as he prepared to knock on the door. Like the golden-haired schoolboy he'd been channeling since I met him, lying, deceiving and breaking with protocol weren't going to be easy for Whitt. He seemed like a very different man to the one he had described to me as we crouched, pinned, in the desert. The alcoholic, the stalker, the restless detective obsessed with hunting the predators who had eluded him. Some part of me admired the fact that, in bringing himself back from rock bottom, Whitt seemed to have fashioned a totally new being out of his self. Somehow, by zooming in and perfecting the smallest tasks—making his bed, ironing his shirts, polishing his shoes—he avoided those big black thoughts. Maybe there was something to learn from his behavior.

The cabin door opened.

"Mr. Linbacher," Whitt said, smiling.

"What? What is it?"

"I was hoping you could accompany me to the chow hall." Whitt straightened his shirtfront. "We're conducting interviews, and as the head of security—"

"Yeah, yeah." The older man waved dismissively, slamming the door of his donga behind him. "Took you idiots long enough to get around to me."

The two men wandered slowly away from the donga. I spied Beth at the second accommodation yard in the distance, moving from cabin to cabin. I slipped through the door of Linebacker's donga and stood in the cool dark.

The small space smelled of boot polish and gun oil, and was as spotless as Whitt's side of our own cabin. I went straight to the closet, running my finger along the shirts and trousers hanging there, the garments hanging longest to shortest, with each coat hanger placed precisely two inches apart on the pole. We'd arranged our uniforms in the very same manner in the police academy. Two sets of shoes on the floor of the cupboard, toes out, gleaming. One pair of brown leather, one pair of black.

If the killer was ex-police, that would explain his knowledge of weapons, and perhaps his marksmanship. It would be difficult in Australia to get training in long-range rifles without being either police or military, or spending wads of cash at one of the few ranges in the country. Even then, without a permit the killer wouldn't have been able to own the kind of weapon capable of killing in the way ours was. It was a good lead.

I rummaged through the top of the cupboard and

brought down a huge black rifle, setting it on the bed. I took a quick photograph on my phone, picked it up and popped out the magazine. It was fully loaded. My skin was on fire with excitement. But even finding the murder weapon in his room wasn't going to be enough to convict Linebacker of the murders. I'd found the underwear of rape victims in the bedrooms of their assailants, and still not managed to get a conviction. I needed everything I could get. I grabbed the first drawer of the desk and dumped its contents on the bed.

Pens, pencils, notebooks, rubber bands, keys. I grabbed the second drawer and dumped it. Photographs of naked women. A magazine called *Gore Porn*. I flipped through it briefly, feeling my upper lip curl. There were two more copies in the drawer. I grabbed a blue manila folder and sifted through the papers stuffed inside.

Birth certificate. Tax return forms. Pay slips. Rental ledgers. And a wad of papers stapled together, marked with a black Australian coat of arms.

I sat on the bed and scanned the document quickly. My eyes locked on bold lettering on the third page.

MEC5 Discharge.

I heard Whitt shouting outside, but before I could stand, Linebacker threw the door of the donga open. I had my gun out of my belt and trained on him as he stood in the doorway, his face darkening.

CHAPTER 74

LINEBACKER GAVE A short, hateful laugh.

"This is your idea of top-secret operations, is it?" he said. "Supersleuthing. You get the nancy boy to lead me away and you pick through my things like a vulture."

Whitt walked into the donga, his shame quickly overcome by shock at the great black rifle lying on the bed.

"Would you care to explain this?" I gestured to the gun.

"It looks like a gun," Linebacker said, smiling unpleasantly.

"Interesting." I smiled back. "Because as I recall, the only weapon you're permitted to have is the one in the guard station."

"Clever girl," Linebacker said.

"Is the one at the guard's station still locked up?"

"Of course it is."

"Then what the *hell* is *this?*" I snapped.

He reached for the gun and I sprang to my feet, actioning my pistol. Whitt had his gun out too, both hands locked on the butt, the barrel almost pressing against Linebacker's ear.

"Don't fucking move!"

"Put your hands in the air!"

"All right." Linebacker froze, his hand inches from the rifle's butt. "Why don't *you* action it then."

I paused. With a sinking feeling, I put my gun down and picked up the rifle. I grabbed the bolt and tried to slide it back, and found it hit nothing. The spring was missing. As my finger naturally slid into the trigger guard, it fumbled and found no trigger. I turned the gun on its side. The trigger slot was empty.

Linebacker was sniggering. I held the rifle in my hands, staring at the glossy black body.

"Not so clever anymore, are you, girlie?"

"Where are the missing pieces?"

"They don't exist," Linebacker sneered. "I have a mate in the army who's feeding the gun back to me piece by piece. Every six weeks he orders a spare part from his armory, so as not to arouse suspicion, and posts the part to me. It's missing the trigger, the firing pin and the bolt spring. In about—oh, maybe three months—I'll have a complete gun, totally off the register."

"Why would you want a gun like this off the register?"

"To sell, you moron! You know how much I can sell an untraceable gun of this size for?" Linebacker squinted at me. "Are you stupid or something?"

I looked at the mess on the bed. Linebacker picked up the rifle and pointed it at my face.

"*Pow!*" he roared, and broke into a hacking laugh.

CHAPTER 75

I STOOD WITH my eyes closed in the blazing sun, looking at the redness it made on the back of my eyelids. Maybe if I stood there long enough, I thought, I could burn the embarrassment away.

"Well, assembling stolen parts and creating unregistered weapons for sale on the black market isn't nothing." Whitt clapped me on the shoulder.

"Fat chance of conviction, given the illegal search." I groaned long and loud. "He'll get rid of it all by the time we make the phone call for a warrant."

"Oh, I know," he sighed. "I was just commending you on your effort. A good effort should never be ignored."

We walked for a long time in silence. I felt the heat of humiliation slowly draining from my neck and face, but my heart was still thundering in my chest.

"I don't like the guy, Whitt." I looked at my partner.

"He had a medical discharge form for the Defense Force. So we know that not only has he got army friends, he was probably army himself. He'd have the training to use a weapon like that, whether he says he's assembling it for sale or not. There was also a copy of *Gore Porn* in there."

"*What* porn?"

"*Gore Porn* magazine," I said. "Don't look so disgusted. It's a pretty popular rag. Contrary to men like yourself who only read *Grammar Weekly* and *Quiches of the World*, guys in groups read pretty sick shit. *Broot* magazine's most popular sections are still the horrific workplace injuries and, of course, the porn. Put the two together and you have *Gore Porn*. Sadism. Plastic surgery gone wrong, birth defects. Execution videos and snuff."

"I don't see the appeal."

"Thing about *Gore Porn* is, it's good for a laugh," I said. "Whenever I've seen the magazine before, that's been the reaction from the owner—*hey, it's good for a laugh*. It's gross and kinky. You find them in policemen's locker rooms and navy messes and sports club back rooms. Female no-go zones."

"I'll take your word for it, Harriet."

"In my experience, though"— I tapped Whitt's shoulder—"there's only ever *one* copy. You can't say someone bought it for a laugh when you've got a collection of them. *In your bedroom*."

"So how many did Linebacker have?"

"At least three. And they were consecutive issues. You know, I'm not trying to make a big deal of something just because I think the guy is an award-winning jerk—

which he clearly is—but you put the gun and the military service together, add in the unpopularity of this guy, all the time he spends alone walking around this place, and witness accounts that he's tortured animals. On top of that, you add private reading material which suggests a strange, violent sort of arousal and what you get is someone who—whoa!"

A miner hurtled past me so fast and so close I was nearly knocked sideways. Two more followed, heading toward the rec room. I heard shouting. Whitt and I locked eyes. I saw terror flash briefly in my partner's face, and then I heard a gunshot rip through the air.

CHAPTER 76

A CROWD HAD gathered at the side of the yard along the fence line, hands gripping the wire. Some men were shouting out, but the majority were silent.

"What the hell is going on?" I grabbed the nearest miner. He had no words, just pointed.

Out in the desert a tall, muscular man in a hard hat stood still, his hands slightly out from his sides. He must have been three hundred meters away. In the distance I spotted a crane.

"What's happening?" Whitt gripped the wire beside me.

The man seemed to take a deep breath, then rushed forward, arms swinging madly as he put all his effort into the sprint. He started to dart sideways as puffs of sand exploded at his feet. Eventually the terror took him and he skidded to a halt.

"Oh, Christ." I drew my gun. "He's got the sniper on him."

I scrambled to the front of the crowd at the gate. The opening wasn't big enough for a car. I pushed through and shut it behind me, locking Whitt on the other side with the crowd so he couldn't stop me if I needed to run out there. I did not want these miners outside the fence line.

There was absolutely no cover out there on the plains. The man standing in the desert had no choice but to try to make a run for it. Wherever the gunshots were coming from, they came whenever he started running. He didn't know whether to stand still or run. He was completely at the mercy of the shooter.

"Fuck, man!" someone near me cried. "Where are the shots coming from?"

"I can't see! There's no sound. Has he got a suppressor?"

"We need to get out there."

"No one's going out there." I watched them push against the locked gate. "Everybody stay calm."

"Lenny! Lenny, run!" a young girl screamed.

"Where's Mick? Mick was out there with him!"

"Everybody shut up!" I could feel the tremors starting at my calves, creeping up my legs. I needed to think. "I want all of you back from the fence. You're all exposed here."

"We can't just stand back and watch them kill him!" someone cried. "We need to get out there!"

I turned to the man in the desert, Lenny, who was gearing up for another sprint at the fence.

He ran, and after ten meters or so the puffs of sand began again. He swerved sideways, stumbled and fell, gripping at his calf. The chatter at the fence stopped just long enough for us to hear his agonized wail.

"Do something!" the girl screamed at me.

Sweat dripped off my upper lip. I needed to know what direction the shots were coming from. The sand seemed to be puffing out to Lenny's right side. But there was nowhere out to the east where the shooter could take cover—unless there was a tunnel entrance I couldn't see, a hole he was slightly popped up from. I squinted into the blinding light, my breath coming in hard gasps.

This is all on you, Blue. They're all watching.

Lenny was crawling, trying to get to his knees. I opened the gate and pushed back through the crowd, pulling it shut behind me.

"She's leaving!" someone cried as I sprinted across the yard. "Don't go, you stupid bitch! Don't leave him there!"

There was a four-wheel drive standing at the edge of the truck yard, the driver's door left open. I leapt into the vehicle and turned the keys.

The machine had all the weight and grip I was after. I floored the accelerator, spun the truck and headed straight for the gate, my horn blaring.

"Get out of the way!"

The fence rushed up against the front of the car, and as the gap closed I pushed the accelerator to the floor.

The gate smashed down in a terrifying roar. A scream escaped my lips. The gunshots started immediately, the driver's side window exploding, a thousand cubes of glass raining over my shoulders and back as I bent almost double at the wheel.

Pock-pock-pock-pock.

I didn't look, but I knew he was littering the side of the vehicle with holes. I heard the telltale rush of air as one of the back tires exploded. I knew a bullet could tear into my insides at any second. I'd been shot before—I knew there'd be a *thump,* a dull heat, and then that sickening wetness running down my side.

Lenny started running. I reached over and threw open the passenger door, slamming on the brakes as I came alongside the miner. He launched himself sidelong into the vehicle, his whole body slamming into mine, his head almost in my lap.

I swung the wheel and let the engine roar, putting my back to the shooter, making a smaller target of the vehicle. I didn't care where we ended up. The man in the vehicle with me was alive. He curled, crying against the dashboard, his fingers gripping the car like claws.

CHAPTER 77

WHEN EVENING FELL Whitt and I retreated to the steps of our donga, having spent most of the day interviewing Lenny Xavier. A quietness settled over us as we thought about what he'd said, about the voice on the radio telling him that a sick game was on.

Out in the desert, Taylor Fink and her team were examining Michael Hibbert's body. Lenny had told us that when the shooting first started, Mick had lain flat on the ground and refused to run. The gunshots had hit the sand all around him, the killer seemingly trying to encourage him to participate in his twisted race.

"I guess he realized Mick wasn't going to play," Lenny had shuddered, sitting hunched over in the corner of the rec room. "Then one final shot came, and the top of Mick's head came clean off. I just bolted after that."

Whitt and I had received word that afternoon that police reinforcements were on their way.

"Will the killer stay, or will he go?" I mused aloud. Whitt brushed off the knees of his trousers, thinking.

"He'll stay," he said finally. "Everything about Lenny's story suggests the killer enjoys the spectacle. He'll want to watch the hornets scurrying around, now that he's well and truly kicked the nest."

"Broad daylight," I said. "Dozens of people watching it unfold. This guy's accelerating."

"You've got that right."

It was only a five-minute rest break, but I still felt guilty that Gabe arrived and found Whitt and me not actively doing anything. I shot up from my seat when I spotted him coming over, his hard hat in his hand.

"Something bite you, Harry?" Gabe asked.

"No." I brushed my hair back. "No, we were just putting our heads together, and I didn't want you to think—"

"I think you look exhausted." Gabe smiled. "Both of you. And the whole camp's talking about you driving out there to save Lenny like a crazy person. You could have both been killed."

I didn't notice Whitt slip away. But when Gabe put his hand on my shoulder, I knew it must have been because we were alone.

"I was terrified when I heard that," he said.

"It was fine."

We walked in silence to the east fence and looked out at the Forensics unit's tents lit up in the distance. My eyes wandered over the black desert until I found a convoy of cars heading toward town, a chain of gold and red rumbling across the horizon.

"Very few will leave," Gabe said.

"Really?"

"Oh yeah." He laughed a little sadly. "There'll be plenty of discussion tonight, but the majority will stay. None of these guys want to look afraid in front of each other."

I watched his big fingers grip the wire.

"I was doing a materials check at three kilometers deep once," Gabe said. "Ride down in the elevator took fifteen minutes. Down that deep it's hot, and the air isn't right for breathing. You've got to wear masks and protective gear. Sweat was pouring down my whole body."

He stared at the sky.

"The earth makes noises—doesn't necessarily mean anything. It rumbles and grumbles all the time. But for some reason it spooked this young miner. There'd been a collapse at a nearby mine the day before, and he must have been extra sensitive. After a really sharp rumble he dropped his tools and shouted, 'It's coming down!'"

"Jesus," I whispered.

"At that depth, in the dark, with the air pressure and the heat, you're right on the edge. Your mind is *ready* to panic. But most of the time you just get on with the job. But this kid's cry. Everyone broke. *Snap!* We were like animals."

He shook his head in disbelief.

"It's times like that you really face your own humanity. Or lack of it. Long story short, these guys are world-class veterans in denying their own fear. They won't leave."

My hands, of their own volition, had crept up and

gripped onto the collar of my shirt, my sweat dampening the fabric. I had been on the edge of that same animalistic panic since Sam was arrested. *It might be years of this,* I'd thought. *It might never go away.*

"How do you live on the edge like that for so long?" I asked.

"You train your mind away from it. It's all about denial. And trust me, place like this? We're so far from anything ordinary that the few little lies you tell yourself to survive are so easy. I mean, it's like a dream, isn't it? Sun rises, sun sets. There are no days, no months, the weather never changes. Same people come and go. Danger and fear are so everyday that they kind of cancel each other out. You know, truth is, if you're twenty meters deep or three thousand meters deep, you're still going to die if it all comes crashing down."

He stared at the horizon.

"So, you spin yourself a web of lies."

CHAPTER 78

WHITT AND I sat on my bunk in the semidarkness, our backs to the cork partition. Around us on the bedcovers lay six or seven notebooks crisscrossed with suspects, their work histories and whereabouts on the mine. We stared at the laptop screen between us. Jaymee the Bilby had snagged the personnel list for us. And emails from my headquarters containing the criminal records of the miners had started rolling in.

Jaymee had also brought me a clear plastic bottle of "Mine Wine." To combat the alcohol restrictions on the camp and high prices in town, plenty of miners had started home-brewing. Like prison hooch, most of the Mine Wine was terrible—the result of unsuccessful experiments with dried fruit and tomatoes, even bread sometimes. Though this batch was terribly sour and filled with sediment, it wasn't all that bad. I kept the bottle between my knees and enjoyed the gentle haze that was settling over me.

"Theodore Ivan Sava," Whitt yawned. "Charged: sexual assault, grievous bodily harm. Conviction recorded. Joseph Doyle. Charged: common assault, common assault... Lots of common assaults. Convictions recorded. Blake Henry Young. Charged: common assault, resisting arrest, being a general scumbag."

"Category three," I said. I wrote the names down on my Category Three list.

"Jessica May Harvey. Charged: burglary, possession of a prohibited substance. Conviction recorded. Oh dear. The next three guys have aggravated sexual assaults, and one had a manslaughter charge."

I picked up my Category One notepad and started writing.

Whitt started laughing suddenly. "David Alistair Burns," he said, smiling. "Possession of a prohibited substance. Three charges."

"That dickhead," I said. "No wonder he didn't want the checks done. Where's Linebacker's? I can't wait to see that guy's rap sheet."

"They're not giving us the files in any particular order." Whitt yawned again.

There was a soft knock at the door, and Taylor Fink poked her head in.

"Ooh," she said. "Slumber party?"

"The password is 'I'm tired and I want to go home.'"

The pathologist wriggled onto the bunk between

Whitt and me. I shifted the laptop to make space for her. She flipped open a scrawl-filled notebook.

"All right." She drew a deep breath. "Let me start you off with what I've just seen out there in the desert. Deceased Caucasian male, mid-forties, mildly obese, one major external injury, likely the cause of death. Head wound, large caliber gun. Took the skullcap clean off. Likely died instantly."

I made notes quietly in my own notebook.

"I also have the findings from the three mine bodies, but I'm paraphrasing here. Amy King was played with a bit. Fingers missing, bullet wound to the knee and hip. Looks like he might have chased her around. Her younger sister died from a single long-range gunshot wound to the back. Hon Lu suffered a number of injuries. He was missing a couple of fingers and an ear. Burn patterns suggest these were also long-range gunshots. Teaser wounds."

"Did your colleagues do the soil analysis of the boots?" Whitt asked.

"They did. Tori and Hon had deep-desert sand uppermost in their boots. So, shortly before death they'd been out there somewhere in the Never Never. Amy's boots were filled with mine sand only. So it looks like she was killed here."

"In the tunnels," I sighed. "He probably hunted her down where she worked, for talking to us. Didn't have time to complete his ritual."

"Here's an interesting tidbit for you," Taylor said. "All three had gun oil on their palms. Hon Lu even had bruise impressions on his right hand consistent with the ribbing on a rifle stock. All three handled a gun shortly before they died."

"What?" I looked at Whitt. "Why would our victims have handled the weapon?"

"No idea. We're not even sure they handled *the* weapon, the one that killed them. They just handled *a* weapon," Taylor said. "The gunshot residue findings are interesting, too. Hon and Tori had very small amounts on them, consistent with handling a gun that had, at some point, been fired. But Amy was covered in the stuff. It looks to me like she might have actually fired the weapon she handled."

We sat in silence for a long time.

"It's a hunt," I said, looking at the others in the dark. "Lenny said that before the shooting started, a voice on the radio told him that if he made it back to the camp he'd be left alive. Think about it. It's like a ritual. You set them up with a challenge and a defense mechanism of their own and then you hunt them, like foxes. What pisses off fox hunters most? When the foxes go to ground. When Michael wouldn't run for his life, he was executed. Maybe the killer gave the others a weapon to make the hunt more interesting. Give them a chance to fight for their survival."

"He didn't give Lenny a gun," Whitt said.

"No, but this time he was hunting in broad daylight with dozens of spectators. The odds were always on Lenny's side that he'd be rescued somehow. The whole spectacle of it would have been titillating enough."

"How do we find this guy?" Whitt murmured, staring at his hands. "How do we get control of the ritual?"

"We stop acting like prey," I said.

CHAPTER 79

I WOKE TO the sound of helicopters, and for a moment lay wondering if another body had been found. But it was the Channel Seven helicopter sending tumbleweeds rolling across the accommodation yard. The miners were walking to and from work like nothing was happening, but I knew there'd be a heavy press turnout at the front gate.

When I arrived at the chow hall, Whitt was sitting with a group of eight uniformed police officers, four men and four women. A black coffee was waiting for me when I sat down.

Whitt introduced me to each of the officers in turn.

"I'd really love to know what we're supposed to be doing out here," one of the men said. "Edward tells us we don't have approval from the mine bosses to search cabins. And Perth seems to be dragging their feet on a warrant."

"We won't get a warrant," I said. "People with this kind of money and influence, they'll have too many friends in the Justice department. There's no way the bosses are going to have cops exposing the mine's drug problem live on the evening news."

"What bullshit," the cop next to me snorted.

"Searches are happening, but they're happening unofficially." I sipped my coffee. "Background checks are also happening, but it's very hush-hush. I've got a list of mine personnel with violent backgrounds or gun offenses. You can help with those. But we don't have approval for any arrests. So if the miners refuse to talk, there's nothing you can do."

"Who are your main suspects?" someone asked.

I took a photocopy of Linebacker's ID card and spread it on the table.

"I don't like this guy," I said. "And yeah, maybe that's influencing me a bit. He's a major creep. But if my instincts are any good, he's someone we should be looking at."

A heavy silence fell over the table.

"OK." I felt my face grow hot. "I know what you're all thinking. What good are this detective's instincts if she couldn't even recognize her own brother as a sexual predator? Well you know what, guys? My brother's guilt or innocence is still on the table. So, as of today, there's no reason to suspect there's anything wrong with my intuition."

"I second Harriet's feelings about this guy." Whitt tapped the picture of Linebacker. "I think we need a couple of our team watching him at all hours."

I unfolded the printout of the shadowy figure at the EarthSoldier camp.

"I've got this image from a group of activists outside the camp. I don't like their leader, either, this Ocean Divine woman."

"Ocean Divine?" a young female cop howled. "Classic!"

"These freaks are wearing the ear tags of dead sheep. Who knows what they're capable of? I don't feel like they're behind these murders. But they're certainly not cooperating with us, and I want to know why."

"Richard Lee Machinna." Whitt laid a picture of Richie on the table. "He's the camp drug lord. Richie and his crew have been violent toward people on the mine. They've been known to rob helpless tourists, and even the weaker members of the mine staff trying to pass through. Now, if that isn't some kind of sick power game, I don't know what is."

"Why have we got a drug syndicate operating openly on the mine?" one cop asked. "Is this guy on payroll?"

"Don't ask," I sighed. "He gets to just wander around. He's part of the furniture."

"We also have prostitutes conducting our searches for us," Whitt said, smiling. "But while they've been very helpful, they've also been responsible for some violence toward miners, too. So they're not completely off our suspect list."

"Welcome to the Outback," someone laughed.

CHAPTER 80

SINCE WE'D SENT them out to search the accommodation areas, the Bilbies had been feeding me back photographs of interesting things they'd found. There were plenty of handguns on the mine. With so much masculinity flying around, it made sense that a few guys had brought in pistols to show off, maybe even take out into the desert and pop off a few cans.

There were rifles among the mix, but so far only classic wooden-stock, low-range rifles without scopes. The type farmers might give their sons to keep the rabbits at bay. None of the men seemed to be hiding their weapons very well. The pictures were of guns leaning against walls and sitting on the ends of beds. There was probably a bit of bragging going on, about what might happen the next time the shooter showed up.

As the day wore on, miners started to approach Whitt

and me as we worked through the criminal records and interviewed security staff who had been on the edges of the mine when Lenny and Mick were targeted. Most could only offer useless leads, rumors and snatches of overheard conversations.

Someone saw a flash from the east accommodation block as Lenny was being shot at.

Someone heard the killings were linked to a sex trafficking ring.

Someone knew an ammunitions guy in Perth who had recently been bought completely out of .50 cal bullets by a man in a snappy suit.

My mood slid downhill dramatically with every new supposed lead. I knew this was what was happening back in Sydney, now that the papers had named their suspect for the Georges River killings. Someone would have overheard my brother in a bar talking about what he'd done to the last victim. Someone would have heard about him dumping evidence behind a warehouse somewhere. Someone's friend's friend would have made a narrow escape from him, having agreed to help him move some items he didn't own into the basement he didn't have.

People wanted to be a part of trauma and terror. I didn't know if it was because they wanted to make sense of the tragedy, to feel better themselves, or if it was just a sick fantasy made real through lies.

The men and women of the mine were nervous and agitated. I suspected that some of them stayed for the reasons Gabe had explained. But, deep down, I also suspected some of them stayed because they feared losing their jobs. These were people from hard lives, who knew security here that they'd never known anywhere else. They stayed for the money, for the beds, for the food. They stayed because maybe home, where angry husbands and wives and parents waited, was just as dangerous.

Many of them held the same suspicions as me about some of their number. I kept hearing about violent things Richie had done to people who'd brought drugs onto the mine that weren't his. The girls seemed particularly afraid of him and his pack of sunbaked dogs.

As our dangerous suspects list grew, Whitt and I wandered between the cabins of the all-stars of violence and gun offenses on the mine. These were dark-eyed, lanky men sitting alone in their dank, stinking accommodation areas or laughing in closely huddled groups in the rec room.

We had no legal right whatsoever to ask these men if we could go through their things. But the implications of refusal were clear. As we confronted them, they looked around the faces at the tables with them and knew a rumor about their guilt could be halfway across the mine within an hour. Whitt and I crawled under beds, pulled boxes down from cupboards, pushed aside bags of clothes.

The day wore on. By midday, the journalists at the gate, having had no luck gaining entry to the mine or comment from the bosses, had begun to creep down the side fences, trying to engage miners in the truck yard and accommodation blocks. No one would talk, but I saw some miners taking business cards. I kept my head low, not wanting to be recognized.

"I wonder if there's money on the table," I murmured, shielding my eyes from the cameras.

"If the miners are smart, they'll wait until three. Reporters will start scrambling for an interview for the six o'clock news."

Two reporters started tailing Whitt and me along the fence line, noticing that we were not in miners' uniforms. With the arrival of the press I'd taken to wearing my black baseball cap, and I pulled it down deeper as they started calling out.

"Hey! Are you guys with the cops?"

"They're good," I murmured.

"It's you," Whitt said. "You've got cop written all over you."

"What? No I don't!" I straightened my shoulders.

"You keep touching your gun," he said. "They're thinking, 'Either that woman's got a gun back there or her jeans don't fit.'"

"No they're not. They're thinking, 'Who's that very ordinary woman and what's she doing with that antiques dealer?'"

Whitt gave a small, weary laugh. I liked the sound of it. I might have enjoyed it for longer if it hadn't been interrupted by gunfire.

CHAPTER 81

THE GUNSHOTS STARTED just as we were rounding the corner to the big empty space before the chow hall. They were rapid shots, splitting the air in painful cracks. Whitt and I hit the edge of the supplies building. I looked over and saw the two journalists were crouching against the fence, the camera already rolling. Along the wire I could see the other journalists were running across the sand toward us.

"Fucking idiots." I drew my gun. The camera turned to me as I waved at them. "Get down! Get down!"

Miners rushed past us. Whitt and I jogged in a crouch toward the chow hall. A young girl ran outside, smacking into the glass door with her shoulder, splintering the glass. I could hear chairs and tables being knocked over.

The gunfire stopped. I could smell cordite in the air, but also the distinct taint of rotten eggs that took me back to my childhood, summer nights and New Year's. I knew even before we burst through the doors of the chow hall that something was wrong. The room was clear.

I walked to the buffet and picked up the spent string of a row of red firecrackers. The giggling and snickering of the men at the far window drew my eye. Three of Richie's crew members, with the snake-eyed man himself standing at the back of the crowd, his phone up, filming. The men bolted as I stood there like a fool, my gun by my side.

"Wow." Whitt took the string from me. "That's pretty low."

A man in plain clothes ran into the chow hall, a huge camera by his side. It seemed I only twitched, but my nerves were so raw, and I was so angry, that the sight of him triggered an animal reaction in me. For half a second, I saw a gun, and then I realized my arm was out and my pistol was aimed at the journalist.

"Whoa!" he said. "I'm sorry! I just hopped the fence. I wanted to see—"

"You hopped the fence?" I put my gun back in my jeans. "Right. Put that thing down. Get out some ID. I'm citing you for trespass."

"You're what?" The cameraman laughed. "You can't be serious."

I knew what I was doing was stupid, and petty, but aside from chasing Richie and his crew down, yelling for them to get back here like a schoolteacher chasing a crew of naughty boys, I had no course of action. I did not know how much longer I was going to be able to stand my inability to act in the face of a cowardly sniper who was picking off people like ducks. I needed to do something. When I gripped the guy's bicep I dug too hard and he yelped.

"You don't have to say anything, but anything you say may be taken into evidence and used against you. I'm escorting you off the premises, where you'll be issued with a citation to appear in court."

Whitt grabbed the camera and popped the memory chip as I led the cameraman out. The crowd of people who had been scared out of the chow hall were watching, along with a dozen journalists. The rage in my chest was so hot and painful I couldn't focus on anything else, couldn't stop myself rushing down this foolish path. I couldn't back down now.

As I was marching the cameraman across the yard, the cameras focused in on my face. I'd drawn attention to myself in the worst way possible.

"Harriet... Harriet Blue?" one of the journalists called. "Hey! Isn't that Detective Harry Blue?"

CHAPTER 82

"CAMERA CREWS INVESTIGATING the murders of several employees at a mine in remote Western Australia were met with police resistance today. An officer involved with the case laid trespassing charges against a cameraman for illegally entering the property," the newsreader said. "Seven Network news cameraman Simon Windell was escorted off mine grounds by lead detective Harriet Jupiter Blue after an incident inside the mine startled reporters in attendance."

Gabe shifted in the bed beside me, sitting up taller against the pillows, his thick arm around my neck.

"What did they just say?"

"They said I arrested a journalist." I exhaled cigarette smoke out the open window beside me. "I did."

"No, they said Harriet Jupiter—"

I glanced sideways at him. "That's my name."

Gabe looked at me in the dark, his eyes sparkling. *"Jupiter?"*

"My mother was a prostitute and a drug addict," I said. "What the hell did you expect?" I punched him in the ribs.

We watched as footage shot from outside the fence showed me leading the cameraman away from the chow hall.

"News crews at the mine were shocked to discover Detective Blue, who has not spoken publicly since her brother Samuel Jacob Blue's arrest this month for the Georges River Three murders."

More footage of me, waving off the cameras after I'd shown Simon Windell out of the mine gates. Reporters hollered at me on the screen but I put my head down and walked off, safe within the boundary of the mine. An image of Sam flashed on the screen. The picture of us together in the sunny garden.

"Samuel Jacob Blue has not yet entered a plea for the murders, nor are police commenting on whether the killings are linked to his sister's investigation in Western Australia."

I grabbed the remote from Gabe and switched off the television at the end of the bed.

"Linked?" I snapped. "If these killings here are linked to the Georges River killings, who the hell do they think's doing them? Sam's in fucking jail!"

"They're just sensationalizing," Gabe yawned. "Murders are more exciting when they're linked."

As the boss of a large crew of miners, Gabe Carter had a small, run-down donga to himself. He'd set the bed up near the dusty window, where he could sit propped against the wall and drink coffee in the morning. I lay on his chest and watched the lights flashing on the big crane in the center of the mine while tapping the ash of a well-earned smoke out the window.

"How could I have been so stupid?" I said. "Now my cover's blown."

"You're being too hard on yourself." He stroked the soft hairs at the nape of my neck. "You were sending a message to the journalists that you're not taking any shit."

"They came out here for footage of a killer being arrested, and what they got was me frog-marching one of their own off the mine for hopping a fence. It looks bad. Not only am I not supporting my brother back in Sydney, I'm not even doing my job here."

"Harry, you're—"

"Killer. Dark. Hunter. Vengeance."

"What?"

"Killer. Dark. Hunter. Vengeance," I said, twisting the hairs on his chest as I thought. "Danny Stanton wrote those words in one of his notebooks. If I can't find the gun, I need to figure out what connects all the victims. Did those words mean something? Are they the key piece of information I'm missing?"

"Yow!" Gabe snatched up my fingers from his chest hairs. "Those are attached!"

"Oh. Sorry."

We lay in silence in the cool sheets, the night outside pulsing with the leftover heat of the day. Initially, the faintest touch of Gabe's skin, even from that very first handshake, offered so much refuge from thoughts of what was happening back home. But that comfort seemed gone now. That first night in the desert, he hadn't known who I was or what was happening in my brother's world. How could he not wonder what I knew, what involvement I had in what Sam had supposedly done? I curled away from him, but he pulled the arm tucked beneath me tight and pressed his lips to my ear.

"Stop thinking about Sydney. You're only out here in the first place because you're trying to stay away from all that trouble back home."

"Are you reading my mind now?"

He reached up and tucked a black curl behind my ear. "If you try hard enough, you can forget anything outside the fences exists. I've been doing it for years. Forget the press. Forget your brother. You can't do anything about that now. Just focus on what's going on here."

I closed my eyes and tried to imagine the mine in the middle of the desert as its own planet in a vast, sandy universe. For a moment, I latched onto that lie, and my big bad world felt slightly smaller.

CHAPTER 83

BY TEN O'CLOCK that night Gabe had fallen asleep beside me, his internal clock matched exactly to the shifts he worked each day in the mine. I crept out of his bed and went back to my own donga to find Whitt. There was a note on his bunk saying he'd gone into town. For a moment, panic racked me, and I stood frozen in the dark. Maybe all the officers on the case had gone into town. Most of the press were probably staying at the hotel there. They'd pressure Whitt and the cops for details on the case. They'd know everything before I even got in the car to leave the mine.

I walked to the car, trying to breathe evenly. This was what I did. Expected the worst. Put no faith in the abilities of others. Of course the other cops wouldn't talk to the press. Of course Whitt would never reveal anything sensitive. These people were professionals.

I spotted Whitt at a table at the back of the pub with two of the female officers.

"Is it true?" he asked. I felt the hairs on the back of my neck stand on end.

"Is what true?"

"Jupiter?" The corner of his mouth twitched. "Is your middle name really Jupiter?"

I sighed. The cops beside him giggled. I sat down and poured myself a glass of wine from the bottle that was on the table and drank it dry in three gulps.

"What's the news of the past few hours?" I asked.

"Well, one of your little working-girl spies came running to us with a very exciting find." The cop's name tag read Beckett. She put her mobile phone in front of me. There was a picture of a black plastic case under a messily made miner's bunk. "Looked good, too. The owner was Ethan Formosa. Food stores guy, worked with Hon. Couple of serious assaults on his record."

"Did you check it out?"

"We did." The shit-eating grin hadn't left Whitt's face. "Plenty of resistance on the part of Formosa. He did not want that case opened in front of the other miners hanging around the donga at the time. No, sir."

"So what was it? Was it a gun?"

The officers around the table paused, looking at each other.

"Goddamn it, Whitt, speak up."

"It was, uh." He cleared his throat. "I believe they call it a *gimp* outfit?"

The other cop, Shae, snorted hard, covered her mouth.

"There was a zipper mask," Whitt said, struggling to maintain his composure. "Some straps and buckles. Some... *implements*. There was a... a pump, of some sort."

"All right." I sat back in my chair and poured another wine. "I get the picture."

"The girls' searches also turned up four other heavy-duty black cases hidden around the mine," Beckett said brightly. "Two flutes, a saxophone and a bassoon. I wouldn't have thought there'd be so much musical talent in a place like this. We could start a band."

"The Dusty Miners," Shae said. "With special guest, the Masked Gimp."

The three burst out laughing. The tension of the past few days had finally cracked in Whitt. The weariness in his features had lifted. I was grateful, suddenly, to the women at his side. In this job, it was impossible to remain bent by the graveness of the situation at all times. That kind of dreariness could kill you. I had seen it do its magic on older officers, when the laughter tank emptied and no joy came, even when times were good. I wasn't there, yet. I knew I had good humor in reserve, but it didn't feel safe to let any of it out yet. If I did, I'd quickly remember what was happening back home, and the guilt would come. Taking solace in Gabe's arms was all I could manage right now.

I went to the bar to get another bottle of wine, without announcing where I was going. I did that when I was deeply involved in a case, started being rude, distant, forgetting the rules of good company. Pops noticed it, called it my "action mode." I missed him desperately all of a sudden, heading toward the bar in the dark hall. And it was in this sorrow cloud that I failed to notice the first arm that reached out from nowhere.

A man in front. A man behind. There was a warm, hard hand that came up around my mouth and another attached to an arm that wound around my waist and dragged me backwards.

CHAPTER 84

THE MUSIC IN the main bar was so loud even I didn't hear my scream. I was being dragged backwards up a tiny staircase and was then shoved forward into one of the musty bedrooms on the first floor.

The bathroom light came on, and with it my defenses. The voices of a hundred rape victims came back to me from across my career. The ones who'd fought and the ones who hadn't, their voices alive in my imagination, reliving those first few moments when their safety was taken away.

Bite. Scratch. Twist. Kick. Gouge. Do whatever your body will allow you to do. Just don't let them get you in the car—the room—the basement.

The moment I started fighting, the man who had me in his arms dropped me heavily on the tiles of the big shower cubicle. The nozzle above me was dripping steadily. The floor under my hands and jeans was wet.

Richie hung in the doorway with my black service pistol in his hand, plucked at the last moment from the back of my pants. Two of his men stood in the bathroom, their eyes flicking to the stubble-covered sink, the stained tub, the cracked mirror and the terrified cop. The musty smell of their male bodies filled the room.

Richie waited as I surveyed my situation. I knew two of his crew were missing, probably guarding the door. The floor was vibrating with the music from below. No one was going to hear me. No one was going to come looking for me. I was unarmed, and outnumbered. This is what pure, wild terror feels like.

"Don't say anything," Richie said, as though I was capable of it. "Just sit and think about all the things we could do to you right now. Be imaginative. Don't just picture us dragging you out there onto the bed, holding you down. Look at the bathtub. Think about me filling it up halfway and drowning you in it. Think about what tools I might have to play with. Can you imagine those things, Bluebird?"

I tried to get air deeper into my lungs. Richie pointed at me. All his gentleman-thief swagger was gone now. His eyes were empty.

"You've caused me a lot of trouble here, woman," he said. "From the moment you came along, you've been a fucking nuisance. People stopped buying. Then more stopped when your little friends arrived yesterday. A stream of cars left here in the past forty-eight hours, and most aren't coming back. These are my roads, yet they all got through without paying the toll. You know why? Because I had two idiot cops sitting on my back like fleas."

Richie crouched before me. One of his crew, a lanky blond man with tattoos on his hands, smiled when I caught his eye.

"My income right now is zero," Richie said. "Somebody's got to pay up."

"Whitt is going to come looking for me," I said.

"Oh yeah. They tell you to say that, don't they?" Richie murmured. "First they say, *Fight for your life. Don't let them get you away from the herd.* Then they say, *Tell 'em you've got a disease. Tell 'em you're pregnant. Tell 'em your boyfriend will be back any minute.* Then they say, *Tell 'em things about yourself. Make yourself a real person, so they won't kill you when they're finished.*"

He laughed. "Well, your boyfriend's not coming, Bluebird. And you ain't no person to me. But I won't hurt you. And neither will my guys. You know why? Because we don't have to. You realize now that all your clever fighter-girl antics—they haven't got you anywhere. You've been strutting around like you're some wildcat cop who doesn't take no shit. Well, look at you now. You're fucked. And I think that for someone like you, that's just about the worst thing I could ever do."

Richie rose and looked down at me.

"Here's what's going to happen, Bluebird," he said. "Pete and Andy here are going to drive you to Perth. You're going to tell your bosses your inquiries led you back there, because you believe the shooter has left the mine. You'll call your poofter boyfriend Whittacker and tell him to come home, and you'll call off the support crew. When you've done all that, I'll think about sending you back your service weapon so you don't look like any more of a complete fuckup than you already do for having lost it."

He tucked the gun into his back pocket and turned away, exchanging a look with the blond man. His two cronies came forward.

"I don't think I have to tell you what'll happen to you if you fuck with me, Detective." He waved a finger around, taking in the apartment, the bathroom, the bed, the beautiful little trap he'd snared me in. "This? This was easier than it should have been."

"There's a problem, though," I said.

I rose steadily, and Pete and Andy backed up just slightly, glancing at their boss. Richie stopped in the doorway as I gathered myself.

"I *am* a wildcat cop who doesn't take no shit."

CHAPTER 85

IT'S BEST TO conserve your energy when you know you're fighting for your life. Start small. Keep light. Strike with precision, and don't waste your swing. The one named Pete smiled and reached for me in the corner of the shower. I slapped his hand away, smiled back. *That's right. It's all fun and games.* Terror sweat was still dripping from my jaw, even as I danced with my attacker. Richie paused in the doorway to see what would happen.

Pete came forward again, and I locked onto his arm with both hands, twisted and shoved. He crumpled slightly against the shower door, making the glass rattle in its frame. I lifted my knee high and shoved my heel down hard on the arm I held, snapping his radius with an audible *crack*. Pete howled. Andy's arm came around my neck from behind. I pushed backwards into him, enough to slacken his grip so that his forearm slipped up around my mouth. I took a nice, deep bite.

The sound of Andy's screaming made my eardrums pulse. I used all my body weight to topple him onto Pete, both men falling through the shower screen and into the cubicle. I half turned to launch myself at Richie in the doorway, but Andy was on me again, trying to bundle me up in his arms. I went with it, let him lift me.

Big mistake, buddy.

I wrapped my body around his head like a cat, digging my fingers into the soft flesh under his jaw, my legs around his waist. We fell into the sink, the tap jutting into my hip, splitting the flesh beneath the jeans. I grabbed fistfuls of Andy's hair and head-butted him hard in the nose.

Pete sat in the corner of the shower where I'd been only moments earlier, clutching his bent and broken arm. Andy had let go of me and slid to the floor beside the toilet. I sat on the edge of the sink and wiped Pete's blood off my chin with the edge of my shirt, crossing one wet leg casually over the other as Richie watched.

One of my shoes was off. The shoulder of my shirt was torn, and my hair was in my face. My pants were soaked, and by now all the terror had been burned away by the adrenaline released in the fight so that, as I took a moment to reconsider my position, I found myself more pissed off than I had ever been before.

Richie lifted my gun and pointed it at me. The gun

clicked. I reached into my other pocket and drew out the magazine I kept there.

"I never keep it loaded when I'm drinking," I said. I beckoned him forward. "Come get it. I won't hurt you."

Richie dropped my gun on the floor and backed out.

CHAPTER 86

"YOUR SKULL MUST be made of lead," Whitt was saying. He tapped me hard above my left eyebrow. "Days after the killer cracks it open for you, you're using it as a weapon."

The nurse was the same humorless woman who'd patched me up outside my donga after I'd almost met my end in the tunnels. I lay on a table in the medical center while she stitched the Y-shaped split in my hip caused by the bathroom tap.

"You know," she said, "there's a link between frontal-lobe trauma and antisocial behavior. Do you go around head-butting people often?"

"I try to keep it to two or three a week."

"It's surprisingly easy to give yourself brain damage." She shrugged as she pulled a stitch through. "Your frontal lobe houses all the neurons that control your emotions. Mess with that, and you can become violent. Reckless."

"Are you advising me to stop head-butting people," I said, "because I might end up wanting to head-butt people?"

The nurse glared at me.

"I guess we can cross Richard Lee Machinna off our list," Whitt sighed. "Why would he bother trying to bundle you off to Perth if he was the killer? He'd have just snuffed you out from a distance like the rest of his targets."

"Maybe he likes me," I said. "Maybe he likes you. Maybe he likes us both, and he wants us out of the way so that he can continue his killing spree without hurting either of us, because we're so delightful."

"No one here likes you," the nurse said.

"I'm not letting him go," I told Whitt. "Could be that this ritual he's got going only involves miners, and we're proving too much of a bother for him. I want to know if we should keep him on the suspect list or boot him off. We'll find out where he stays and then we'll know just how serious this guy is."

"The whole crew's got a couple of caravans off the mine, about ten kilometers' drive," Whitt said. "I suspect we'll have the same kind of trouble getting a search warrant for there as we've had for here. We can think about it in the morning. Set up a distraction or something."

"What about Aaron Linbacher's criminal record?" I said. "Has it come in yet?"

"No," Whitt said, "not when I checked last, which was

a couple of hours ago at least. I'll check again when we get back to the donga."

My partner stretched in the plastic chair, and I heard his neck crack. It felt good to see him a little less fatigued. At least one of us was operating at an effective level of tension. I knew I was too wound up. But I always had been, even before I'd joined the force. Being this hyper was going to get me into trouble in times of war or peace. Richie had been right. I was wild.

"Go to bed," I told Whitt. "I'll be here a while longer I reckon."

He agreed reluctantly and slouched off into the night. While my friendly nurse searched for an appropriate painkiller in her outer office, I sat thinking about Danny Stanton.

"Killer. Dark. Hunter. Vengeance," I murmured.

I knew I was close to finding the killer. I could feel his presence on the mine. He was going to give me more of a fight than Richie and his goons—one I wasn't sure I would survive.

CHAPTER 87

"THIS IS GOING to be great," I told Whitt. "Not a soul around. We'll be in and out without even having to draw them away from there."

We lay on our bellies on a ridge in the blazing desert sun, watching Richie's lot through binoculars. The camp consisted of two battered white caravans and a gray 1980s model Hyundai Sonata up on bricks, the tiny rectangle of shade it provided stuffed full of lantana and desert grass. In the half hour we'd lain watching, nothing on the camp had moved. I was sure Richie and his crew had at least another couple of hours in lockup in Perth. I wondered quietly whether he had been worried or relieved when the "common assault of a police officer" charge came down, knowing I could quite easily have taken him up on an attempted-murder charge.

Across the rocky landscape, a pair of emus wandered, the man-sized birds dipping now and then to inspect the ground under their massive feet.

"Right," I cleared my throat. "Carry on."

We searched the caravan from top to bottom. There were no weapons of any kind. We locked the second caravan behind us and stood in the sweltering sun.

"A bitter disappointment," I said.

"Maybe not." Something had caught Whitt's eye. He wandered over to the disemboweled car. A huge sand-colored lizard broke cover from the dry grass and fled toward the rocky ridge.

On one side of the vehicle, the hard grass and shrubs had been cut back so that a person could happily slide beneath the car to what was underneath. Whitt reached through the glassless windows, tried to shift the front and passenger seats, but to no avail. He'd need to get on his belly and crawl under the car. When he did, he started furiously brushing sand away.

"I'm going in!" he cried happily.

I listened to the twist and *thunk* of something opening, and then watched his legs disappear as he shifted around to lower them down a capsule opening.

I grabbed the circular edge of the opening, pushing aside the heavy fiberglass lid of the submerged capsule. When I dragged myself forward and looked down, I saw Whitt standing on the floor of a fifteen-foot-deep space, the walls lined with homemade shelves. There was enough room for Whitt to stand alone comfortably. He looked up at me and smiled.

"Get in here," he said.

CHAPTER 89

I STEPPED OFF the tiny ladder and stood beside Whitt, our chests almost touching. Around us three shelves crowded, stuffed with drugs. The bottom two layers were almost full of tightly packed bricks of what was probably cocaine and heroin wrapped in black plastic and brown tape. The two shelves above them were crammed with boxes of prescription drugs.

"Wow." I took a couple of boxes off the shelves and read their contents. "Look at all the steroids. All the antidepressants!"

"Yeah, I can't imagine the guys out here being too happy seeing the doctor about their depression." Whitt studied the boxes. "It's probably just easier for them to get their meds from Richie. Not so many questions and checks."

"Painkillers." I moved to the shelf on the left. "This whole shelf is all Oxy. There must be hundreds of boxes."

"Oh, shit." Whitt gave a little excited laugh. He'd dragged a huge vacuum-sealed bag of weed from an upper shelf. "It weighs as much as a child."

On the uppermost shelves were the items the boys needed quickly, things they could lean down from the roof hole and grab without necessarily having to climb all the way in. I reached up and took down a few stacks of green and yellow bills. Whitt and I smiled at each other, weighing the money in our hands. We were going a bit silly in the presence of so much wealth. I fanned the bills in his face, held them to my nose and sniffed. I'd never held so much money. Not even on the drug raids I'd participated in as a young recruit. It was shocking, and strangely amusing, that people lived like this. Stacking bricks of heroin in an underground bunker like they were preparing for the apocalypse.

The fun was abruptly halted by a scraping sound outside. Whitt and I looked at each other, and I watched the shadow of the bunker lid slide across his face.

"No," he cried, looking up. "No!"

CHAPTER 90

FOR A MOMENT we simply stood there, the two of us, shouting. Shouting at whoever had locked us in. Shouting at each other. In the panic and darkness I was pushed into the shelves behind me, the stitches on my hip pulling tight beneath the bandage. Pill boxes clattered to the floor.

"Fuck," Whitt yelled. "Fuck!"

"You're deafening me!" I shouted.

"You're deafening *me!*"

"Climb up there." I shoved at him. "Go."

Whitt took the three ladder steps required to reach the roof opening and pushed hard against the lid. It didn't budge. I listened in the complete blackness as his fingers fumbled at the rubber rim that sealed the opening tight. My own breath seemed thunderously loud in the tiny space. Though the capsule was submerged and therefore cooler than the desert outside, sweat was already breaking out all over me. There was barely enough room for the two of us to stand. Whitt thumped his fist against the inside of the lid.

"Help! Help!"

"Whoever's done this isn't going to help," I snapped. "If they were going to help they wouldn't have sealed us in in the first place."

"Do you think it's him?" Whitt asked, climbing down beside me.

"Probably. Who else would be watching us and know we're out here?" I checked my mobile phone, but of course there was no coverage. Whitt did the same. I reached behind the boxes and thumped the walls of the capsule.

"I think this thing is an old water tank. Which means it's airtight. We could die in here."

"Your constant positivity astounds me, Harry," Whitt sneered. "You're always looking on the bright side, aren't you?"

I frowned in the dark. "Who's this nasty Edward Whittacker? I haven't seen this side of you. Are you claustrophobic or something?"

"Possibly." His voice was small in the dark.

"Well, sit down and cover your ears," I said, taking out my gun. "This'll help."

I wedged one of my ears against my shoulder, but there was no saving the other one from the sound of my gun blasting at the ceiling. Light spilled down over us from two perfect holes in the tank lid, illuminating Whitt's grave features. I climbed back up and pushed

against the lid, hoping the holes might have weakened it. But, looking through them, I could see the fiberglass was an inch thick.

I slid down to the floor of the tank in front of Whitt, our legs interlocked. His shirt was already sticking to him with sweat. I looked around, and grabbed a box from the bottom shelf.

"Valium!" I shook the box at him.

My partner crunched a Valium quietly, his breath coming in long, even streams. For a while we simply sat together and tried not to panic. We wouldn't run out of air, not with two holes punctured in the lid of the water tank. But it was possible we'd be killed when Richie and his crew returned. Or if they didn't return, that dehydration and heat exhaustion would kill us. There were no liquids in the tank whatsoever. Only enough cash to buy us a small island, and enough drugs to kill us many times over.

"I've got to warn you," I said. "Things get much worse, I'm lighting a joint."

CHAPTER 91

WE TOOK TURNS standing at the top of the ladder, listening for sounds in the desert outside, periodically yelling for help. Both of us were drenched in sweat within an hour. The holes in the top of the tank provided air, but that air was hot, and soon condensation was dripping down the ribbed walls. Now and then wind brought red sand raining down.

While Whitt seemed beaten by the structure, I was convinced there was a way out. I tried turning the lid of the water tank, but it seemed levered shut with something and would only shift by mere millimeters. I found a knife on the uppermost shelf and went about carving up the black rubber rim of the lid, dropping pieces down on my increasingly angry partner.

"This is the stupidest thing I've ever experienced," h

said, wiping sweat from his face. "Why didn't he just kill us?"

"Because that's no fun?" I said, jabbing at the lid with my knife. There had been plenty of opportunities for the killer to take either of us out since we arrived in Bandya. There were only two reasons I could think of for leaving us alive. One, his victims were very specifically chosen, and he was unwilling to kill anyone other than them. Or two, that Whitt and I upped the stakes of the hunt, put a couple more predators on the field as competition in his pursuit of his quarry. I cut out all of the rubber lining of the lid of the tank and found it made no difference to its operation. Still, I felt some weird satisfaction knowing Richie and his crew were going to have to reline their tank.

"Let's keep working on connections between the victims. We know there's no age connection, or racial motive. But they've got to be connected somehow. Where did Danny Stanton work?"

"Construction," Whitt said. "Under Gabe Carter."

"Hon worked in food stores," I mused. "Tori and Amy in electrical, and Lenny and Mick on the diggers. So it's not their placement on the mine that connects them all."

"No." Whitt perked up, seemingly happy to have something to distract him. "No, that's not the line of connection. Hon was single and looking online for girls back in his hometown. Tori had a boyfriend, and Danny was in some sort of relationship with that purple-haired girl. So it's not a love triangle or anything like that."

"Danny and Shamma," I murmured, leaning back on the ladder. "Danny would have been visiting the

EarthSoldiers a lot if he was familiar enough with that girl to become infatuated with her. Amy said Tori used to go out there a lot, so maybe Amy went there too. That's half of our victims right there."

"And the other half show no connection to the EarthSoldiers whatsoever," Whitt said. "Hon was no weed smoker. He was straight as an arrow. Mick and Lenny looked a bit past it, didn't they?"

"If the victims were selected deliberately, something must connect them all," I insisted. "What else could get all of these totally disconnected characters together? I mean, they vary in age from nineteen to fifty. What did they all *do* that might have put them in the path of the killer? What activity unites them?"

"Mining," Whitt said.

I sighed at him and slid down to the bottom of the tank. The silence stretched for an hour or more, in which we waited, sweated. When the email alert tone on my phone sang it startled us both.

"You can get emails?" Whitt grabbed at the lit screen in my hands. "Why didn't you say anything?"

"I didn't know I could get emails!" We fought stupidly for the phone in the dark. "Give it to me!"

I checked my coverage. Still nothing. How could an email possibly get through? I composed a message directly to Pops, the subject header "URGENT! HELP!" My fingers trembled as I described our situation. When I pressed send, it went straight into my outbox, and a message appeared on the screen.

"Network coverage error?" I read. "What the fuck?"

"You must have just had coverage for a second or two,"

Whitt said. "Must have been a satellite going over or something."

I opened the email I'd received. It was from a journalist. She'd attached a photo of the front page of the *Herald*.

We'd love to be the first interview on this, Harry, she wrote. *Any comments? Just one will do!*

The cover was a picture of my brother, his hollow-cheeked face as he passed between doorways at police headquarters. The headline read BLUE GIVES FULL CONFESSION.

"Anything important?" Whitt yawned.

"No." I tucked the phone away. "Nothing."

Sitting in the dark, listening to my partner's breathing in what was possibly going to be my death chamber, I wondered if it was OK to cry yet.

CHAPTER 92

WHEN THE NOISES came, it was dark. Whitt was humming, trying to take his mind off how much he needed to pee, he told me.

"Shut up! Shut up! Listen!"

"Oi!" someone shouted on the wind. "Oiiiiii!"

"Help!" I cried. I shimmied up the ladder as fast as I could, my whole body tingling and numb from sitting cramped in the heat. "Help! We're in here!"

I thumped the inside of the tank lid. Whitt stood up and bashed the ladder onto which I clung.

"Are you sure we should do this? What if it's them?"

"I don't care if it's them, I'm getting out of here," I said. "Help! Help!"

There was silence. I kept wailing, hoping the visitor could hear me. Sand dripped from the bullet holes in a steady stream. I thumped and thumped, listening to the sickening quiet between my efforts.

"Where the hell are you?" a girl said.

"Oh God, we're in here!" I cried. "Help! We're under the car!"

Two voices, curious and a little frightened. Then the sound of sand being pulled and scratched away from the lid. I was surprised how much had blown in while we'd been trapped. After a minute or so, a single blue eye appeared, staring in at me.

"What the fuck is this?"

Shamma lifted the rock out from where it had jammed the lid shut. She twisted off the covering and fell back as I scrambled out of the tank.

"Oh God, thank you. Thank you so much." I sprawled on the sand beside the young EarthSoldier's friend. "Oh, you're the best people in the whole world."

"What the hell were you doing in there?" Shamma asked. "Where's Richie?"

"He's been arrested." I breathed the clean desert air. "He'll be back soon. We went down there to snoop and got trapped. What the hell are *you* doing here?"

"We came to get weed, what else?" Shamma laughed. "We can't get onto the mine. Something's gone down."

"What's gone down?" I asked.

"I dunno." The girl shrugged, curling a purple dreadlock around her ear. "The alarms have been going off all afternoon."

CHAPTER 93

THE CAR WE'D borrowed from the mine rumbled and bumped over dry rocks on the way back to the mine. Darkness was falling, lighting the horizon bloodred and sending plumes of tiny desert birds up from the spinifex toward the rolling clouds. Whitt sat beside me in the dimly lit cabin, going through his missed calls and emails. On the camp in the distance I could see lights gathered at the gates, more than there should have been. The press camp had grown.

"Linebacker's criminal record came back," Whitt said. "Clear."

"I'll bet his military service record isn't," I said. "Have you got that yet?"

"Not yet."

At the gates the media swarmed around the car, absurdly glamorous women with hard, sculpted hair battered by the desert winds, their silken shirts clinging to their bodies with sweat. I heard the alerts as soon as the gates shut behind us, pumping through the camp's PA system.

"Harriet Blue and Edward Whittacker, contact the administration office immediately. Valerie Beckett and Julia Shae, contact the administration office immediately."

"Beckett and Shae." I glanced at Whitt. "Those are the two—"

"The two officers we assigned to Linebacker," he said. His face was hard.

I pulled the car onto the dirt strip in front of the administration office. David Burns burst out of the doors of the building just as we exited the car and came striding toward us. For once, he looked ruffled and mildly stressed. I was almost pleased.

"Where have you been?" he snapped. "Two of your officers are missing. There are another four in there who are just about beside themselves."

I didn't bother explaining what had happened to Whitt and me in the desert. I wanted to know what had happened to my officers. Hanging nervously around the counter I found three of the men and one of the women who had been sent from Perth to assist us. A cop named Hellier grabbed me by the arm as soon as I got within reach.

"Where are Beckett and Shae?" His words were so fast they were almost slurred.

"You tell me," I said. "You've tried them on radio?"

"They stopped responding to radio and phone around midday," the woman, Doyle, said. "They were assigned to

Aaron Linbacher. We've talked to Mitch and Sully, they're on their way back from Perth. They dropped your assault charges there."

"I know. I know." I tried to breathe. "No one's seen Beckett and Shae? They didn't say anything before they went missing?"

"They reported to me at about eleven-thirty." Hellier was pacing. "Everyone did. We thought you must be out with the EarthSoldiers or something. They said everything was fine, they were just observing Linbacher on his rounds. Where were you? We called and called."

"You shouldn't have left." David Burns puffed his chest out at me. "If anything happens to those officers it's your head, Detective. Not mine."

CHAPTER 94

IT WAS GETTING harder, but the climax of combat was like that. A soldier was tested in many different ways. His patience was tested. His mind was tested. And he was tested on what he was willing to sacrifice in order to take the campaign to the next step. If he faltered, if he hesitated, he proved himself ineffective to command—and, like fathers, the sole important goal of command was to raise the future generation and pick out the runts.

The Soldier found it easier if he didn't think. If he only acted, diligently and fiercely, when the time came.

He'd hung around the group idly the night before, listening to their chatter, identifying them all. He knew their weaknesses. Now, after securing Detective Harriet Blue and her partner in the tank in the desert, the Soldier had gone back to the mine to hunt the two female police officers, Beckett and Shae. With his main quarry delayed for the final mission, his last task before entering the next glorious phase of his plan was to eliminate the two women. They weren't a threat to him, of course, but what their demise would do to Detective Blue's mindset would be profound. Vulnerable women had become her mission. Her life's purpose. To strike two of them down right under her nose would continue his program of shattering the delicate strands of his adversary's confidence. Mind games. They were so important.

A sneak attack would do it. There was no need to lull these two into a false sense of security. He'd found the two of them leaning against a transport truck in the cool shade of the yard, lazy sentries laughing quietly together, one of them looking at the screen of her phone with serious interest.

The Soldier had climbed stealthily up the narrow ladder on the back of the truck and crept across the aluminum top of the vehicle, pausing at the edge to listen to his victims, to smell their cigarette smoke.

"Can you imagine that?" Beckett was saying. "You wake up one morning and open the newspaper and *whammo!* Good morning! Your brother is a fucking sicko murderer."

"I don't have a brother."

"Your sister, then." Beckett slapped her partner. "Your boyfriend. Your mother, for fuck's sake. Play the game with me! Shit!"

"It's gotta suck. But what's the difference between that, right, and thinking your husband loves you and then finding out he's got, like, three other wives?"

"Or that he's gay," Beckett snickered. "You're married

to him twenty years and you've got three kids and then suddenly he tells you he likes guys. Whoops, sorry, I forgot to mention it!"

"I guess everybody thinks that, at the very least, there are some people who they *know*. Truth is, nobody knows anybody."

"That's right," Beckett said. "Nobody knows anybody. Isn't that terrifying?"

The Soldier slid the wire garrote from the pocket of his trousers and let it uncurl, the natural twists in the weave straightening his makeshift weapon on the truck top. One half of the wire was insulated with plastic coating that would protect his hands, but the Soldier wasn't taking any chances—he pulled on a pair of electrician's gloves and made a wide wire loop that would accommodate the width of a human head. He crept to the edge of the truck and looked down at the two women. The neat, identical parts in their straight blond hair reminded him of two angelic children. There was something about the top of the head, the vulnerability of that crown, the ease with which an adult might stroke or cup the top of a child's head with their hands as they passed at waist height. For a second, he had to steel himself. This was war. There was no place for thoughts of children here.

The Soldier lowered the wire carefully so that it hung just an inch or two above Beckett's unknowing forehead. The loop bulged and sat out, ready to ensnare her. Holding both ends of the wire in one hand, the Soldier slid his hunting knife out from his pocket, gripped the very tip of the handle. He stretched his arm out, aiming carefully, the shining blade dangling down like a pendulum above Shae's head.

He closed his eyes, counted to three, and let the knife go. It sailed silently downward and, with hardly a sound, lodged handle up in Shae's skull.

"Direct hit," he murmured. "Target down."

Beckett was still talking as an unfeeling, unseeing Shae fell to her knees and flopped forward on the sand. The Soldier gave Beckett a second, no more, to wonder what was happening.

Then he lowered the loop as swiftly as he could and pulled backwards and up, hooking the wire beneath the officer's jaw and tightening it around her throat.

He gripped the wire, wound it around his hands, and pulled.

CHAPTER 95

BURNS FOLLOWED US doggedly, his tie caught in the desert wind. Now and then he rambled to himself about our incompetence, lawsuits and the media. We ignored him, passing through the center of the mine to try to avoid the press cameras at the fence. The PA announcements were still ringing every few minutes for us and the two female officers.

My phone had exploded with messages and missed calls as soon as I'd come within range of the mine's mobile and internet servers. I glanced at the screen as we walked. For once, journalists weren't bothering me about Sam. The messages were mostly the same, desperate writers trying to get something of value out before the evening newsreel.

Channel Nine reporting you're missing on the mine?! Call us!

Harry Blue hav u gone 2 ground? On way back 2 Sydney? Comments plz!

Harry, has Mine Killer killed you? If no text back, will assume yes! This is Joe @ the Enquirer.

We found Linebacker by his security hut, filling out forms, the furrows in his brow darkened by tiny particles of red desert dust. As we approached he put one foot inside the doorway, leaning his body closer to where his gun was propped. Whitt reached out, his hand barely brushing my shoulder as I picked up speed.

"Harriet, keep it together now..."

I smacked the clipboard and pen out of Linebacker's hands and grabbed his shirt, dragging him out of the security hut and throwing him away from me. He stumbled, his face almost purple with rage.

"Where are my officers?" I howled.

"Hey? Running back to me about your fucking mess-ups again, are you, copper!" Linebacker spat on the ground at my feet. "I should have expected this, shouldn't I?"

I drew my gun and pointed it at him. David Burns, who had been jogging after us, put his hands in the air like an action-movie hostage.

"Oh God!" He looked around, trying to decide where to run. "Oh God, please! Don't shoot him!"

"Tell me where my officers are, Linbacher, or I'll shoot."

"This is excessive force!" Linebacker pointed a bent finger at me. "I'm not threatening you right now. Help! Help!" He took a few big steps backwards to put himself in view of the press down a small corridor between the buildings. "I'm unarmed, and a police officer has a gun on me!"

"I'm gonna give you five seconds," I said. "And then I'm gonna put one right in your guts."

"Help!" Linebacker called toward the press. "I'm unarmed!"

"Five." I actioned the pistol.

"Harry, Jesus, put the gun down!" Whitt yelled.

"Four."

"Harry, I can't let you do this!" I heard Whitt draw his weapon. "Put it down!"

"Three."

"Help me! Someone!"

"Please don't!"

"Two."

"Harry!"

"One."

CHAPTER 96

A SCREAM SPLIT the air, so high and shrill that it almost shocked me into pulling my trigger. I turned and saw Whitt with the eye of his gun on me. I holstered my gun and ran toward the sound, Whitt coming into line beside me. Miners who had been watching my standoff with Linebacker from the corners of buildings darted out of the way.

The screaming woman was Officer Doyle. She was kneeling in the sand between two trucks, dressed in jeans and a sweat-stained shirt. Officer Shae was lying on her front, the black leather handle of what must have been a large knife protruding from the top of her head like a single radio aerial. There was no blood, but as I neared I could see Shae was certainly dead, all the color drained from her face and her hands curled inward in the awkward claws of someone with a traumatic brain injury.

Officer Beckett was slumped on her side next to Shae's feet. I ran over. Her death hadn't been so quick. A wire garrote, it looked like, had been pulled tight around her neck, and she'd fought for her life silently while the wire gouged right through the skin to her windpipe. I followed the angry red welt up behind her ears to the rear of her skull. She'd been kneeling, maybe, and the killer had pulled upward, hung her against himself. Or she'd been standing, and had been hung from above.

I looked at the tops of the trucks on either side of us. There were dents and scratches above Beckett, where she'd kicked frantically. The lividity in both women, the purple clouds of color where their bodies touched the sand, told me they'd been dead three, maybe four hours. Not long after Whitt and I had been locked away.

It had taken that long for someone to find them, or for someone who had found them to report it. There were plenty of footprints in the sand around the kill zone. The miners had probably come and seen the women here and decided they didn't want to be the ones to raise the alarm. They didn't want to be suspected.

Whitt stood nearby, unsure of where to look. Eventually he grabbed the crying officer and dragged her away. At the ends of the alley created by the trucks, miners came into view, staring, openmouthed or grave-faced. They came, saw and rushed away, making room for others. I sat on the sand between the two dead officers and watched them.

"Get a good look," I snapped. "Yep! Make room! Come and have a gawk, you fucking sickos!"

I pulled the collar of Beckett's shirt up to hide her face

from the crowd. Her final seconds had frozen the pain and terror of her murder on her features.

Whitt returned and crouched by me. "Will we just arrest him now?" he wondered aloud.

"No." I rubbed my eyes. "The lividity."

"Right." Whitt bent down to look. "Four hours? Five?"

"Plenty of time to have a shower. Ditch the garrote. Ice his palms so they don't bruise. I don't want to bring this guy in only to have them set him free six hours later." I stood and looked down at my fallen colleagues. "I think I've got a plan."

CHAPTER 97

AARON LINBACHER STARED out the slatted window of his donga, watching the journalists at the fence line. The huge lamps they carried looked like the torches of a monster-hunting mob, throwing their shadows on the sand inside the property. He sipped a coffee he'd made at his personal machine and squinted as two EarthSoldiers approached the media pack, striking up a conversation with a couple of cameramen.

"Terrorists," he sneered. He felt the muscles in his shoulders tighten around old wounds, familiar rivers of pain zinging through his frayed nerves. All the old trauma was there, always within grasp. The twitching in his fingers had already started. "Insurgents. Rats."

The media swarmed around the little pair of terrorists, gold lights falling on their youthful features.

Linbacher had been in Afghanistan on special assignment when the planes hit the towers. He remembered people yelling in the night, running toward mosques, the patter of their hurried footsteps in the dirt the first soft sounds of what would become a hellish orchestra of war. A siren that rang even in his quietest moments now, even in his dreams.

Before the attacks, he remembered the gentle creep of danger in the streets, the rise of traitors and men with dark hearts, the seemingly disconnected instances of rebellion. After that, there were press cameras. Horrified faces of women and girls, running, shooting, and gold-lit faces on street corners watching planes quietly traverse the sky. Linbacher had learned to recognize the signs. He'd even tried to convince people, the blind ones, but no one ever listened to him. He was too old, and the worst thing was, his personal experience of the war excluded him from having any kind of opinion on it. Imagine that! People had decided somewhere along the line that those who were least trustworthy in conversations about war were the ones who had *been there*. They'd been on the ground, shaken by the explosions, pierced by the shrapnel, face-to-face with the terrorists—both the black-bearded kind and the baby-faced kind. And all of that horror had marked them. There was no way they could get their heads out of the dust cloud and see what was really going on. The subtle movements of chess pieces on a vast, crowded chessboard. No, soldiers were only pawns. They didn't know how things worked.

"Bullshit," Linbacher snarled. He clenched his shaking fist. "Bull. Shit."

Because he had been there, because he had smelled the gunpowder and seen the shadows creeping in the night, he could see that it was happening again. You had to notice the little things. The baby-faced terrorists were on the television. In the newspapers. They were on the trains and in the shops. Hundreds of them. Suddenly the insurgents weren't black-bearded men but white-haired grandmothers. Their hunting grounds were universities, cafés, forests in Tasmania.

They disguised themselves, and they disguised their cause.

Today, it was feminism. Capitalism. The *environment*.

Tomorrow, people would scream and towers would fall.

Aaron was ready. If no one else wanted to join him, that was fine. He'd lived alone long enough, surrounded by people. He'd still be alone when all the people were gone.

"Terrorists," he found himself muttering, taking his coffee cup to the tiny kitchenette by the back window of his donga. "Creeping, creeping, creeping."

Almost as though they'd been conjured from his words, Linbacher looked up and saw two black-clad figures slipping between the trucks behind his donga, pausing at the bull bar of a white van parked on the corner. They waited for something, probably a signal, and then darted away again into the night.

The EarthSoldiers.

Linbacher dumped his cup in the sink and ran to the door.

CHAPTER 98

WHITT AND I got to the bottom of the huge tower crane, running so fast through the camp grounds we almost slammed into each other as we came to a stop. Above us, fourteen stories of dark red scaffolding stretched into the black sky, the whole thing creaking and yawning, the monstrous song of an impossibly large beast. The balaclava I had borrowed from the Earth-Soldiers was already itching on my brow and cheeks. This was no place for heavy wool. I gripped the first ladder with my padded gloves and looked back at the masked figure of my partner.

"You think he took the bait?" I huffed. "Should we wait for him?"

"Go." Whitt pushed at my back. "He'll come."

I climbed the first ladder shakily, trying to reason with

the terror in my chest. If I kept trembling, if I kept panting, I was going to fall. And if I fell I would likely take my partner with me. I glanced down at the camp as we came above the level of the demountable buildings. Already, the height was terrifying.

We rushed across the first platform and leapt onto the second ladder, Whitt reaching the bars first this time.

Using the crane had been his idea. Get him away from the miners, from his victims, not into the desert—which we knew was his hunting ground—but up into the air, into our birdcage. We paused on the third ladder and listened to the creaking and ticking of the massive structure. A muffled padding. Footsteps on the first platform. A lightning bolt of fear crackled through my chest, racing over my scalp. I reached up and pushed at Whitt's feet.

"Go, go," I whispered. "He's coming."

CHAPTER 99

LINBACHER POPPED HIS head up over the top of the third ladder and surveyed the platform, the waist-high rails that lined the five-meter-square space. No one there. The intruders must have been continuing upward. Yes—he could hear their footfall. He heaved his rifle onto the platform and pushed himself up, reaching for the butt of the weapon as he steadied himself.

"Hands off," someone said.

He paused, fingers inches from the black steel, and looked up.

There they were. Two lean, strong ghouls in black, pointing pistols at him. He didn't move. Didn't continue toward the gun, or straighten. It took precious seconds to assess the situation, and in those white-hot seconds, his fingers started their furious trembling again.

The one nearest him ripped off her balaclava and threw it on the ground.

"I'm not one of those fucking hippies," she said. "I *will* shoot you dead."

Linbacher straightened. The woman was dressed like a cat burglar. He had known she was a traitor the moment he laid eyes on her. Her partner, the nancy boy, pulled his balaclava up and tightened his grip on the pistol.

"You were so close to slipping away from us," Detective Blue said. "Fuck, man. I thought we were never going to catch you."

"What are you talking about, you stupid bitch?" Linbacher was surprised by the hate in his own voice. *Keep it together, Lieutenant.*

"Your civilian criminal record was empty," Harriet said. "You've never had so much as a speeding ticket. Even your army service record was clean. We had to bust into the medical records to find out what you'd done in Afghanistan. The medical reports stated that because of the trauma you'd experienced in one particular village outside Yemen, you were no longer capable of serving. But what happened there? We only found out when we went into your psych records. I guess the command team cleared all that up for you, didn't they? The things you did over there."

Linbacher snorted. Words failed him. He was so enraged that it was almost tipping over into a kind of sadness. It was all so ridiculous. So juvenile.

"The village was so small it didn't even have a name," Detective Blue said. "Forty-eight people. You had orders to cleanse the town of terrorists. But they were all terrorists to you after a while, weren't they? You ordered them all into the pit. You made them turn away from you, so you couldn't see their faces."

He took a step toward his rifle.

"Don't," Whittacker warned, his gun following Linbacher's movements. "Just don't."

"You told the psychiatrist that you see them in your dreams. The backs of their heads. You're terrified of their faces. In the dreams, they start to turn around. You wake up screaming."

"You pathetic little shits," Linbacher said. "You think I haven't killed you yet because I can't? I want to hear more of your stupid story about me. Go on. I dare you."

"You never leave this place," Detective Blue said. "Even when they make you go home. You're always in the desert. Your mind is always here. Because this is what you're familiar with. The sand hills. The enemies they hide. You use your imagination, and they're all here. Your victims."

Linbacher was trembling all over now.

"One of the EarthSoldiers described someone in the camp spitting on her, just like you spat at me this afternoon. She thought you said 'harshee.' But it was '*hajji*,' from the word Muslims use for those who have traveled to Mecca. The coalition forces had plenty of slurs for the locals over there. But *hajji* was the most common, wasn't it?"

Linbacher shook his head in disgust.

"This place was perfect for you." Detective Blue nodded at the camp, the lights below. "It was so easy for you to envision the mine as your base. You, after all, are the head of security. Keep the miners safe, and keep the *hajji* out. Take down those within the camp who betray the security of the people. Hon, who let the EarthSoldiers raid the food stores. Danny, who fraternized with them, and Tori, who traded with them. Amy, who sided with us against you."

"You're so blind," Linbacher sneered. "So fucking blind."

"Lenny and Mick were just target practice, weren't they?" Harriet said. "Sharpen your skills. Complete your drills. Protecting this place is your mission, isn't it, Aaron? It's all you have left."

"You're right." The old man's face cracked, and a soft smile crept over his lips. "This is all I have left. And I'm not gonna let you take it away from me."

CHAPTER 100

HE WAS FAST. That was the only reason he'd made it to lieutenant. He decided things quickly, he acted quickly, and he was never wrong. Linbacher reached for the gun with one hand, drawing their eyes away, and with his other hand grabbed a fistful of the sand he'd poured into his pocket before he climbed up the crane. The wind was perfect. He needed only the lightest underarm swing. It exploded out of his fingers and sailed across the platform into their eyes. The officers gripped at their faces. He snatched up his weapon and cocked it.

It was his last action on Earth. The bullet that took him snapped off the lights in his cold, war-torn world.

CHAPTER 101

I THOUGHT FOR a second that it was my bullet that had taken out Linbacher. I'd squeezed the trigger, but not far enough, and the gun hadn't kicked in my fingers. There'd been no blast sound, no muzzle flash from Whitt's gun. There'd been a *whoosh,* a *thump,* and Linbacher's head had exploded.

The old man slumped to the iron mesh on the bottom of the platform, most of his skull missing. I felt his blood spray onto my face, a warm mist on my fingers and the front of my shirt.

"Oh, Christ," Whitt said softly. The wind picked up and howled around us. "Oh shit, it's not him."

"What?" I staggered, barely comprehending what was happening.

A bang, a spray of yellow sparks above us. I thought for a second something electrical was going wrong with the crane. Another bang as a second gunshot hit the lamp hanging above the third platform. We flattened, both of us, onto the bloody floor.

"It's not him!" Whitt was wailing. "It's not him!"

A sickness swelled in my stomach, not at the mess of Linbacher's head that I was lying in but at the sudden realization that we were hundreds of meters up in the sky and the killer was not here with us, was not the dead man lying before me. A volley of gunshots whooshed and banged at the rail, the steel struts above us, the top of the ladder. The killer wasn't playing now.

Through the iron grille beneath my hands, I saw people running, taking cover. A scream. The sound of an engine firing and a car screeching away.

"We're trapped," I shouted. The bullets kept raining around us. "We're trapped!"

"Don't panic." Whitt reached out and grabbed my hand. The mesh had made a bloody tattoo of diamonds on his cheek. "He can't get us, or he would have. He'll move to get a better shot. And when he does, we go."

"It wasn't him," I stammered, the panic rising hot and painful into my throat. "We were wrong. We were wrong!"

"We can do a full postmortem of our fuckups later." Whitt flattened against the floor as a bullet slammed into the rail behind us. "Right now, let's try to get down from here alive."

CHAPTER 102

I WATCHED THROUGH the platform floor as our officers took up their positions, one trying to calm the nearest donga of screaming female miners and positioning himself in the window, his pistol at the ready. Two others were sticking together, disappearing into the bowels of the crane's bottom floor. Whitt and I lay twitching at every shot that blasted near us, some nicking harmlessly off the structure of the crane, others showering us in sparks. Whitt's poker face was better than mine—I could feel shock coming on quickly, and those familiar in-action symptoms were starting. My teeth were chattering. The shivers had started in my legs. But even in his straight-faced denial of all that was happening around us, his hand squeezed mine way too hard.

"Any second now," he muttered. And as he did, the firing stopped.

We waited, half a second or more. Then he sprang to his feet, half-sunk in a crouch.

"Let's go, Harriet," he said.

I should have anticipated that, caught up in all his old-world chivalry, he'd be the one to dive first into the danger. But I was still surprised when he passed me on the path to the ladder. We couldn't be sure the gunman was shifting position, or had run out of ammo, the way we'd hoped. If one of us was going to sacrifice themselves to test the theory, Whitt was going to make sure it was him.

He slid over the edge of the platform like a snake, pivoting on his belly, and grabbed the rungs of the ladder.

"It's OK," he said, glancing at me. "Come on."

The gunshot took him high in the back. He slammed forward into the ladder, and then slumped downward out of sight.

I screamed, the sound coming out as a hard, high yelp, cut off by my own determination to launch forward and grab him. But by the time I'd reached the ladder he was out of sight. I heard him hit the first platform with a sickening thud. A second thud coming as he hit the sand.

CHAPTER 103

I CRAWLED MORE than climbed down the ladder to platform two. My whole world was shaking. My limbs didn't work. Before I could account for what I was doing, the danger I was putting myself in, I was sliding across platform one to the final ladder. I couldn't hear whether the gunshots were still coming. There was a ringing in my ears, a low hum that drowned out everything.

Whitt lay motionless on the sand, his knees up and his arms sprawled outward from his sides. I gripped the ladder, stumbled and grabbed at an upright pylon, just trying to keep myself from falling face-first on the sand. I felt drunk.

No one was coming into the vast, bare space beneath the crane where my partner lay. The gunshots had driven them back, so that they could only watch, wondering if he was dead, wondering if I was going to follow him.

I didn't care. I was going for my partner.

CHAPTER 104

I LET GO of the pylon and stumbled across the sand, trying to make my lips say his name. I didn't see Gabe coming until his body slammed into mine, at once knocking me down, gathering me up and carrying me out of the danger like a child.

"No, no, no!" I cried. "Whitt! Whitt!"

Was it my partner lying there on the sand, or my brother? A young man was down, sprawled, bleeding. A man I cared for, a man it was my duty to protect, needed me. I crawled at the air, twisted, tried to get free.

"Please, please, I have to save him!"

"You're going to get yourself killed," he growled, setting me on the ground. He didn't stop his momentum, his arm around my shoulders like the boom of a sailboat, carrying me forward with impossible strength. "I won't let you do this."

He shoved me into the harsh fluorescent light of the rec room. I tumbled onto the couch before the huge television set, which seemed to be paused on a video game. This wasn't me. I didn't run from the fight. I gripped the couch, turned, tried to get up. Where was my gun? Had I dropped my gun? I needed to find the shooter, to take him down, to save my partner, my brother. To save everyone.

"Stay here," Gabe said from the doorway, miners running past him in the night. "The shooting's stopped. I'll see what's going on."

I couldn't get air into my lungs. My eyes wandered over the walls; a huge poster of a naked girl lying on her side, one leg up, her hair tumbling down her skinny wrist. Her image marked the territory of the couch corner, the television and gaming console as a men-only zone. Beside the poster girl, a pair of notebook pages had been taped together and scrawled messily with words beside a column of numbers, the figures crisscrossed, written over and circled triumphantly.

I read the names in a panicked daze.

SergeantKill.

ShooterAce99.

LetTheBodiesHitTheFloor.

HajjiHunter71.

VengeanceIsMine.

I shifted on the couch, and under my hands a plastic case crumpled and cracked. I picked it up. It was for a video game. On the cover, two soldiers crouched in a muddy trench while a mushroom cloud lit up the sunburned horizon.

"Duty and Honor III," I read aloud, turning the case over with trembling fingers. I read the game description in a daze, my eyes flicking now and then to the images at the bottom of the case: a desert landscape, the first-person gamer imagined only by the gun he held in front of him. Crosshairs positioned over graphics of bearded men. Women in black shrouds holding the hands of little computerized children, running for cover in some sort of virtual marketplace.

I ripped open the case and found a glossy booklet held together with staples. More of the same images. Bearded men with gaping mouths, blood droplets spraying the screen as they twitched and danced under gunfire. Everywhere, slogans written in spatters of enemy blood.

Protect your base. Weed out the terrorists. Fight for your honor.

"War is a game," I read, my voice trembling.

And the only way to win is to be mentally, physically, and strategically strong. In Duty and Honor III, *you won't just face enemies in the deserts of Afghanistan, the ice fields of Russia and the jungles of Africa—you'll find them inside your own unit!*

The hands that lifted the controller from the couch felt like lead. I had to control my shaking, push down hard on the buttons to shift through the menu on the television screen. I went to the game's leaderboard, where a bulky soldier in sunglasses stood beside a list of names, his arms crossed across his impossibly large chest. The names from the list on the wall were all there.

SergeantKill was on the top of the leaderboard, with a

kill score that outdistanced the other players by several digits. I opened the player's profile and saw a webcam photo of Gabe.

He was all around me suddenly, his huge hands on my arms, lifting me up from the couch.

"We've gotta go, Harry," Gabe said, shoving me toward the door. "We'll follow Whitt in the ambulance to town."

I stumbled out of the rec room in the direction of the van, Gabe's arm around my shoulders. I was still holding the game booklet. My eyes never left it.

Follow the path of your personalized character right through training and into the field. Serve your commander through a series of tough missions, and earn points toward your overall rank. Conduct missions in which you stalk, hunt and mess with the minds of realistic enemies! Make Commander, and lead your team! The war experience has never been more immersive!

Gabe pushed me into the van, got in, and started driving.

I clung to the windowsill in the dark vehicle, watching the media pack as they passed by us. We were out of the camp before I could utter a word of protest.

CHAPTER 105

THE VAN TUMBLED along the sand hills, now and then traversing huge dry plains where rocks made the whole vehicle clatter and shiver. The numbness in my limbs was slowly easing, but I didn't speak. I watched the dark horizon approaching us, a smooth line that marked the distinction between starred dark and empty dark.

In the rearview mirror, the mine shrank to a handful of gold sparkles, and then was gone.

I held the booklet in my hands and looked at Gabe. He was focused on the road. Though I'd watched his handsome, gentle profile from beside him as he slept, he seemed an unfamiliar figure now. He looked pointed. A man on a mission. He glanced at the booklet, and then my eyes.

"So you've figured it all out, then," he said.

"I don't know," I said. "But I'm not feeling good. Tell me I'm wrong, Gabe. Tell me this isn't... this isn't you."

I turned the booklet, showed him the picture of a virtual soldier spraying machine-gun fire on cowering digital civilians, their mouths a little too big, their eyes a little too white.

It made sense. Gabe never left the mine. He'd told me himself that living a lie, a fantasy, forgetting about the real world was the only way he got through life here. The only way he could possibly have gotten the score he did on the video game, the kill figures that stretched sickly across the screen, was by spending hours upon hours inside the game.

"I'm sorry," he said.

I gripped my seat as the realization of what he really was shuddered through me. I felt sick. When had I lost my ability to see monsters behind the masks they wore, of friendly, harmless men? My instincts were failing me, terribly. I'd lain beside a vicious killer, given up my secrets to him, laughed and held him in the moonlight, trailed my fingers over his murderous body. If I could be so completely dazzled by Gabe's lies, did this mean that I was wrong about my brother, too? *What the hell was wrong with me?*

Gabe glanced at me with empty eyes as I sat wrestling with my thoughts.

I said nothing. He gave me some time, his face taut in the dim light from the dials in the console before us.

"I think that night, when I told you about my wife, I was trying to explain it," he said. "How this place—it's like another world. An escape world. A place where you come to mark out your own horizons, and you sort of say, 'All right. This is it. Everything outside, it's gone now.'"

I looked at the desert before us. The repeated patterns of spinier, dry grass, rocky ridges running under our tires. Something bolted out in front of us, rocketing away from the light. A rabbit?

"I can control things here," Gabe said, pointing toward the windscreen. "In the game, and in the Never Never. You have to understand how great that is. I mean, you're all about control, right, Harry? I knew that the first time I looked at you."

"Do you actually have any kids?" I asked. "Your room. I should have noticed. No photos of kids." My voice was hollow. Why was that my first question?

"Kids? What? No, no, no," he said. "It's all part of the game. I was creating myself. My profile. I knew a vulnerable divorcé would speak to you. Someone who wanted desperately to be with his kids, but who never could be. The family shattered. You know? Strategy." He looked embarrassed. "All strategy."

"Why are you doing this?" I asked. "How have you kept this secret from me?"

"The game is bleeding," he said, his voice thin, almost panicked. "It's been hard to see the edges sometimes. It's like ink leaking out. At night I have dreams from inside the game, and when I wake up, it's like I have to try to remember who I am. Am I SergeantKill? Or Gabe Carter?"

He ran a hand through his sweaty hair, almost laughed.

"Who do I want to be? Who gives me more purpose? Who makes me feel more real?"

"Gabe, I—"

"Who's playing a role, and who isn't?" He gestured helplessly to his reflection in the windscreen. "I can't tell the difference anymore."

We were a long way from the mine. He stopped the van and looked at me, his eyes wider than they should have been. He reached for me, and I jolted in my seat.

"Do you get it?" he asked. He reached out and knocked against the inside of the windscreen, the glass making a loud tonking sound under his huge fist. "I mean, are we *in here,* or are we *out there?*"

"We're out there," I said, my voice trembling. "This isn't a mission. This isn't a game. You've killed real people, Gabe. You've murdered real men and women. Edward Whittacker is a real man. He might be dead. I'm a real person."

"Yeah, maybe." Gabe looked skeptically at the windscreen, the edges of it, cast his eyes through it toward the blackened horizon. "Maybe. Maybe. Listen, jump out, would you? We're on the clock here."

CHAPTER 106

"WE'RE NOT ON any clock," I said as he wrenched open my door. "Gabe, look at me. Look at my eyes. You can trust me, OK? You can trust what I'm saying."

"That's what they all say," Gabe smirked, grabbing my wrist. "You can trust me. I'm one of the team. I'm one of the good guys. Yeah. Yeah. And they all turn against us in the end, don't they? I mean, Danny—he spent more time out there with the EarthSoldiers than he did on the camp. I should have known by the way he performed in the missions. Fucking backstabber. Fucking glory hog."

Gabe locked the van and walked around to the back doors, flung them open, annoyed.

I stood in the sand, holding the game booklet, numb.

"Killer. Dark. Hunter. Vengeance," I murmured. "The names in his notebook. He was trying to pick a game name."

"VengeanceIsMine," Gabe snorted, rummaging in the back of the van. "Really? Wow."

"But he wasn't your first."

"No."

"Hon," I said. "He was your first victim. You'd been out here alone in the desert, stalking the EarthSoldiers, but you couldn't get near them because of the cameras. You were fantasizing about the mine being an army base. The EarthSoldiers being insurgents. The enemy. When Hon allowed them to raid the food stores, he was betraying you. Betraying the mine."

"You're very good, Harry," Gabe said, a little sadly.

"Hon mustn't have given you what you wanted. A challenge. A proper fight. Danny was next," I said. "Hon you hunted in the tunnels. But Danny you took out into the desert."

"He'd been in the game," Gabe sighed, looking at the stars. "We'd fought together, in the desert, in Afghanistan. We'd cleared villages together. I thought he'd be in his fucking element out here. But he was a coward. An idiot. That Shamma girl ruined him. Made him soft. Same with Tori. She had spunk. I thought she might have put up a good fight. But she was a dulled blade. Back and forth to the enemy camp all the time, hungry for weed. I should have known."

"Gabe." I grabbed at him. "Gabe, listen to me. This is the real world. The camp is not a base. It's a fucking uranium mine. You hear me? I'm not your enemy. I'm not. I'm not."

Tears were welling in my eyes. But I could not show weakness now. It might be the difference between living and dying. He seemed to want to shake away an anger that kept rising. Adrenaline for the start of the hunt was beginning to leak into his veins. Maybe if I could just keep him calm, I'd have a chance.

"Gabe, listen to me, you don't have to do this."

"Look, Harry, I might have time to get a hold of things eventually, get some downtime and figure out exactly who I can trust. But not right now."

I tightened my hands on his arms, tried to hold on, but with his brute strength he brushed me off like a fly.

"You're good," he said. "But you're not that good. You were a special mission from the start, Detective Blue. You were always going to take extra planning. Extra strategy. Lure, subdue, capture and gather intel. Those were the objectives for you. I thought you were out of my league for a while there. But I got you in the end. And now we reach the final challenge. I'm sorry it has to be this way."

He lifted a pair of black goggles onto the top of his head, a complicated band of instruments encased in rubber. Only when he flicked the night-vision lenses down over his eyes did I realize what the headset was.

"On a bearing of zero-five-one, at a distance of one-point-nine-one kilometers, your weapon is waiting," he said coldly. He pointed over my shoulder, the green glass over his eyes making him look like an alien visitor. He swiveled, and pointed to the northwest. "On a bearing of three-two-eight, at a distance of one-point-eight-seven kilometers, my weapon is waiting. The camp lies at true north."

"Gabe," I begged. "Please."

For a moment he seemed to break from his robotic ritual, his green alien eyes turning down toward me. At the corners of his lips, a pleasurable smile twitched.

"Because you're a special mission, Harry, I'm going to have to even the odds a little. I didn't do this for the others. But you're no ordinary case."

Before I could speak, he swung his fist back and then forward, sinking it deep into my stomach. I doubled and fell to the sand even before the pain had a chance to swell through me, stealing the breath from my lungs.

"We're green-lighted, soldier," Gabe said from above me. "Move out!"

CHAPTER 107

WAKE UP, TIGER!

I gripped the sand with my fists, tried to suck air into my lungs. Both felt flattened against my back, the punch having destroyed everything between my lower ribs, hollowing me out. When I did finally gasp, I got a lungful of sand for my troubles. It was a good hit. But I'd taken worse.

Get up! Pops was there with me, roaring, spitting with rage and exhilaration, kicking at my side as I rolled on the mat. *This is round fucking two!*

I glanced at the stars and tried to steady myself against the rocking, spinning world. I stumbled, staggered, then fell into a hunched run. I didn't know where I was going. But I was getting the hell out of here.

Hands up. Head down. Breathe, Tiger. Remember to breathe.

I looked at the stars as I ran, and their secrets began to speak, single stars emerging from the mess of lights. I remembered Gabe holding my hand, pointing toward them, linking them together, a huge black map stretched over the Earth.

That's Venus. That's Saturn. And that one is the Square of Pegasus.

I put my head down and sprinted through the dark.

CHAPTER 108

GABE TROTTED STIFFLY across the rocky plains, rising and falling skillfully over the landscape. His boots thudded between sharp desert plants, avoiding long cracks in the earth. These were his hunting grounds. He knew them intimately, as was his duty. The rifle wavered in front of him, bobbing back and forth with his steps, a rhythm he'd become accustomed to over the long months as his body shifted from fat, muscle and bone to killing machine.

It had been a long journey. There had been plenty of failures out here in the dark. He should never have buried Danny. It was laziness, cockiness—a shortcut he'd taken after a long night on the mission that had almost cut his game short.

There would always be failures, but what was important was that he kept leveling up, kept learning and getting stronger. He had to do his research. He had to weed out the traitors. Complete the special missions and outsmart the idiots who currently had command.

One day soon, he knew, he'd be ready for the final campaign—the eradication of the EarthSoldier camp. He didn't have the power yet, but when he did, he'd rain hell on them. His reconnaissance missions told him that they were the only ones out here with the training and equipment to challenge him. They had the resources to destroy his base, and they'd threatened his people more than once. They'd shown their mental and physical strength just by surviving the dust storms, the dry heat, the sun-scorched land. Their cause never wavered.

The EarthSoldiers couldn't be underestimated. They were cunning as foxes, and it would take a well-planned attack to wipe them out.

He drew a deep breath and let it out slowly as he headed up over a ridge. He mustn't get ahead of himself, lose himself in dreams. He needed to be strong. Grounded. Only one thing stood in his way, and she was just coming into sight now, a tiny figure moving on the horizon.

Harriet Blue was the ultimate test of his loyalty, his commitment to the mission. In another life, he might have liked to be with a woman like Harry. Like the EarthSoldiers, she was resilient. She didn't bend to the winds of trouble, but stood strong and tall like a tree. But wasn't that just the key to it all, exactly what made her so dangerous? She was *like* the EarthSoldiers. She was powerful, and resourceful, like them.

She was the enemy. Gabe couldn't afford to be sucked in.

The Soldier watched Harriet running along the bottom of a shallow valley toward the gun he'd left for her, propped upright against a round rock. The moonlight lit up the weapon like a torch.

He stopped running and settled into a crouch, watched the bright green shape of her slow briefly before snatching up the weapon and turning slightly on her path.

Gabe frowned. He lifted the rifle and set the lens of his night-vision goggles against the scope. And watched Harriet bolting with all her strength southward, in entirely the wrong direction.

She was heading out into the desert. Away from the camp.

CHAPTER 109

MY BREATH CAME in loud, harsh yelps. Every step rocked pain up through my hips, into my stomach. The rifle was enormous. I carried it in both hands, stumbling and almost falling now and then as my boots fell crookedly upon the desert sand.

A *whoosh* above my head. He'd started firing.

I ducked and kept running, sailing between two huge boulders. Gunshots puckered and popped against them as I passed, showering me in dust. I screamed and rolled, staggered to my feet again. The sand before me went up in rapid puffs.

He was going to nick me. Wound me just a little—take off a foot. Blast at a knee. That was his way. I knew, somehow, that he would slow me down, and he'd follow my warm blood in the sand until he found me crawling in the desert, where he could finish me at his leisure.

That was his plan, anyway. It wasn't mine.

There was no way I was leading him back to the camp, not while he was this disconnected to reality, this dangerous. He couldn't tell the difference between real people and his enemies in the game. There would be nothing stopping him from taking out dozens of miners as they came to my aid. No, I was alone now. I was going to escape, or he was going to kill me out here in the dark.

I shifted the enormous rifle up against my shoulder as I ran, and tried to unscrew the suppressor without slowing. If we were going to battle it out, I wasn't going to have any unsuspecting EarthSoldiers who might be wandering around in the dark getting mixed up. I needed to take Gabe down swiftly and safely. I hoped a bit of gunfire might scare away any innocent bystanders.

One of Gabe's bullets zinged past my shoulder, scaring me into a stagger, and then a fall.

"I'm not going to die like this," I promised myself, gathering up the gun.

I wrenched the suppressor off the barrel and let it fly out of my hands. The weapon was like a heavy child in my arms, clumsy, almost wanting to slip from me and fall. The glow before me was getting brighter. I pointed the gun in the general direction I thought Gabe was.

My arms shook with the gunfire, and for a moment the sand before me was lit white with flashes. I sent out another volley of shots, my ears ringing with their noise. It rippled out across the flat land like thunder.

I'd make him go to ground, and then I'd think of something. If I could just get some distance between us, I hoped I might survive.

CHAPTER 110

GABE WATCHED AS the green figure that was Harry fired to the left of him, still running, an explosion of white streaming upward from her gun in his night vision. She'd ditched the suppressor. What the hell was she doing? Stupid woman, wasting her ammo trying to scare him into hiding.

He picked up speed, firing off a couple of shots near her now and then as he ran, just to remind her he was on her tail and wasn't backing down. He glanced toward the mine, a distant collection of smoke lit dimly from below, the top of the massive crane just visible as a blinking eye overlooking a collection of boulders. It was a mere three kilometers to the mine. She might have made it if she'd run hard enough. But no. Not Detective Blue. She'd never bring the danger back to the base just to save her own hide. She'd die out here before that happened. He smiled as he ran. Blue was definitely worth bonus points. A decorated hero, sacrificing herself for her people? She was going to be a good kill.

His smile disappeared as the lights appeared on the hill.

CHAPTER III

IT WAS RICHIE and his crew. Gabe snarled, slowed to a stop. Harry's gunfire had piqued their curiosity rather than driving them away. They'd jumped in the car, and were coming for her. He glanced at the stars. Yes, they were just north of their camp. The young men must have been driving back from Perth after their arrests.

The Soldier almost laughed. Stupid girl. Gabe had known Harry would be his biggest challenge, and she was living up to his expectations. Just when he thought she was sacrificing herself, making his mission easier, she threw hazards in his way. Her death was going to be almost too much for him to bear—a tragic but honorable end to a worthy adversary.

Gabe would have to slow her while he dealt with the new players. He aimed carefully at the graceful deer galloping across the horizon. She was waving her arms frantically, trying to warn the men away. He fired, and watched her fall, heard her scream carried toward him on the wind.

Richie's headlights swung around to Harry, a hundred meters out. She stumbled to her feet, dropped the massive gun, knew that slowing her momentum and going back for it was too dangerous. Gabe gave a few potshots to confirm her suspicions, and watched her sprint headlong for the car.

"Don't stop!" she was screaming, waving her arms. "Don't stop!"

The men in the car didn't think she was waving them away. They saw the blood, and thought she was beckoning them.

Gabe stopped running as the car came to a halt, and let his gun spray into the vehicle.

CHAPTER 112

I HURLED MYSELF to the ground behind the four-wheel drive, hardly coming to a stop, the inertia of my run making me roll and skid on the gravel. The windows and tires exploded as bullets hammered into the car, and I heard the men inside screaming, throwing themselves at the doors. Between the hammering rounds, their voices came to me. I tucked my body into a tight ball, my hands around my head, listening.

"What the fu— What the fuck!"

"Go! Richie! Drive, man, drive!"

All of them ducked as the gunshots came again. I worked my shaking hands down the back of my right arm, feeling the damage done by the bullet that had whizzed behind me. It had blasted into the back of my bicep, taking a fist-sized piece of meat with it. I fancied I could feel bone, and when that thought took root in my frantic brain the retching started. I gagged and tried to breathe, wiping my blood-soaked hands on my shirt.

When the gunfire stopped, the men in the car were silent.

I got up and yanked open the driver's side door. Richie slumped out of the car, hitting the ground with a thud.

"Oh fuck," he groaned. He didn't seem to have been hit, but the terror had paralyzed him. I shoved him flat against the sand.

"Play dead, idiot," I said, trying with all of my might to shove the driver's seat back. I grabbed the gun hidden there and fell on the ground. I could hear footsteps on the rocks. One of the men in the car sent up a pitiful wail.

CHAPTER 113

GABE APPROACHED THE car and looked in at the bloody, tangled mess of men. The wounds were superficial—a finger taken off here and a chunk of flesh missing there—but they'd all flopped onto each other, numbed with fear, the eyes of the closest man wide and staring at the back of the seat in front of him. Gabe had seen this reaction in plenty of massacres he'd participated in. People fight, or they go limp. He lifted the rifle and pointed it at the nearest young man's face, wondering if the barrel inches from his cheek would rouse him. He could smell piss. Someone had lost all control of their faculties.

"Pathetic," he said. He wandered around the side of the car and looked at the blood there, great pools of it from the wound he'd given Harry on the run. Richie himself was there, lying on his stomach, his head turned away toward the ridge. He looked dead. Gabe followed the marks and blood in the sand and saw the very tip of one of Harry's boots poking out from behind the right front tire of the vehicle. She must have been lying on her back. He felt disappointment sweep through him.

Gabe reloaded his rifle and slammed the magazine shut.

"Get up, Harry," he said. "Get to your feet and face me."

CHAPTER 114

I WALKED AROUND the back of the four-wheel drive, watching Gabe as he took in the sight of Richie sprawled on the ground, the blood I'd left there congealing in the sand. I closed my eyes and wondered if he was going to shoot Richie. At this range, there'd be no surviving it. Was it a good enough performance? I heard the magazine sliding back into place with a sickening snap. He'd spotted my boot at the front of the car. Richie was safe.

"Get up, Harry," Gabe said. "Get to your feet and face me."

I stumbled forward in my remaining boot, rising behind the man I had trusted, the man I had slept beside, who had been my one and only consolation in this dark and terrible desert. I lifted the huge Smith & Wesson revolver and pointed it at his head.

"Hey, SergeantKill," I said, watching him stiffen at the sound of my voice. I waited, and when he'd turned enough to catch my eye, I forced a tired smile.

"Game over."

I shot him dead.

CHAPTER 115

I LOOKED DOWN at my feet propped against the old leather padded footrest behind the front row of the gallery. I'd had to borrow the black patent heels from my neighbor, as I didn't own any. The pointed tip of the shoes was crushing my pinkie toes. Why did women do this to themselves?

I looked up, glanced around, and met a hundred sets of eyes all staring back at me. *Better to just focus on the shoes, Harry,* I told myself. Forget about the packed courtroom. The media murmuring and whispering in their dozens on the mezzanine level like a collection of crows. The victims' families and friends cuddling and sobbing on the other side of the gallery, now and then throwing hateful glances at me. The gawkers—law students and retirees with nothing better to do—filling up the uppermost level, standing room only for the hungry public.

I'd never been as physically and emotionally uncomfortable as I was now. Not even out there in the desert, where the sweat rolled constantly and the sun sheered off every surface into my eyes, where my only allies were men I couldn't trust. My outfit had been a poor choice. I'd wanted to look professional, so I'd abandoned my usual jeans and T-shirt for a pencil skirt and sleeveless blouse, completely forgetting about the fresh red scars that littered my right upper arm like lightning strikes.

Yes, yes, this is where a piece of my bicep went missing, and was replaced by a chunk of my calf. It's nicely shaped, yes, but it's the wrong color. Yes, it still hurts. It has only been five weeks. No, my partner wasn't so lucky.

I rubbed my scars self-consciously and waited for my brother to arrive. The old desire to cry was still there, but since returning to the city I'd not yet found the right moment to give in to it. Maybe now was the time, here in the court, right in front of a pair of gawkers who had been murmuring too loudly about me from the moment I arrived.

"What the hell was she doing out there, anyway?"

"Getting an incredible tan, by the looks of it."

"Do you think she knew about the brother?"

"Pfft. You serious? How could she not know?"

There was a tapping sound, and the courtroom rose as one, shuffling feet and adjusting skirts and flipping back freshly flat-ironed hair. The heavy, brooding judge walked into the court and climbed the stairs behind his bench. No one spoke, not until a second door opened at the side of the room and a great hulking guard brought my brother into the court.

He was dressed in the bottle-green tracksuit of Silverwater Remand Center, and he looked tired. His eyes caught mine, and for a second he seemed not to recognize me.

Before I knew what I was doing I'd rushed along the pew, almost knocking over the only other person who'd dared to sit in the same row as me, and flung myself at my chained and hunched brother. He smelled the same. After all this time, he smelled the same.

"Sam, Sam, Sam, Sam," I gasped, squeezed him, crushed him to me.

"Oh my God, Harry," he said. "Harry, I didn't do this."

I pulled him away from me, held his face in my hands. The guard was flapping at me, wanting to pull me off but not wanting to manhandle me in front of the hundreds in attendance.

"But you—" I fought for breath, locked onto my brother's eyes. "The papers said you confe—"

"I didn't do this," Sam told me, reaching for me with the hands chained at his belt.

The audience thrummed with excited gasps and murmurs. I turned and pushed my way through the crowd at the doors and ran out into the hall. I couldn't breathe. I grabbed at the collar of my stupid blouse, the bra that seemed wire-tight around my rib cage.

"I can't do this," I gasped, trying to get air down into my lungs, trying to keep myself upright. I put my hands against the cold sandstone wall nearest me, tried to get a grip on reality. "I can't. I can't. I ca—"

"Harry?" a voice said.

I turned.

Edward Whittacker was standing there watching me. His left shoulder was still immobilized, strapped up in a huge dark-blue sling to protect the muscles and bone that had been shattered by the bullet that entered his back. The last time I'd seen my partner he was still unable to walk, his first week in hospital filled with drugs and pain. I'd left him in Perth, a wounded creature confined to a hospital, to face my family battle in Sydney alone.

"Oh." I wiped my eyes desperately. "Shit! Edward, what . . . what . . ."

"I'm sorry I'm late." He glanced at the door beside us. "Have they started yet?"

I walked toward him, and though we'd never hugged each other, his good arm seemed to know what to do. It rose and enveloped me as I sank into him. I heard his surprised exhalation above me as I buried my face in his hard, warm chest.

There in the dark of his shirt, my face hidden from the terrible world, it seemed safe, finally, to cry.

ABOUT THE AUTHORS

JAMES PATTERSON received the Literarian Award for Outstanding Service to the American Literary Community at the 2015 National Book Awards. He holds the Guinness World Record for the most #1 *New York Times* bestsellers, and his books have sold more than 350 million copies worldwide. A tireless champion of the power of books and reading, Patterson created a new children's book imprint, JIMMY Patterson, whose mission is simple: "We want every kid who finishes a JIMMY Book to say, 'PLEASE GIVE ME ANOTHER BOOK.'" He has donated more than one million books to students and soldiers and funds over four hundred Teacher Education Scholarships at twenty-four colleges and universities. He has also donated millions to independent bookstores and school libraries. Patterson invests proceeds from the sales of JIMMY Patterson Books in pro-reading initiatives.

CANDICE FOX is the author of *Hades,* which won the Ned Kelly Award for best debut in 2014. The sequel, *Eden,* won the Ned Kelly Award for best crime novel in

2015, making Fox only the second author to win these accolades back-to-back. *Fall,* the third Archer and Bennett novel, was released in 2015.

Fox lectures in writing at the University of Notre Dame, Sydney, Australia, while undertaking a PhD in literary censorship and terrorism.

BOOKS BY JAMES PATTERSON

FEATURING ALEX CROSS

Cross the Line • *Cross Justice* • *Hope to Die* • *Cross My Heart* • *Alex Cross, Run* • *Merry Christmas, Alex Cross* • *Kill Alex Cross* • *Cross Fire* • *I, Alex Cross* • *Alex Cross's* Trial (with Richard DiLallo) • *Cross Country* • *Double Cross* • *Cross* (also published as *Alex Cross*) • *Mary, Mary* • *London Bridges* • *The Big Bad Wolf* • *Four Blind Mice* • *Violets Are Blue* • *Roses Are Red* • *Pop Goes the Weasel* • *Cat & Mouse* • *Jack & Jill* • *Kiss the Girls* • *Along Came a Spider*

THE WOMEN'S MURDER CLUB

16th Seduction (with Maxine Paetro) • *15th Affair* (with Maxine Paetro) • *14th Deadly Sin* (with Maxine Paetro) • *Unlucky 13* (with Maxine Paetro) • *12th of Never* (with Maxine Paetro) • *11th Hour* (with Maxine Paetro) • *10th Anniversary* (with Maxine Paetro) • *The 9th Judgment* (with Maxine Paetro) • *The 8th Confession* (with Maxine Paetro) • *7th Heaven* (with Maxine Paetro) • *The 6th Target* (with Maxine Paetro) • *The 5th Horseman* (with Maxine Paetro) • *4th of July* (with Maxine Paetro) • *3rd Degree* (with Andrew Gross) • *2nd Chance* (with Andrew Gross) • *1st to Die*

FEATURING MICHAEL BENNETT

Bullseye (with Michael Ledwidge) • *Alert* (with Michael Ledwidge) • *Burn* (with Michael Ledwidge) • *Gone* (with

Michael Ledwidge) • *I, Michael Bennett* (with Michael Ledwidge) • *Tick Tock* (with Michael Ledwidge) • *Worst Case* (with Michael Ledwidge) • *Run for Your Life* (with Michael Ledwidge) • *Step on a Crack* (with Michael Ledwidge)

THE PRIVATE NOVELS

Missing (with Kathryn Fox) • *The Games* (with Mark Sullivan) • *Private Paris* (with Mark Sullivan) • *Private Vegas* (with Maxine Paetro) • *Private India: City on Fire* (with Ashwin Sanghi) • *Private Down Under* (with Michael White) • *Private L.A.* (with Mark Sullivan) • *Private Berlin* (with Mark Sullivan) • *Private London* (with Mark Pearson) • *Private Games* (with Mark Sullivan) • *Private: #1 Suspect* (with Maxine Paetro) • *Private* (with Maxine Paetro)

NYPD RED NOVELS

NYPD Red 4 (with Marshall Karp) • *NYPD Red 3* (with Marshall Karp) • *NYPD Red 2* (with Marshall Karp) • *NYPD Red* (with Marshall Karp)

SUMMER NOVELS

Second Honeymoon (with Howard Roughan) • *Now You See Her* (with Michael Ledwidge) • *Swimsuit* (with Maxine Paetro) • *Sail* (with Howard Roughan) • *Beach Road* (with Peter de Jonge) • *Lifeguard* (with Andrew Gross) • *Honeymoon* (with Howard Roughan) • *The Beach House* (with Peter de Jonge)

STAND-ALONE BOOKS

The Moores are Missing (with Loren D. Estleman, Sam Hawken, Ed Chatterton) • *Triple Threat* (with Max DiLallo, Andrew Bourrelle) • *Murder Games* (with Howard Roughan) • *Penguins of America* (with Jack Patterson with Florence Yue) • *Two from the Heart* (with Frank Constantini, Emily Raymond, Brian Sitts) • *The Black Book* (with David Ellis) • *Humans, Bow Down* (with Emily Raymond) • *Never Never* (with Candice Fox) • *Woman of God* (with Maxine Paetro) • *Filthy Rich* (with John Connolly and Timothy Malloy) • *The Murder House* (with David Ellis) • *Truth or Die* (with Howard Roughan) • *Miracle at Augusta* (with Peter de Jonge) • *Invisible* (with David Ellis) • *First Love* (with Emily Raymond) • *Mistress* (with David Ellis) • *Zoo* (with Michael Ledwidge) • *Guilty Wives* (with David Ellis) • *The Christmas Wedding* (with Richard DiLallo) • *Kill Me If You Can* (with Marshall Karp) • *Toys* (with Neil McMahon) • *Don't Blink* (with Howard Roughan) • *The Postcard Killers* (with Liza Marklund) • *The Murder of King Tut* (with Martin Dugard) • *Against Medical Advice* (with Hal Friedman) • *Sundays at Tiffany's* (with Gabrielle Charbonnet) • *You've Been Warned* (with Howard Roughan) • *The Quickie* (with Michael Ledwidge) • *Judge & Jury* (with Andrew Gross) • *Sam's Letters to Jennifer* • *The Lake House* • *The Jester* (with Andrew Gross) • *Suzanne's Diary for Nicholas* • *Cradle and All* • *When the Wind Blows* • *Miracle on the 17th Green* (with Peter de Jonge) • *Hide & Seek* • *The Midnight Club* • *Black Friday* (originally published as *Black Market*) • *See How They Run* • *Season of the Machete* • *The Thomas Berryman Number*

BOOK**SHOTS**

Black Dress Affair (with Susan DiLallo) • *The Killer's Wife* (with Max DiLallo) • *Scott Free* (with Rob Hart) • *The Dolls* (with Kecia Bal) • *Detective Cross* • *Nooners* (with Tim Arnold) • *Stealing Gulfstreams* (with Max DiLallo) • *Diary of a Succubus* (with Derek Nikitas) • *Night Sniper* (with Christopher Charles) • *Juror #3* (with Nancy Allen) • *The Shut-In* (with Duane Swierczynski) • *French Twist* (with Richard DiLallo) • *Malicious* (with James O. Born) • *Hidden* (with James O. Born) • *The House Husband* (with Duane Swierczynski) • *The Christmas Mystery* (with Richard DiLallo) • *Black & Blue* (with Candice Fox) • *Come and Get Us* (with Shan Serafin) • *Private: The Royals* (with Rees Jones) • *Taking the Titanic* (with Scott Slaven) • *Killer Chef* (with Jeffrey J. Keyes) • *French Kiss* (with Richard DiLallo) • *$10,000,000 Marriage Proposal* (with Hilary Liftin) • *Hunted* (with Andrew Holmes) • *113 Minutes* (with Max DiLallo) • *Chase* (with Michael Ledwidge) • *Let's Play Make-Believe* (with James O. Born) • *The Trial* (with Maxine Paetro) • *Little Black Dress* (with Emily Raymond) • *Cross Kill* • *Zoo II* (with Max DiLallo)

A Princess in Maine by Jen McLaughlin • *Sabotage: An Under Covers Story* by Jessica Linden • *Love Me Tender* by Laurie Horowitz • *Bedding the Highlander* by Sabrina York • *The Wedding Florist* by T.J. Kline • *A Wedding in Maine* by Jen McLaughlin • *Radiant* by Elizabeth Hayley • *Hot Winter*

Nights by Codi Gray • *Bodyguard* by Jessica Linden • *Dazzling* by Elizabeth Hayley • *The Mating Season* by Laurie Horowitz • *Sacking the Quarterback* by Samantha Towle • *Learning to Ride* by Erin Knightley • *The McCullagh Inn in Maine* by Jen McLaughlin

FOR READERS OF ALL AGES

Maximum Ride

Maximum Ride Forever • *Nevermore: The Final Maximum Ride Adventure* • *Angel: A Maximum Ride Novel* • *Fang: A Maximum Ride Novel* • *Max: A Maximum Ride Novel* • *The Final Warning: A Maximum Ride Novel* • *Saving the World and Other Extreme Sports: A Maximum Ride Novel* • *School's Out—Forever: A Maximum Ride Novel* • *The Angel Experiment: A Maximum Ride Novel*

Daniel X

Daniel X: Lights Out (with Chris Grabenstein) • *Daniel X: Armageddon* (with Chris Grabenstein) • *Daniel X: Game Over* (with Ned Rust) • *Daniel X: Demons and Druids* (with Adam Sadler) • *Daniel X: Watch the Skies* (with Ned Rust) • *The Dangerous Days of Daniel X* (with Michael Ledwidge)

Witch & Wizard

Witch & Wizard: The Lost (with Emily Raymond) • *Witch & Wizard: The Kiss* (with Jill Dembowski) • *Witch & Wizard: The Fire* (with Jill Dembowski) • *Witch & Wizard: The Gift* (with Ned Rust) • *Witch & Wizard* (with Gabrielle Charbonnet)

Confessions

Confessions: The Murder of an Angel (with Maxine Paetro) • *Confessions: The Paris Mysteries* (with Maxine Paetro) • *Confessions: The Private School Murders* (with Maxine Paetro) • *Confessions of a Murder Suspect* (with Maxine Paetro)

Middle School

Middle School: Escape to Australia (with Martin Chatterton, illustrated by Daniel Griffo) • *Middle School: Dog's Best Friend* (with Chris Tebbetts, illustrated by Jomike Tejido) • *Middle School: Just My Rotten Luck* (with Chris Tebbetts, illustrated by Laura Park) • *Middle School: Save Rafe!* (with Chris Tebbetts, illustrated by Laura Park) • *Middle School: Ultimate Showdown* (with Julia Bergen, illustrated by Alec Longstreth) • *Middle School: How I Survived Bullies, Broccoli, and Snake Hill* (with Chris Tebbetts, illustrated by Laura Park) • *Middle School: My Brother Is a Big, Fat Liar* (with Lisa Papademetriou, illustrated by Neil Swaab) • *Middle School: Get Me Out of Here!* (with Chris Tebbetts, illustrated by Laura Park) • *Middle School, The Worst Years of My Life* (with Chris Tebbetts, illustrated by Laura Park)

I Funny

I Funny: School of Laughs (with Chris Grabenstein, illustrated by Jomike Tejido) • *I Funny TV* (with Chris Grabenstein, illustrated by Laura Park) • *I Totally Funniest: A Middle School Story* (with Chris Grabenstein, illustrated by Laura Park) • *I Even Funnier: A Middle School Story* (with Chris Grabenstein, illustrated by Laura Park) • *I Funny: A Middle School Story* (with Chris Grabenstein, illustrated by Laura Park)

Treasure Hunters

Treasure Hunters: Peril at the Top of the World (with Chris Grabenstein, illustrated by Juliana Neufeld) • *Treasure Hunters: Secret of the Forbidden City* (with Chris Grabenstein, illustrated by Juliana Neufeld) • *Treasure Hunters: Danger Down the Nile* (with Chris Grabenstein, illustrated by Juliana Neufeld) • *Treasure Hunters* (with Chris Grabenstein, illustrated by Juliana Neufeld)

OTHER BOOKS FOR READERS OF ALL AGES

Pottymouth and Stoopid (with Chris Grabenstein) • *Crazy House* (with Gabrielle Charbonnet) • *House of Robots: Robot Revolution* (with Chris Grabenstein, illustrated by Juliana Neufeld) • *Word of Mouse* (with Chris Grabenstein, illustrated by Joe Sutphin) • *Give Please a Chance* (with Bill O'Reilly) • *Jacky Ha-Ha* (with Chris Grabenstein, illustrated by Kerascoët) • *House of Robots: Robots Go Wild!* (with Chris Grabenstein, illustrated by Juliana Neufeld) • *Public School Superhero* (with Chris Tebbetts, illustrated by Cory Thomas) • *House of Robots* (with Chris Grabenstein, illustrated by Juliana Neufeld) • *Homeroom Diaries* (with Lisa Papademetriou, illustrated by Keino) • *Med Head* (with Hal Friedman) • *santaKid* (illustrated by Michael Garland)

For previews and information about the author, visit JamesPatterson.com or find him on Facebook or at your app store.

JAMES PATTERSON *RECOMMENDS*

Don't tell Alex Cross and Michael Bennett this, but I might have a bit of a soft spot for Lindsay Boxer and the Women's Murder Club. Why? Because Lindsay, Cindy, Claire, and Jill always get their man. And by "man," I mean the criminal they're hunting. As some of the most respected professionals in the San Francisco justice system, they were sick and tired of tip-toeing around their male bosses to get the job done. So they banded together, shared information, and closed more cases.

Meet the first ladies of crime fighting: the Women's Murder Club.

JAMES PATTERSON

"Patterson has mastered the art of writing page-turning bestsellers."
—*Chicago Sun-Times*

1ST TO DIE

#1 *NEW YORK TIMES* BESTSELLING AUTHOR

A WOMEN'S MURDER CLUB NOVEL

1ST TO DIE

Three sets of murdered newlyweds, bureaucratic red tape, and a truly terrible diagnosis from the doctor—Detective Lindsay Boxer has her hands full in 1ST TO DIE, the book that launched the Women's Murder Club series. She's one tough cookie, though, and a heck of a character to get to know: fierce, determined, smart, and unstoppable. In short, she's my kind of woman. She'll need to keep her wits—and her WMC friends—about her, though, because the killer is the last person anyone would ever see coming.

JAMES PATTERSON

"Unquestionably the best book in the series."
—BookReporter.com

and Maxine Paetro

#1 NEW YORK TIMES BESTSELLER

4TH OF JULY

A WOMEN'S MURDER CLUB NOVEL

4TH OF JULY

As an author, I love shaking things up and seeing how characters grow—or, in my books, if they even make it to the end of the story. The most interesting thing to test? Loyalty. Lindsay Boxer has dedicated her life to upholding the law. But after a routine arrest goes terribly wrong, she finds herself facing judge, jury, a very public trial, and a brutal murderer slashing through her sister's once-peaceful hometown. I turned Lindsay's life upside down in this book. And that's not all of it. Read what happens because I put a twist in this book that's pretty killer.

JAMES PATTERSON

"Patterson's books might as well come with movie tickets as a bonus feature."
—*New York Times*

AND MAXINE PAETRO

7TH HEAVEN

#1 *NEW YORK TIMES* BESTSELLING AUTHOR

A WOMEN'S MURDER CLUB NOVEL

7TH HEAVEN

San Francisco. Beautiful weather. Beautiful people. Beautiful architecture. It's the perfect setting for everything to go wrong. And, boy, does everything go terribly wrong. Lindsay and the WMC face two of their biggest cases yet: the politically charged disappearance of the mayor's son and a string of devastating fires that destroy some of the city's most iconic homes—with their wealthy owners inside. When the pressure is on, the WMC is at its best, and that's what they need to be in this book. Because when everything converges in 7TH HEAVEN, it's nothing short of explosive.

THE WORLD'S #1 BESTSELLING WRITER

JAMES PATTERSON

& MAXINE PAETRO

OF NEVER

12TH OF NEVER

When I think of a newborn baby, I think "nesting" and desperately trying to sneak in a few moments of precious sleep. Lindsay Boxer, detective and newly minted mom, doesn't experience any of those in 12TH OF NEVER. After only a week of baby bliss, a string of murders pulls Lindsay out of the nursery and onto the streets of San Francisco. I've always been amazed at how working moms juggle families and careers. But on top of finding lost socks, Lindsay also has to find a missing body from the morgue. And that's just the beginning. The shocker I have lined up at the end? Mind-blowing.